Mailboat

Cade Haddock Strong

About the Author

Cade spent many years working in the airline industry, and she and her wife have traveled all over the world. When not writing, she loves to be outside, especially skiing, hiking, biking, and playing golf. She grew up in Upstate New York but has lived all over the US and abroad, from the mountains of Vermont and Colorado to the bustling cities of DC, Chicago, and Amsterdam.

Find Cade here:

Website: cadehaddockstrong.com
Twitter: @CHaddockStrong
Email: cadehaddockstrong@gmail.com

Praise for the works of Cade Haddock Strong

Jackpot

This is my first time reading a Cade Haddock Strong book, and I must say if they are all as good as this then I shall be looking for more. What I really loved about this book is that it starts at the beginning for both Ty and Karla, it's not a story of they meet and flash back. It starts at the beginning and you get to read their story as they move along. There are many layers to this sweet story which is well written and kept me keen.

-Cathy W., *NetGalley*

The Schuyler House

...is a story about learning valuable life lessons from painful circumstances, opening one's heart to love and making positive changes in one's life. This story captivated me on so many levels because I was taken on a wild journey with Mattie! The numerous twists and turns in the plot kept me wondering about what was going to happen next. I also entertained insane thoughts of just forgoing sleep so I could continue to read on to satisfy my curiosity. If you enjoy a storyline with unique twists and angst filled situations coupled with a dash of slow burning romance, then this is certainly the story for you!

-*The Lesbian Review*

Fare Game

The author nails intrigue/thriller and romance in this book...The whistle-blowing storyline is plausible, logical, tense and interesting, the romance believable and sweet, the ending satisfying. With all other elements done well, this one makes a second good book by Haddock Strong. I liked it, and will definitely check out her next offering.

-Pin's Reviews, goodreads

This author is new to me but I'll be looking for more of her work because I really liked this story. It's a romantic thriller with two likeable leads, some well-done minor characters and very interesting plot that kept me interested from start to finish.

-Emma A., NetGalley

My belief is that when readers pick up this book, they will be enamored by a carefully and skillfully plotted story line that's also well written and doesn't sacrifice moral complexity to the demands of a fast-moving narrative. Ms. Haddock Strong does such a great job...

-Diane W., NetGalley

The plot has many layers—lust, a whirlwind relationship, intrigue (where is the money going?)—and desperate characters on both sides of the law.

-Ginger O., NetGalley

I loved how Haddock Strong gets her readers into the story. Her writing is clear and persuasive, and she manages to explain airline financial irregularities, price-fixing, and whistleblowing without ruffling a single one of my feathers. She introduces them slowly as part of the story, mostly in dialogue, and they become one of the many layers of the story. Likewise, the relationship between Kay and Riley is also layered, their professional and personal lives, their exploration of each other and their difficulties. It is beautifully done. This book is a must for readers like me that need a bit of something on the side of their romance. It gives a good read, good romance as well as some very hot sexy moments. An excellent combination.

-The Lesbian Review

Other Bella Books by Cade Haddock Strong

Jackpot
The Schuyler House
Fare Game
On the Fence

Mailboat

Cade Haddock Strong

BELLA
B O O K S
2022

Bella Books, Inc.
P.O. Box 10543
Tallahassee, FL 32302

Printed in the United States of America on acid-free paper.

First Edition - 2022

Editor: Alissa McGowan
Cover Designer: Kayla Mancuso

ISBN: 978-1-64247-374-2

Acknowledgments

Although *Mailboat* is my fifth book, I wrote it over the course of the GCLS Writing Academy—a great place for new and not so new writers alike! My WA teachers, including Finn Burnett, Karelia Stetz-Waters, and Anna Burke, were not only amazing but supportive and generally awesome. Ditto for my WA mentor, Susan Meagher, who painstakingly read my MS more than once.

My WA classmates made the experience all the more rewarding. We split into small critique groups, and I was paired with fellow authors Rita Potter, Lori G. Matthews, Nan Campbell, and Michele Brower. They all read multiple early chapters of *Mailboat*, and beta read the completed draft. Two of my tried-and-true beta readers, Tagan Shepard and Celeste Castro, also read *Mailboat*. I cannot thank you all enough. Because of you, this story is way better. You're part of what makes the writing community so incredible.

Mailboat is set in Coopersville, a fictional town on the banks of the St. Lawrence River in the Thousand Islands. For those of you who have never visited the area (or heard of the place) it's stunningly beautiful and has a rich history. I've visited, but I am no expert on life there, especially in the colder months. Lucky for me, my friend Jane's parents own two islands along the US/Canada border, which runs through the middle of the river. They were kind enough to answer all my questions about the intricacies of life on the islands. Thank you, Ian and Eve Tatlock! I recall you describing the early spring, when you hear the first loon or spot the first oriole and I worked hard to incorporate that kind of detail into *Mailboat*'s setting.

Thanks also to my editor, Alissa McGowan. Sorry I'm terrible at grammar and thank you for catching all those inconsistencies and gaffes I let slip through.

I am so grateful to be part of the Bella Books family. Thank you for nurturing me and for believing in me.

And! Thank you to my wife, Lisa. You are my sunshine.

CHAPTER ONE

When she neared the rocky shore of Owl Island, Wen pulled back on the throttle and the boat lowered in the water as it slowed. From her vantage point, only the red metal roof of the main house was visible. A wide wooden dock jutted out into the water, but rather than approach it, she circled the island, searching for any sign of life.

Owl Island, summer home to the illustrious Gage family, was the largest private island on the US side of the Saint Lawrence River. By Wen's estimate, it measured almost a half a mile in circumference. Soaring trees fringed its shoreline, and a long rolling lawn—one ready-made for croquet—surrounded the now dormant gardens and a three-bay boathouse. Aside from a small cluster of pine trees, the limbs of the trees were bare, and small patches of snow remained in their shadows. Even from the water, Wen could smell the thawing earth under the afternoon sun.

When the hulking, white-shingled house came into view, Wen thought she detected movement in the widow's watch perched atop its roof, but she might have imagined it. It was probably way too early in the season for any member of the Gage family to be up in the islands, and it wouldn't be the first time her mind had played tricks on her. Being out on the water all alone each day could do that to a person.

Just as she completed her loop of the island, the boat's inboard engine sputtered.

"Dammit." She patted its fiberglass turtle shell. "Come on, baby, don't fail me now."

The engine ignored her pleas and stalled out, leaving her adrift in the river's swift current. She turned the key in the ignition. Nothing.

She let out a low growl. "Why am I stuck running this damn mailboat?"

No time to dwell on that now. The boat drifted dangerously close to a shoal on her starboard side. She counted to three, held her breath, and turned the key again. The engine choked to life.

"That's my girl."

But when she nudged the throttle forward, it died again. No matter how many curse words she uttered, it would not restart.

* * *

Estelle Gage stood in the widow's watch and peered out over the water. She'd come up to the islands to focus on her writing, but all she'd succeeded in doing thus far was freeze her ass off. *Maybe I should have stayed in New York...*

Commotion on the water pulled her from her thoughts. A woman—it looked like a woman—waved her hands in the air, and even from her perch in the widow's watch, Estelle could hear her profanity-laced tirade. What in the world? She welcomed the sight of another human being, but this one appeared to be on the verge of a meltdown. And her boat was drifting toward the shoal off Owl Island. Although they weren't visible until you were right on top of them, rocks loomed inches below the water's surface. She watched as the woman scurried to the bow and hurled an anchor into the water. Was she in trouble? Estelle got her answer when the woman lifted the engine's cover and peered inside. She took off down the stairs and snagged a coat from a hook near the back door.

When she got outside, she hollered across the water, "Do you need help?"

What a stupid question, of course she needs help...

"Engine croaked," the woman replied without looking up.

Estelle ran toward the boathouse, forgetting that none of her family's vessels were in the water yet.

"Fuck."

A rubber Zodiac dinghy rested in the hoist above one of the boat slips. It would have to do. She lowered it into the water and grabbed a life preserver from a hook on the wall. The door to the boathouse creaked as it rolled open. She fastened the buckles on the life vest and jumped in the Zodiac. It rocked heavily from side to side, forcing her to grab onto the nearby deck to keep from falling in the water. The small chunks of ice floating in the river were a grim reminder that this was no time to take a swim, unintended or not. She plunked herself on the wooden bench flanking the Zodiac's stern, pulled the choke on the engine, and tugged the start cord. The little outboard started on the first pull. Estelle reversed out of the boathouse, shifted into forward, and steered toward the woman in her disabled craft.

"On my way," she yelled as she closed the distance between them. The large wooden boat engulfed her dinky dinghy in its shadow.

The woman peeked up from the engine compartment and gave Estelle a broad smile. "Quite a mighty vessel you have there."

Heat rose up Estelle's neck, but not because she was embarrassed. She hadn't been prepared for the soft blue eyes that stared down at her.

"Come on around by the stern and I'll help you aboard," the woman said. Under the circumstances she was amazingly calm. Her anchor seemed to be holding, at least for the time being, but the current was unrelenting, and if she drifted even a few feet, her boat would be on the rocks.

Estelle maneuvered the dinghy along the hull of the bigger boat. A large wooden platform jutted off its back, right beneath the name *MATHILDE* stenciled in thick gold letters. Two strong hands reached out. She latched onto them and slid out of the dinghy and onto the platform.

The woman tied the Zodiac's line to a cleat and nodded toward *Mathilde*'s helm. "The darn thing won't start for me. Why don't you give it a shot? Maybe you'll have better luck."

Estelle swung her legs over the back of the boat, stepped inside, and strode toward the helm. The boat rumbled to life on the first turn. The woman pumped her hand in the air and lowered the cover over the engine. Once she'd hoisted the anchor back aboard, Estelle stepped aside to let her take the wheel. They turned toward shore, and the woman flawlessly landed the large boat, bringing it perfectly parallel to the island's dock on her first try.

Estelle jumped ashore and wound the bow and stern lines around the big metal cleats. "Would you like to come in for a cup of tea?" she hollered over the hum of the engine.

The woman nodded and killed the engine. The raw weather had rendered her round cheeks rosy. When she joined Estelle on the dock, she tugged off her wool cap, sending a cascade of blond hair down her back.

Estelle stumbled backward. *Dear God.* The lesbian fairies were shining on her. Thirty minutes earlier, she'd been shivering in the widow's watch, cursing her decision to come up to the islands alone in the off-season. And now, a tall, handsome mailboat captain stood on her dock. *Ooh, la la.* Having a deserted island at her disposal might come in handy. She took a deep breath and extended her hand.

"I'm Estelle Gage, by the way."

* * *

Wen knew who she was. Although they'd never formally met—townies and the summer folk rarely mingled—she'd long admired Estelle from afar, swooning over her on the rare occasions when she ventured into town during the summer season.

Wen wiped her own hand on her canvas workpants and shook Estelle's perfectly manicured one. "Wen Apollo. Mailboat captain extraordinaire, except of course when my engine dies. Thanks for coming to my rescue."

"You're welcome," Estelle said, "although I'm not sure how much I did. You probably would have gotten her started on your own."

"I don't know. The old girl only decided to cooperate when you came aboard." Wen patted the hull of her boat. "*Mathilde* and I both appreciate you venturing into these icy waters on our behalf."

"Speaking of which, it's awfully cold out." Estelle tugged her coat around her lean frame. "How about that tea I promised?"

"If you're sure you don't mind." Surely, Estelle wasn't on the island alone. "I don't want to intrude."

"You wouldn't be intruding at all. I'd love the company."

"All right then," Wen said, "but before I forget, I've got a package for you. That's why I was out this way."

She jumped back onto the boat and squinted into a pile of boxes next to the helm. The package she sought wasn't hard to find. It was large and oddly shaped. Thick block letters scrawled on its brown packaging read: *Estelle Gage, Owl Island.*

"Careful," she said as she handed the package to Estelle. "It's heavy."

Estelle took the package and effortlessly hoisted it over her shoulder. "Thank you."

Wen threw two dense rubber bumpers over the side of her boat and climbed back ashore. "Would you like a hand with that?"

Estelle shook her head. "Nah, I've got it, but thanks." She turned and led Wen up the wide stone steps to the front porch of the house. A lone white wicker rocking chair occupied its narrow gray floorboards. The wooden door creaked when Estelle pushed it open and a blast of warm air hit Wen's face when she stepped into the house's grand foyer. Why people referred to these island homes as "cottages," she'd never understand. True, they served strictly as summer homes, partially because they were virtually unreachable during the long, brutal winters, but nonetheless, "estate" or "manse" seemed more apt.

It was barely forty degrees outside, and places like these were rarely insulated. Yet the house was toasty, enough so that Wen's numb fingers began to tingle. A peek into the living room explained why. A fire raged behind the window of the jukebox-sized wood-burning stove at the far end of the room. The bin next to it overflowed with firewood. If Wen had to guess, Estelle had not been in residence for long. A musty smell permeated the air, as if the house had just been roused from its long winter's nap.

Wen shrugged out of her wool-lined Carhartt jacket and combed her fingers through her long blond hair. She held up her coat and asked, "Where should I hang this?"

Estelle's intense brown eyes were on her, and Wen quickly diverted her gaze.

"You can just toss it on the couch," Estelle said as she lowered the package to the floor.

"Are you sure?" Wen eyed the sofa's plaid upholstery. "I'd hate to mess it up."

Estelle waved her off and continued across the living room, so Wen gently laid her jacket on the back of the couch and hurried after her.

"This is my favorite part of the house," Estelle said when they crossed into the adjoining room.

"I can see why."

A slightly warped wooden ping-pong table sat in the middle of the floor, and shelves full of board games and books lined the walls. Wooden tennis rackets—encased in dusty racket presses—and a croquet set were tucked in the corner. She ran a hand over some of the book spines. No surprise, all the classics were there. Did the Gage family sit around at night and discuss Homer and Brontë? Probably. A far cry from the conversations around the dinner table at the Apollo household.

"During the summer, we kids spend every night in here," Estelle said. "I'm the residing Yahtzee champion."

Wen chuckled. She pegged Estelle to be in her early thirties, so it was funny to hear her refer to herself as a kid, although Estelle's mother was legendary in town. Rumor had it that she ruled the Gage family roost with an iron fist.

A wide hallway led back to the kitchen, one side lined with a well-stocked bar. Its glass shelves held dozens of bottles of brown liquids and crystal glasses of various sizes and shapes. Wen generally stuck to beer, preferably IPA, the hoppier the better, but if she had a bar like that at home, she might be inclined to toss back a splash of bourbon.

The kitchen was enormous and more updated than Wen expected given the state of the rest of the house. Gleaming stainless appliances, two deep white porcelain sinks, and a light gray granite island that was big enough to ballroom dance on. Did the Gages actually cook their own meals?

Estelle set the kettle on the stove, fired up the burner, and pulled two mugs from the cupboard.

Wen nodded toward the ornate silver tea set atop a nearby butler's table. "You mean you aren't going to serve us with that?"

Estelle laughed. "I don't think anyone has used that since my grandmother died. My mother just can't bring herself to get rid of it."

While the water heated and Estelle busied herself arranging cookies on a plate, Wen took the opportunity to steal a few glances. She was even more beautiful than Wen remembered. Her long, dark lashes fluttered when she blinked, and her fair skin bore evidence of having recently spent time in a warmer climate. If Wen had to guess, she was close to six feet tall and had probably grown up playing tennis and soccer and every other sport under the sun. Light streaks ran through her otherwise dark brown hair. A few strands had come loose from her ponytail and hung down alongside her face.

After their tea steeped, Estelle said, "Why don't we go back into the living room. It's the warmest place in the house."

Wen followed her back the way they'd come. "Would you like me to add wood to the fire?" she asked.

Estelle smiled. "Yes, thank you. I swear that stove goes through wood like you wouldn't believe."

"Oh, I believe it. We've got one at home, albeit a lot smaller than yours. They sure do crank out the heat, though."

Two leather chairs flanked the wood-burning stove and after Wen tended the fire, Estelle gestured for her to take a seat. The silky-smooth leather crinkled when Wen lowered herself into the chair. A footstool, topped with a bulging needlepoint cushion, sat in front of each chair. Estelle propped her feet up on the one in front of her.

"Cute shoes." Wen gestured toward Estelle's black Converse high-tops. "I've got a pair just like them."

She focused on the needlepoint stool in front of her chair. It looked dainty next to her steel-toed Timberlands. Unlike Estelle, she opted to keep her feet on the floor. She'd hate to dirty the stool. It had probably been needlepointed by Estelle's great-grandmother or something. *Shit, where are my manners?*

"Oh, jeez, I'm sorry. Would you like me to remove my boots? I should have asked."

"Don't be silly," Estelle said. "We're very informal at the cottage."

Wen stifled a smirk. She lifted the mug of tea to her lips and took in her surroundings. The room probably looked the same as it had when the prior generation of Gages had summered here. An Apple laptop on the side table next to Estelle was the only indication that they were living in the twenty-first century. A patchwork of well-worn, braided wool rugs covered the pine floors, and photos of sun-kissed children and framed nautical charts hung on the walls. Wen paused at a collection of photos to the left of the wood stove.

"Are those all woodies your family has owned?" she asked. The classic antique wooden boats were a jewel in the river's rich boating heritage.

Estelle nodded. "We still have two of them, although one is in much better condition than the other."

"My dad's got a wooden Chris-Craft in our garage," Wen said, "but it's in crappy shape. I don't think it even warrants being called a woodie. It would probably sink to the bottom of the river if he actually put it in the water. My dream is to fix it up one day." Wen laughed. "*Mathilde* is a solid old girl, but she's not exactly the belle of the ball."

"If you ask me, *Mathilde* is a fine vessel," Estelle said, "but I have to agree, no boat is as beautiful as the old woodies." She paused to take a sip of tea. "My father was a trustee of the Antique Boat Museum and restoring old Chris-Crafts was a lifelong hobby of his. When I was a child, I considered it the most boring activity in the world, but I've grown to appreciate it. It requires a lot of love and patience, but the finished product—a beautifully restored woodie—makes the hard work well worth it."

Estelle set her mug on the table next to her chair and stood. Her perfectly shaped, white-tipped fingernail tapped the glass on one of the photos and she gave Wen a brief history of the boat in the picture.

Aside from the mammoth silver Rolex hanging around her wrist, her hands bore no jewelry. Interesting that there was no wedding ring. The townies loved to gossip about the wealthy families who owned the private islands, and Wen recalled Estelle marrying another New York debutante a few years back.

She jammed her chapped and calloused hands into the pockets of her hoodie and joined Estelle in front of the photo to get a closer look at the boat.

They stood inches apart as they moved along the row of photographs. Wen tugged at the neck of her sweatshirt. Heat rose up her torso, and she was fairly certain it had nothing to do with her proximity to the wood stove.

When they returned to their seats in front of the fire, Estelle asked, "You might be wondering what I'm doing up here all alone this time of year?"

"I'll admit, it's a bit, um, unusual."

Estelle crossed her ankles on the needlepoint stool. "I'm an author, and I've had a rotten case of writer's block. I thought a change of scene would help. I came here to do one thing: finish my manuscript, come hell or high water."

"Wow," Wen replied. "I had no idea you were an author." She knew very little about Estelle except that she was very rich and very beautiful.

Wen shifted in her seat, suddenly self-conscious about the smears of grease and dirt on her pants. Why hadn't she put on clean Carhartts this morning? *Because you didn't know you'd be sitting here chatting with Estelle-fucking-Gage.*

"I've let life get in the way of my writing for too long," Estelle said, "and now I've decided to make it a priority." She picked at a thread on her sleeve. "Took countless hours of therapy, but I'm finally learning to devote more time to the things that are important to me and not feel guilty about it."

Their conversation up until now had been mostly superficial. And this sudden shift to a topic of a more personal nature would have been fine under normal circumstances, but the circumstances were anything but normal. Townies didn't come to tea at places like the Gage residence, and when they did interact with the summer folk, they stuck to cursory topics, like the weather. Wen wasn't always one to follow conventions, but she knew her place.

There was a lull in the conversation, and she realized she needed to say something in response. She sensed that there was more to the story about why Estelle was up on Owl Island all alone in early April—still borderline winter in this neck of the woods—but she didn't want to pry.

"Um, good for you…If nothing else, it sure is quiet up here this time of year. Even though the river has mostly thawed, most people still consider it way too cold."

"I know the calendar says it's spring," Estelle said, "but you could have fooled me. Are you aware it's forecasted to snow tonight? Hopefully I won't freeze to death."

Wen leaned forward and rested her elbows on her knees. "I'd be happy to check in on you over the weekend if you like." She pulled her phone from her coat pocket. "And here, let me give you my number. Feel free to call me if you need anything at all. If I can't help, I'm sure I know someone in town who can."

"That's very kind of you, Wen, thank you." Estelle jotted down her number and asked, "Did you grow up here in Coopersville?"

"I did. My family has been here for five generations."

"Sounds like maybe it should be called Apollosville instead of Coopersville."

"Ha, yeah, maybe I should bring that up with the mayor," Wen said. "He might entertain it, especially because there's been talk about naming the new community center after my father. He helped raise most of the money for it."

"Your father sounds like a miracle worker," Estelle said. "Raising money isn't for the faint of heart under any circumstance."

"He's an incredible guy. That, and he adores the town."

"With good reason. It's a beautiful place, and it seems to be full of decent, hardworking people."

"It is."

"I'm sensing maybe you don't have the same enthusiasm for Coopersville as your father does."

"Oh, I do," Wen said. "It's just, I've been here my whole life and—this is kind of embarrassing—the furthest I've ever been from home is Ohio. I'm itching to go someplace else. You know, maybe experience another culture. I'm trying to teach myself Spanish, but it's hard. Everyone in town who speaks it fluently probably wishes I'd get abducted by aliens because I constantly pester them to help me practice."

"I hope you get a chance to explore the world outside of Coopersville," Estelle said, "but it appears as though you have a lot going for you here. These days, there aren't many people who can say their family has lived in the same place for generations, and from the sounds of it, you know nearly everyone in town."

"Pretty much," Wen said, "which is great. But growing up, if I so much as peered in the window of the tattoo parlor or, God forbid, sneezed without tucking my nose into my elbow, it got back to my parents."

Estelle laughed. "Makes sense. A small town like this, no surprise everyone is in your business. I grew up in New York. There's so much anonymity there. You can get away with a lot, which isn't always a good thing."

"I suppose not," Wen said. "But it had to be a heck of a lot of fun to grow up there."

"It was." Estelle cocked her head and smiled. "But of course, I never did anything mischievous."

"Oh, of course not." Wen couldn't tell if she was kidding or not. Even though Estelle sat across from her in Converse sneakers and jeans and had been nothing but friendly toward her, she still had this image of the Gages conjured up in her head. Stuffy, refined, and well-bred.

"But I'll spare you the details of my youth," Estelle said.

When she didn't say anything further, Wen panicked. Had she overstayed her welcome? Maybe their conversation had gotten too personal?

She sprang to her feet. "I'm sorry, I've taken up enough of your time. It's bad enough that you had to come out and rescue me from the shoal. I should let you get back to your writing."

Estelle stood. "No need to apologize. I've enjoyed your company. You're easy to talk to. I'm the one who should probably apologize. I talked your ear off."

"Not at all," Wen said. She walked over to the couch and slipped on her coat and hat. "And anyway, I'm always happy to listen."

It was true. She often made deliveries to some of the year-round residents, and for many of them, she was the only person they'd seen in days or maybe even weeks. In her line of work, being a good listener was almost as important as knowing how to captain the boat. Although, no one else on her route was as beautiful and intriguing as Estelle. Wen would happily sit there all day and listen to her talk.

CHAPTER TWO

After her last delivery that afternoon, Wen turned the boat toward home. The diesel engine shuddered when she pushed the throttle forward, causing the entire vessel to seize until the boat finally leveled out. Wen leaned against the rail and guided *Mathilde* through the channel. Flurries swirled in the air, and she laughed as she tried to catch them on her tongue. The weather forecast said they could get up to six inches. If so, it wouldn't be the first time they'd had to shovel the walk prior to Easter services.

She eased the boat into her slip at the marina and killed the engine. It was so quiet she could almost hear the snow hit the ground. She gathered up her bow line, and her fingers, numb from the cold, struggled to wind it around the cleat on the dock. Her stern line had fallen in the water as she'd left the final stop on her route, and it was now encrusted in a thin layer of ice. She had to tuck it under her armpit for almost a minute before it was pliable enough to snake around the second cleat.

Once the boat was secure, she gathered up her lunch pail and thermos, stepped up onto the rail, and jumped to the dock below. The heavy soles of her boots skidded across the slick surface, and she nearly joined the few remaining chunks of ice floating in the river. She took baby steps as she made her way toward shore and patted *Mathilde*'s bow before she clambered up the ramp to solid ground. "See you tomorrow, old girl."

Her battered blue pickup truck was the only one in the lot. Mercifully, its engine roared to life on the first turn. Wen whistled while she waited for it to warm up. She wasn't prone to whistling, but then again, it wasn't every day that she had tea with Estelle Gage. Her best friend, Ruby, would flip when Wen told her she'd spent the better part of the afternoon sipping Earl Grey on Owl Island. Shit, Wen was still flipping out about it herself. She put the truck in gear and tapped the steering wheel to the beat of the Elton John song on the radio as she headed into town.

As she coasted down Main Street, the streetlights flickered to life. Snowflakes that, a moment ago, had faded into the gray sky, now danced in abundance around the tall, frosted glass lamps. Wen had promised her mother she'd stop by the fish market on her way home to pick up haddock for dinner. Few cars lined the street, and rather than drive around to the parking lot behind the strip of old storefronts, she parked along the curb and jumped out onto the sidewalk. Ursula, the proprietor of Ursula's Books, was locking up and gave Wen a wave hello.

"I have to wonder if we'll ever see the daffodils," Ursula said.

Wen dragged her work boot through the dusting of snow on the pavement. "You're right to wonder."

Ursula gestured toward Wen's feet and then put her hand on her hip. "Wen Apollo, please tell me you weren't out on the boat today."

"I was. No choice. People out on the islands need supplies, and if I don't deliver them, no one will."

Ursula patted her on the back. "You're a good kid, Wen. Covering for your uncle while he's laid up in bed."

Wen was about to reply that she had only begrudgingly assumed her uncle's duties but held back. Captaining the mailboat was an important job, one she should be honored to do. Although the boat carried little actual mail nowadays, many islanders relied on it for vital supplies. Everything from prescription drugs and pet food to plumbing supplies and engine parts. Sure, taking over the boat while her uncle recuperated meant she'd had to leave her job as an ESL teacher at the community center, but it would be there when she needed it back—they were always desperate for teachers.

To shift the conversation away from the mailboat, she pointed toward the vacant storefront neighboring Ursula's Books. "What happened to old man Ken?"

"He went out of business," Ursula stated flatly. "I'm actually surprised he hung on as long as he did."

"That's too bad. I used to love weeding through his stacks of old comic books. Any idea if the landlord's got another tenant lined up?"

"I doubt it. Running a business in this town is far from easy, and the new superstore they're building out on Route 401 certainly won't help matters." Ursula rubbed her gloved hands together. "I need to run. It was nice to see you, Wen."

"You too. I'll be by the shop soon. I'm nearly finished with that book on the Rwandan genocide you suggested. Not exactly a light read, but I'm learning a lot."

They said their goodbyes, and Wen hurried off toward the fish market. When she emerged ten minutes later, fresh snow had already covered her and Ursula's footprints.

"Hey, Ma," she called when she walked in the back door of the house.

Her mother ducked into the mudroom. "Hi, honey." She cast a glare at Wen's Timberlands. "Take those things off before you come inside. I don't want you tracking snow and God knows what else into the house."

Wen handed her mother the paper-wrapped haddock, untied her boots, and set them on the rubber mat by the door. Before she stepped into the kitchen, she pulled out her phone and hammered off a text to Ruby. *Drinks later? You will not believe who I saw today.*

Ruby replied almost immediately. *Twist my arm. The Igloo @ 8? Can I have a hint?*

Wen typed, *Okay, see you then.* And then added, *Tall, sexy and beautiful*, but she erased the second part before hitting send. She wanted to wait until they were sitting face-to-face. Only then would she give Ruby every last detail about her encounter with Estelle Gage.

"How was school?" Wen asked when she joined her mother in the kitchen.

"Never a dull moment," her mother quipped. She was principal of the local school, Coopersville Central. "I swear to God, that Sawyer boy will be the death of me. I should have expelled him when I had the chance."

Wen unwrapped the fish and laid it out on a platter. "What did Tommy Sawyer do this time?"

Wen's mother ran a hand through her short salt-and-pepper hair. "He knocked over a can of bright pink paint in the gymnasium—he and a bunch of other students were making posters for the upcoming women's march—and rather than try and clean up the mess, he stepped in the paint and proceeded to run circles around the basketball court."

Wen laughed. "That's actually kinda funny."

Wen's mother gave her a stern look. "It absolutely was not. I made Tommy stay after school to help the poor janitor clean it up. They'll probably be there half the night."

"Hey, kiddo," Wen's dad said as he wheeled himself into the kitchen. "How'd it go out on the boat today? Engine give you any trouble?"

"It got a little chilly when the storm started to move in," she said, "but otherwise all was A-okay." Wen opted not to tell her father that the engine had conked out again. He worried enough about her and the boat. And it had started back up again, albeit just in the nick of time. "Although…I did make one especially interesting delivery today."

Her father maneuvered his wheelchair up next to her and his eyes opened wide in anticipation. "Oh, really? What was that?"

Wen told her parents about her visit to Owl Island.

"Strange for a member of the Gage family to be up in the islands this time of year," her mother said. "But how nice of Estelle to have you in for tea."

"Sure was," Wen said. "I'm still reeling from it."

"What's she like?" her mother asked.

"Interesting. Nice." Wen's face cracked into a smile. "Beautiful."

Her mother put a hand on her hip. "That whole Gage family looks like they belong on the cover of a magazine."

"Any idea what was in the package?" her father asked.

"No idea," Wen said. "But it weighed a ton, and it had a strange, pentagonal, cone-like shape, so I doubt it was books, or canned goods, or anything like that."

"I don't want you hurting yourself lifting heavy packages." Her father patted the stump that was his left leg. "I wish it was me out there instead of you."

Wen bent to place a kiss on his head. "I know, Dad."

It killed him not to be able to run the boat anymore. Since his accident, they'd engineered a way to get him in and out of the boat, and he liked to tag along on occasion, but he simply wasn't capable of operating the route on his own. A lot of the packages the boat captain delivered were heavy, like the one she'd given Estelle today, and many of the island residents—seasonal and year-round alike—were elderly. In some cases, it was necessary to run deliveries up to the house rather than leave them on the dock.

"Speaking of which," he said. "I talked to your Uncle Mark today. Sounds like he's on the mend."

"Any idea when he'll be well enough to take back over for Wen?" her mother asked, giving Wen a sympathetic look. "I'd hate for the boat to interfere with her trip to Barcelona."

Her father leaned back into his wheelchair. "No, but hopefully he'll be strong enough soon."

Wen hoped so too. Going to Barcelona for six weeks over the summer was a vital step toward her plan for the future.

* * *

Wen strolled into the Igloo at eight o'clock on the dot, said hello to a couple of friends in a booth near the door, and spotted Ruby on the far side of the horseshoe bar. Her short black hair had that cool, perfectly imperfect messy look, and her green and blue checkered flannel was rolled up to her elbows, exposing her light brown tattooed forearms. The peanut shells strewn across the wood floor crunched under Wen's boots as she crossed the room.

Ruby greeted her with a warm hug and patted the red-vinyl-topped stool next her. "Whaddya want to drink, Apollo?"

Wen climbed up on the stool. "I'm dying to try the new Lawson IPA, Little Sip of—"

"Sunshine," Monique, the bartender interjected.

"Yep, that's the one."

As soon as Monique set the beer in front of her, Ruby pounced. "So? Are you going to tell me who you saw today?"

Wen took a sip of her beer and set it back down on the bar. "You know who the Gage family is, right?"

"Duh, of course." Ruby punched Wen lightly in the arm. "You've had a massive crush on one of the Gage daughters—I forget her name—since we were like twelve."

"Estelle."

"Yeah, Estelle. That's the one. Shit, girl, I remember when we saw her crossing the street last summer. You almost rear-ended the car in front of you."

Wen rested her elbow on the bar and smiled like a Cheshire Cat. "It just so happens I saw her today."

"Saw who?"

"Estelle, dumbass." Wen sat up and feigned straightening her collar. "We had tea."

Ruby burst out laughing. "Right, and I had mince pies with the prime minister of New Zealand."

"I'm not kidding," Wen said. "For some reason, she's up in the islands. I had a package for her, and when I went to deliver it, she invited me in for tea."

"No shit. For real?"

"Uh-huh. Well, after she came to my rescue. *Mathilde*'s engine is acting up again, and it decided to call it quits right in front of the Gage place."

"Isn't that a coincidence," Ruby said with a smirk.

"It was a total coincidence. I swear. I didn't even know Estelle was there until *after* my engine died. And I looked like an idiot. Like I didn't even know how to captain a boat."

"Okay, fine. So what's she like?"

"More laid-back than I expected. I actually enjoyed spending time with her."

Ruby winked. "I bet you did."

"I mean it. We had a nice conversation." A smile inched across Wen's face. "And up close, she's even more beautiful. Like out of this world hot."

"Isn't she a little old for you?"

"Nah, I bet she's only five years older than we are. Thirty-two or thirty-three, tops."

"Okay, well then isn't she a little too rich for you? I'm pretty sure you have to be born with a silver spoon in your mouth to hang out with someone like her."

Wen slumped in her seat. "Probably. It's just, I can't get her out of my mind. I'm literally praying I get another package to deliver to her, soon, like maybe tomorrow. I also gave her my number, you know, in case she needs anything over the weekend."

"If a storm blows in like they're saying, no way you're going out in that boat tomorrow, even if it's to chase after some chick."

Wen rolled her eyes. "Oh, and get this, Estelle wasn't wearing a wedding band. I remember hearing a few years back that the oldest Gage daughter had married a Rockefeller or something."

"Huh," Ruby said. "Now that you mention it, that rings a bell. The town was abuzz because she married a woman."

"Yep, so at least we know she likes the ladies. There may be hope for me yet."

Ruby squeezed Wen's hand. "My dear, sweet Wen. The woman of your dreams is out there somewhere."

"Yeah," Wen said. "And she resides on Owl Island."

"Did Estelle say why she was up here? That house has got to be freezing this time of year."

"Apparently she's an author—news to me—and she's got writer's block. She thought escaping the city would help to cure it."

"After the storm clears out, maybe you could bring her a few of the chocolate croissants from Bella's," Ruby said, referring to the café she owned in town. "A writer's group that meets there each week swears they help the creative juices flow."

"Not a bad idea, my friend. Although, I'd feel better about dropping by if I had a package to deliver too. I mean, I hardly know her, and I don't want her to think I'm a creep."

"I doubt anyone would think you're a creep, but suit yourself...Speaking of delivering packages, any idea how much longer Uncle Mark will be out of commission?"

Wen took a long sip of her beer before she responded. She was trying hard to be a good sport about having to take over the mailboat while her uncle recovered, but the truth was, she hadn't had much choice in the matter. Her family had operated the mail route for four generations, five if you counted her, and right now she was the only able-bodied adult member of the Apollo family who was available. Wen's older sister, Laura, was a hot-shot lawyer in Washington, DC, and her younger sister, Bethany, had just given birth to her third child. Wen lived in Coopersville, she was single, and although she'd had to give up her job to take on the boat, she didn't yet have a full-fledged "career."

"It sounds like he's doing better," she said finally, "but still no idea when he'll be strong enough to do the route on his own."

"Why is it taking him so long to get back on his feet?" Ruby asked.

"I'm not sure. We all have a hunch that there's more going on with his health than he's letting on."

"Are you worried that running the mailboat will mess up your plans to go to Barcelona?"

"I'm trying not to think too much about it, but yeah, I'd be lying if I said I wasn't a little anxious about it. If my uncle isn't better by early summer, there's a good chance Barcelona will be off the table, and if I can't go…no way my Spanish will be up to snuff."

For years, Wen had dreamt of volunteering in the Peace Corps, but getting accepted was crazy competitive. She needed all the help she could get, and being fluent in a second language would give her a small leg up. She'd spent months saving up for the immersion program in Spain and had even exchanged a few messages with the woman who'd been assigned to be her dorm mate in Barcelona.

"I'm sure it'll all work out." Ruby tapped her beer against Wen's. "And I, for one, think you are super brave to want to fly off to Spain all by yourself. Fuck, no way I'd ever have the guts to do that."

"You run your own business. That takes way more moxie than traveling solo to Europe. And don't be fooled, I'm petrified. As eager as I am to get away from our homogenous-as-they-come hometown, I'll have to bottle up a lot of courage to step onto that plane."

"You cross over into Canada in the boat sometimes. That's gotta count for something."

"I don't know about that. The only thing that separates us from Canada is some imaginary line that weaves around the islands in the river. It's not exactly an exotic country."

Ruby gave Wen a broad smile. "You'll get your chance to be Dora the Explorer, I promise."

"I hope you're right." Wen signaled to Monique for another beer and shifted on her stool to face Ruby. "I'll admit, I do love being out on the water. And you know I love it here in Coopersville as much as you do. It's just, there's a whole big world out there. A world I really want to see."

CHAPTER THREE

Estelle sipped her morning coffee and ran her hand over the leather chair Wen had occupied two days earlier. In the short time the handsome boat captain had been at the house, she'd managed to touch something deep inside Estelle. It was a feeling she hadn't had for a long time, and she wasn't quite sure what to make of it. Sure, she was a little lonely on the island all by herself, but that alone didn't explain why she'd been so drawn to Wen.

Out on the water, Wen was clearly in control and in her element. When Estelle had motored out to help her, Wen had handled the situation like a seasoned boat captain. Although her boat was adrift and her engine had died, she'd been calm, and, without preamble, had given Estelle a task. But once they'd gotten to shore, Wen's personality had changed. She became reserved, borderline shy.

Estelle was intrigued by the juxtaposition. Often, when you met someone who was competent and accomplished at what they did, they were arrogant and cocky. Not Wen. Although an intelligence loomed behind her wide-set blue eyes, there was nothing brash about her. And when she'd tugged off her wool cap, sending tousled, wavy, blond hair spilling over her shoulders... Jesus, Estelle's legs had gone weak.

At almost six feet herself, Estelle had a few inches on Wen, but that was often the case with women she encountered. Although Estelle considered herself to be in excellent physical shape, Wen could probably bench twice the weight she could. The way she'd hoisted the heavy package like it held nothing but feathers... Estelle licked her lips. Fortunately, she expected another package soon, and it seemed likely Wen would be the one to deliver it. Until then, one thing was for certain, Wen would continue to dominate her thoughts.

She slipped into her black puffy down jacket and dug around in the bin near the back door for a hat. Her hand came up with a real classic—a bubble gum pink hat with a lime green pom-pom. She pulled it over her long, dark hair and laughed at her reflection in the mirror. Why hadn't this hat been culled for Goodwill ages ago? Estelle couldn't even remember the last time she'd worn it. Freshman year at boarding school? No one was around to see her, so she left it on and made her way up the back staircase. When she reached the second floor, she crossed the landing, opened a small wooden door with a silver-dollar-sized metal handle, and continued up the narrow steps to the widow's watch.

Even before she reached the top, she had to shield her eyes from the sunlight. Last week's storm was now long gone and there wasn't a cloud in the sky. The widow's watch itself measured only about eight feet by eight feet, but with its wraparound paned windows, it felt much larger. Mist rose from the river and Estelle could see a massive cargo ship gliding through the channel in the distance. Owl Island sat in a section of the river that was nearly five miles wide, and snow-covered islands dotted the water as far as the eye could see. The largest islands held dozens of homes, while others were mere specks in the frothy water.

The heat from the wood stove in the living room didn't reach the widow's watch. She could see her breath in the frigid air. Still, she loved to come up here with her morning coffee, and when the weather warmed up, she planned to make it a makeshift office. There was just enough room to add a desk, and thanks to the thoughtful electrician who'd installed electric lights in the house years before, it had an outlet where she could charge her laptop, and heck, maybe even plug in a space heater.

Estelle leaned against the windowsill and sipped her coffee. Birds soared and swooped over the water and a lone fishing boat bobbed in the river. The ping of her cell phone broke the silence. It was Francesca, her roommate at Dartmouth and closest friend, no doubt calling to check up on her. She set down her mug and accepted the call.

"Hi, sweetie," Fran said. "How's island life?"

"Quiet, but nice. Exactly what I needed."

"You aren't going stir-crazy yet?"

"It hasn't even been a week," Estelle said. "Happy Easter, by the way."

"Same to you. Any big plans?"

"Church is out, obviously," Estelle said, "but I've got an Easter egg hunt planned for this afternoon. I hid some eggs last night after I polished off a bottle of wine, so I haven't the foggiest idea where I placed them."

Fran's deep laugh echoed through the phone. "That's classic, but what will your mother say when she hears you skipped church on Easter?"

"It's not like I have a choice. Our woodies are still winterized, and even if they weren't, they aren't suitable transport with so much ice still floating in the river."

"Seems like a reasonable excuse to me," Fran said. "Any word from Claudia?"

Estelle pinched her eyes shut at the mention of her ex-wife. "No, much to my relief, she hasn't called even once."

"I take that as a good sign. Perhaps she's ready to let go."

"I'm not holding my breath."

"How about writing? Are the words flowing?" Fran asked.

"A little. Not as much as I'd hoped."

"If you haven't been writing much, what the hell have you been doing? You're on a remote island all by yourself, for crying out loud, and isn't the Internet up there virtually nonexistent?"

"It's bad by New York standards," Estelle said, "but when your sole purpose in life is to pretend the outside world doesn't exist, it's fine. And I have other ways to occupy my time. For instance, I've done two puzzles, stripped the varnish off a large section of my dad's old boat—oh, and I had a visitor the other day."

"Really?" Fran asked. "You mean there are other people crazy enough to be up there this time of year?"

"The woman who came by is a local. She lives on the mainland and operates a boat that delivers packages and supplies to the islands."

"Is it an ice boat?"

"Very funny. The river is nearly thawed by now and can be navigated if one has the proper vessel. At any rate, this woman had a package for me, and, on a whim, I invited her in for tea."

"I see. Rubbing elbows with the locals, are we?"

"There's nothing wrong with the locals, Fran. They're good people, and well, the woman who came by"—Estelle placed a hand on her chest—"the truth is, I can't stop thinking about her."

Fran chuckled. "You're just horny and lonely."

"True, but Wen—that's her name, by the way—charmed the pants off of me..." Estelle laughed. "That came out wrong. I don't mean literally. What I'm trying to say is, and this is going to sound incredibly corny, she made me feel all warm and tingly inside."

"Whoa. This, coming from a woman who has refused to go on a *single* date since she got divorced. A woman who won't even dare return an admiring glance."

"What? I never said I'd sworn off women for good, but God knows I didn't come up here expecting to see another living soul, let alone meet an enchanting woman."

"All righty then. This Wen person, what's she like? And Wen, that's a unique name. What is it, Scandinavian or Chinese?"

"I have no idea," Estelle said. "Wen is blond, so perhaps Scandinavian. Or maybe it's short for something. I went to summer camp with a girl named Wen. In her case it was short for Wentworth." Estelle took a sip of coffee before she continued,

"Anyway, hmmm, how would I describe Wen?" *Beautiful, sexy.* "She's strong, but slender. A little on the butch side, but she moves like a lion—deliberate and graceful—and although she obviously spends much of her life outdoors, her cheeks are round and smooth, and I imagine, would be soft to the touch. Beautiful blue eyes, and based on my, uh, assessment, ample breasts."

"So under her flannel is the body of a goddess," Fran said with a snicker. "That could make cold nights by the fire a whole lot more stimulating."

Estelle groaned.

"In all seriousness, sweetie, it's good to hear you're on the hunt."

"Let's not get ahead of ourselves. Wen and I have only had tea, and I don't even know for certain that she's into women."

"If not, fingers crossed she's open to persuasion. It's been a year since you and Claudia officially split. You need to get out from under her shadow."

"I know."

"A fling with the sexy boat captain could be exactly what the doctor ordered."

"I don't disagree. A beautiful mailboat captain showing up at my dock not even three days after I arrived on the island. That's got to be a good omen, right?"

"No question," Fran said. "Keep me posted on your conquest."

"Oh, don't worry, I shall."

CHAPTER FOUR

It took Wen almost thirty minutes to clear all the snow off *Mathilde* on Monday morning, and then the boat refused to start. She growled at the engine, begging it to turn over. The fact that she had a mountain of packages to deliver, and none addressed to Estelle Gage among them, did nothing to help her mood. Still, she hoped to swing by Owl Island anyway. After careful deliberation—a.k.a obsessing—about dropping in to check on Estelle after the storm, Wen concluded that a visit was warranted and would in fact be the considerate thing to do. Although, if the darn boat didn't start soon, that plan would go out the window, especially because her delivery docket for the day didn't include any destinations near the Gage cottage. Instead of answering her prayers, it was like the package gods were conspiring against her.

The boat finally choked to life. Wen hooted and hollered and whispered sweet nothings to the engine before she took her position behind the helm. She surveyed all her gauges, zipped her jacket tight against her neck, and reversed *Mathilde* out of the slip. Just as she cleared the dock, a lanky teenager ran toward her.

"Hold up, Wen," he hollered. "Got one more package here for you."

Wen inched *Mathilde* back toward the slip, put her in neutral, and reached out to snatch the box from the kid's hands. A wave rocked the boat—a jackass ignoring the "no wake" rule in the marina—and the package almost landed in the water. Wen bobbled it but managed to pull it to safety. The neat script on the package nearly caused her to drop it again. *Estelle Gage, Owl Island*. Well, how about that? Unlike the first package Wen had delivered to Estelle, this one was no bigger than her hand. She slipped it in her pocket and whistled as she guided the boat toward the channel.

The list of deliveries for the day stretched multiple pages, and as Wen did every morning before she set out, she'd mapped the most efficient order in which to deliver them. After a few weeks of running the boat for her uncle, she'd reviewed the route's finances with her father. He'd remarked at how much lower fuel costs were as compared to the same period the previous year. This came as no surprise to Wen. Regarding the business, she was a lot more methodical than her uncle. Not only did she devise the optimal route, but she arranged the packages on the boat in the general order she planned to deliver them. That, and she drove the boat more conservatively.

Based on the route she'd plotted for the day, it made sense to deliver Estelle's package either first or last. First meant she could head there directly, but in the off chance that Estelle invited her in for tea again, she opted to put the delivery at the tail end of her list. That way, if the opportunity presented itself, she could linger.

When she reached Owl Island at the end of the day, Estelle greeted her on the dock, but this time, rather than emerging from the main house as she had before, Estelle appeared from inside the large wooden boathouse perched on the island's peninsula. The package Wen was there to deliver was so small, she didn't even really need to tie up. Technically, she could pass it off and be on her way, but Estelle gestured toward *Mathilde*'s bow and said, "Toss me your line."

Who was Wen to argue? As the saying goes, the customer is always right!

Once *Mathilde* was secured, Wen stepped ashore and pulled the box from her coat pocket. "I've got a small one for you today."

Estelle took the box, turned it in her hand, and gave Wen a sideways glance. "Thank you."

Her beautiful brown eyes held Wen's in a gaze that was so intense it caused her to trip over her own feet.

Smooth, Apollo, real smooth.

"My last delivery of the day," she mumbled, and then cringed internally. She might as well come out and ask to be invited inside.

Try to be a little less obvious, you nincompoop.

Estelle pulled her phone out of the back pocket of her jeans. "It's not even four o'clock. We've got at least a few more hours of daylight. Would you like another cup of tea? Or heck, perhaps a beer?"

Wen stared down at the dock and pretended to contemplate her answer. "Um, sure. A beer would be great."

She followed Estelle up the steps to the house. Her jeans hung low on her hips, and if not for the black leather belt holding them in place, they looked like they would fall off. Her pants and her black leather work boots were splattered with what looked like brown paint, and sawdust clung to her rear pockets, not that Wen was scrutinizing her ass.

As before, a fire raged behind the glass door of the wood-burning stove in the living room. The house no longer smelled musty. Instead, Wen's nostrils were accosted with a much more pleasant scent.

"Did you just bake bread?"

Estelle's lips curled into a smile. "I did. Come back to the kitchen and I'll cut you a piece."

Wen salivated at the proposition.

"I bet I can even scrounge up some cheese to go along with it."

Estelle's head disappeared into the cavernous fridge, and when she emerged, one hand was curled around the neck of two Heinekens and the other held something round and wrapped in red and blue polka-dotted paper, a clear indication it had come from the Coopersville Deli. Estelle arranged the cheese and bread on a small orange pottery platter and popped the tops off the beers.

"I've been cooped up in the boathouse all day." Estelle hoisted the Heinekens. "Any chance I could lure you up to the widow's watch to enjoy these? The view from up there is astounding, and the sun's been beating through the windows all day so it shouldn't be too cold."

"Sure," Wen said. "That sounds great." She hesitated before adding, "To tell you the truth, I admire the widow's watch every time I pass by the island. It looks so majestic perched atop the house, and I've always wondered what the view from up there is like."

"Well, here's your chance to find out." Estelle handed her a beer and grabbed the cheese plate.

The air grew cooler as they made their way up the steep, narrow staircase that ascended from the rear of the kitchen—no doubt built for "the help," as the island owners benevolently called the teams of people who toiled in their kitchens, scrubbed their toilets, and tended to their children. But Wen felt the warmth of the sun as they neared the top of the house. Her beer bottle nearly slipped from her hand when they reached the widow's watch. The view from its window-framed chamber was even more magnificent than she'd imagined.

She squinted and spun on the heel of her boot. "Oh, my God. It's 360 degrees of breathtaking." A light breeze rustled through the bare tree branches and the sun shimmied off the water. "Cool. You can even see the shipping channel."

Estelle came up beside her at the window. "Yes. I love to watch the enormous ships glide by. My favorite game is to try to guess what's packed inside all the containers piled high on their decks."

Wen smiled. "I totally do the same thing whenever I see a cargo ship." She pointed to an island in the distance. A large red house enveloped most of its rocky surface. "I delivered a package to Gig Island right before I came here."

"To Mrs. Key?"

"Yep."

"I played with her granddaughter when I was a child," Estelle said.

"She's a delightful woman, but jeez, she's as stubborn as they come. She's got to be approaching ninety, but still refuses to leave Gig for the winter. It's a miracle she doesn't freeze to death. One tough cookie, that's for sure, and you've got to love her spunk. Whenever I have a delivery for her, I always try and bring her a little treat. A book from the library, or some of my dad's fresh baked bread. Although she won't admit it, I know she's lonely."

"That's kind of you," Estelle said. "Do you deliver food and supplies to her all winter long?"

"In the dead of winter, my uncle—he's the mail route's primary operator; I'm just filling in for him—uses a snowmobile to deliver goods. In Mrs. Key's case, that also includes bottled water. Like most of the small islands, Gig doesn't have a well, and her water pump must be pulled from the river before it freezes over." Wen laughed. "Mrs. Key once told me that when she was younger, come winter, she simply cut a hole in the ice and drug buckets of water inside."

"You're right," Estelle said, "she is a tough cookie."

Wen turned toward her and nodded. Her eyes fell on Estelle's round, rose-colored lips. She swallowed the lump in her throat and stared back out the window, pretending to be fascinated by a ship in the distance.

"I've never seen the river completely frozen over," Estelle said after a beat. "It must be magical."

"Depends on who you ask. The snowmobilers and cross-country skiers love it. The cargo ship captains, not so much.

And when the wind howls, no matter how many layers you wrap yourself in, the bone chilling cold seeps in."

"A townie, um, I mean a local person, once told me that the Coast Guard often has to use cutter vessels to break the ice before the channel can open in the spring," Estelle said. "That must be quite the sight." She reached for her beer on the window ledge, brushing Wen's hand in the process.

A tingle shot up Wen's arm. *Was that an accident?* She cleared her throat. "Um, yeah, it's amazing to watch the cutters in action, although some people in town wish they'd wait for the ice to melt naturally before opening the channel. They worry about the environmental impact of smashing through the ice, but a stronger, more powerful voice argues to get the channel open in early spring, insisting it's imperative from an economic standpoint."

"What about you? Which side are you on?" Estelle asked.

Wen took a sip of beer and then gestured toward the window. "Personally, I don't think it's ever a good idea to mess with Mother Nature. If the winter she bestows on us causes the ice on the river to be extra thick, she probably has a good reason."

Estelle clinked her bottle against Wen's. "To Mother Nature."

Wen nibbled on a piece of bread and cheese as she scanned the horizon. "If I lived here, I'd never leave this widow's watch. The view out these windows is way better than any movie or TV show I've ever seen."

"I couldn't agree more. In fact, I plan to bring a chair and desk up here. Talk about the perfect home office. If I can't write here, there's no hope for me." Estelle hugged her torso and rubbed her hands over her arms. "Too bad I can't bring the wood stove up too."

"What sort of things do you write?" Wen asked.

"Fiction, mostly. Suspense and a little romance, although lately I haven't been writing much of anything. My agent, Harrison, is none too pleased with me at the moment. As I mentioned the other day, it's the reason I came up to the river.

To write. If I'd stayed in New York, I'd never get my manuscript done. I love the city, but it can feel suffocating at times and to be completely honest, my ex-wife wasn't helping matters…"

Wen's face heated at the mention of Estelle's wife, or rather ex-wife. She stared down at her boots. "Oh, gosh, I'm sorry to hear that. I didn't realize you were, uh, divorced."

"It's okay. It was for the best. Claudia and I split a year ago. It hasn't been easy, but she's had a harder time coming to grips with it than I have. It's a long story…"

Estelle blinked a few times, and Wen wondered if she was crying. Without thinking, she reached out and squeezed her hand. It was warm and soft, and she didn't want to let go.

"At any rate," Estelle said. "For a multitude of reasons, I can't wait to turn the widow's watch into a writing nook. Writing grounds me, and for the first time in a long time, being here on the island will allow me to devote my whole self to it."

Wen peered down the steps that led up to the widow's watch. "Where's the desk?" she asked.

"What desk?"

"The one you want to bring up here."

"Oh, it's in one of the bedrooms on the second floor."

"Let's go get it. I'll help you carry it up."

Estelle's face lit up. "Okay. That would be wonderful. Thank you."

The staircase up to the widow's watch was narrow and steep, making it difficult to maneuver the dense wood desk up it. Partway to the top, they set it down to rest. Wen unbuttoned her thick flannel shirt and stripped down to the thin cotton T-shirt she wore beneath.

Estelle gasped and muttered something that sounded like "Oh, my." Wen looked up at her and smiled. Her face was flushed. Was it from moving the desk or from their proximity? Wen hoped it was the latter.

Once they finally got the desk in place, Wen willed the sun to stop sinking lower in the sky. Here she was, ensconced in the widow's watch with Estelle Gage. What if they never got another moment alone like this? She had to make the most of it. Dial up the charm. It was unlikely that a woman like Estelle would ever be interested in her, but a girl could dream. They'd shared a few lingering glances, hadn't they? Or had it been wishful thinking on her part?

"Would you like another beer?"

Is the pope Catholic? "Oh, gosh, thank you, but I've probably already overstayed my welcome."

Estelle shook her head. "I'm going to grab another beer, and I bet it would taste better if you joined me."

Wen tried to judge her sincerity as Estelle held her gaze. Okay, so maybe it wasn't wishful thinking. "Um, okay, then, yes, please. I'll take another beer."

Together they watched the sun set. Estelle peppered Wen with questions about growing up in Coopersville and life on the river.

"As I said the other day," Wen said, "living here, at least year-round, can feel very insular, but people here look out for each other. Whenever someone falls on bad times, the town always rallies around them. Part of me…" Wen waved her hand through the air. "Never mind, you don't want to hear all this."

"Yes, I do. What is it you were going to say?"

"I love Coopersville and the people who live here, but like I told you, I'm chomping at the bit to go somewhere new. It's just hard because I have certain family obligations. There are people who depend on me."

"This may be hard to believe," Estelle said, "but I can sort of relate, at least partially. My family has, at times, put an extraordinary amount of pressure on me to meet their expectations. You're right, it's hard. To know when you need to step up and do what's expected of you but also to know when you need to draw the line and instead tend to your own needs."

Wen thought about Estelle's words. Finally, she said, "You're pretty articulate, you know that?"

Estelle tossed back her head and laughed. "I don't know about that, but thanks."

Wen drained her beer bottle. "I best get *Mathilde* back to the marina."

"Are you sure you're okay to be out on the water after dark?"

"Yeah, I know the river like the back of my hand." She nodded toward the window. "And there's a little bit of moonlight."

"All right, well, the least I can do is walk you down to the dock."

"Thanks for the beer and bread and cheese," Wen said as they made their way down the large stone front steps.

"You're welcome, and thank you for helping me with the desk. I would have been hard-pressed to move it up there on my own."

Before Wen released *Mathilde*'s lines, she jumped aboard to start the engine. She turned the key in the ignition…nothing. Nada. Usually, the engine at least let out a sputter, a signal that it was making an effort to start. Wen tried the key again. Still nothing. How freakin' embarrassing.

She peeked up at Estelle and forced a smile. "It appears the engine has clocked out for the day."

"Who can blame it? It's quite late. Way past quitting time." Estelle climbed aboard and patted the engine compartment in the middle of the boat. "Mind if I take a peek?"

Wen tried to hide her surprise at the request. "No, of course not." She unlatched the hooks on the floor and hoisted the wobbly fiberglass cover. The faint lamps on the dock reflected off the hulking, oil-stained engine beneath. Surrounding it were tubes and pipes and what seemed like miles of rubber-encased electrical wires.

"Hold on," Wen said. "Let me grab a flashlight."

"Do you have a rubber band or something?" Estelle asked.

Wen couldn't imagine how a rubber band would help get her engine started, but she dug one out of a cubbyhole near the helm.

Estelle used the elastic to pull her dark hair back into a ponytail and bent over the engine compartment.

Wen held the flashlight and watched as Estelle poked and prodded the various lines that ran into the engine. Did she actually know what she was doing?

"Um, any idea what's wrong?"

Over the years, Wen had seen her father and uncle tinker with boat engines, and she knew basic stuff like how to check the oil and replace a dead battery, but her mechanical prowess ended there.

Estelle lifted her head. She had a long streak of grease on her cheek. It was an odd complement to her tweed jacket.

Wen grabbed a rag from another cubby and held it up. "Come here. You've got grease on your face." She gently dabbed the splotch from Estelle's high cheekbone. "There, all gone, or at least partially."

Estelle smiled. "Thanks." She wiped a hand on her designer jeans and nodded toward the boathouse. "I'll be right back. I need to grab some tools."

"Um, okay."

"Don't worry," Estelle said. "I know what I'm doing. My undergrad was in mechanical engineering."

Of course it was.

"And I know my way around engines," Estelle added as she stepped ashore and headed into the boathouse.

Didn't all debutantes? Wen might need to get the word "idiot" tattooed on her forehead. Here she was, the big, tough mailboat captain—albeit on a temporary basis—and a New York City socialite was about to school her on engine repair.

Estelle returned a few minutes later with a small metal toolbox, a handful of socket wrenches, and a contraption that resembled a red lunchbox tucked under her arm. Wen's breath hitched at the sight of her. The dock lights caught the highlights in her hair, and she looked hardcore hot as shit with the tools in her hand and the trace of engine grease on her face. Even in her fancy clothes, she almost resembled a normal person. Not at all the prissy rich girl Wen had always assumed she was.

Estelle handed Wen the toolbox and twirled a socket wrench in her manicured hand. "You'll likely need a new alternator. Nothing I can do about that at the moment."

"You mean you don't keep a supply of backup alternators handy?" Wen asked.

Estelle laughed. "Unfortunately, no. Some mechanic I am, huh?" She gestured toward the engine with her wrench.

"The other issue is your alternator belt. It's loose, and that is something I can fix, at least temporarily, but it also needs to be replaced."

"I'm sorry, come again?"

"A loose alternator belt might indicate your battery isn't getting enough power. By chance was your battery warning light illuminated or have there been occasions where the lights on the boat dimmed?"

"No on the dimming lights, at least not that I noticed, but the battery warning light does flicker on and off. I mentioned it to my uncle, and he said that happens all the time and not to worry about it."

"You might want to ask someone else for mechanical advice next time around." Estelle picked up the red lunchbox-looking gadget. "This is a portable battery charger. I'll charge your battery while I tighten the alternator belt. That should get you back to the marina tonight." She used the back of her hand to brush a loose strand from her face. "Although, I'd feel better if you stayed here for the night and made the trip when it was light."

A sleepover. Wen could get into that. "Thanks for the offer, but I couldn't impose. I'm sure I'll be fine."

"Suit yourself, but promise me you'll have a mechanic check the engine over before you head back out on the water again." She shrugged off her tweed coat, set it on the rail of the boat, and rolled up the sleeves of her shirt.

"I will, I promise," Wen said.

She picked up the flashlight again and held it for Estelle while she worked on the engine. The muscles in her arms flexed when she cranked the socket wrench, and the tips of her fingers became black with grease.

When Estelle gave her the cue, Wen tried the ignition again and the engine roared to life on the first try.

"I can't thank you enough." She handed Estelle the rag. "Looks like you'll need this again."

Estelle gave Wen her cell phone number. "Please, text me as soon as you get back to the marina so I know you made it safe and sound."

Wen drove away with a smile plastered on her face. Wait until Ruby heard about her latest adventures on Owl Island. There was a lot more to Estelle Gage than met the eye, that was for sure.

CHAPTER FIVE

Estelle was half awake when her phone vibrated on the nightstand. The sun had just crested the horizon, casting an orange glow over the room. She rolled over and groaned at the name on her caller ID. What the heck did Claudia want at 6:19 a.m.? This couldn't be good.

She snatched up the phone. "Good morning, Claudia."

"Ralph died."

Estelle sat up in bed. "What did you say?"

"You heard me, Estelle. Ralph crashed his Ferrari on the Henry Hudson. It flipped over and caught on fire. He died on the way to the hospital."

"Oh my God. That's awful." Estelle had not always seen eye to eye with Claudia's business partner, but still, she was upset to hear he'd died. Leave it to Ralph to die in the same dramatic fashion as he'd lived.

"You have to come back to New York, immediately."

Estelle ran a hand through her hair and slumped back against the plush down pillows. So much for her escape to Owl Island.

Of course, she didn't *have* to go back to New York, but in the brief time she'd known Ralph, he'd become a good friend, albeit one akin to a bombastic and often irritating uncle. It would be disrespectful, not to mention coldhearted if she didn't attend his funeral.

"I'll get there as soon as I can," she said.

"Now. You've got to come back *now*."

Estelle tried to keep her voice even. "I said I'll be there as quickly as I can."

"But the business," Claudia shrieked. "What am I going to do without Ralph? I need your help."

"Everything will be okay. We'll figure it out, I promise. I'll phone you when I get to New York." After a brief discussion about the services for Ralph, they ended the call.

Estelle kicked off the comforter, swung her feet to the floor, and hunched over, resting her elbows on her knees. It was bad to speak ill of the dead, but Ralph had picked an unfortunate time to crash his stupid Ferrari.

It had barely been a week since she'd arrived in the islands, but the change in her mental state was already evident. A fog no longer smothered her brain, and she was writing again. Moving her desk to the widow's watch had been a stroke of genius. Perched up there, her hands flew over the keyboard, filling page after beautiful page with words. Her mind had been untethered from the stress of life in New York, allowing it to bustle with ideas—plot twists and colorful characters. But now she'd have to shut it all down again to rush back to New York.

She stood, grabbed her robe off the chair near the foot of the bed, and strode into the bathroom. While she brushed her teeth, she made one promise to herself. No matter what Claudia said or did, Estelle would only stay in New York for seventy-two hours, not a moment longer. Once she was dressed, she went downstairs, added wood to the stove, and started the coffeepot. All she had to do now was arrange transportation to Coopersville where her car was parked. The island's caretaker had ferried her across the river when she'd first arrived, but her mind immediately went to Wen. Although she ran a delivery boat, not a water taxi, Estelle assumed she occasionally transported people to and from the mainland.

Yanking her phone from her back pocket, Estelle scrolled through her messages and found Wen's number. Should she give her a call? It was now after seven. Surely she'd be up. She tapped the phone icon next to Wen's number and held her breath while she waited for the call to connect.

Wen sounded winded when she answered. "Hello."

"Hi, Wen. It's Estelle Gage. I hope I'm not bothering you."

"Oh, hi. No, no, not at all. I just wasn't expecting you to call. Are you waiting on a package? I'm sorry I wasn't able to get out for deliveries yesterday. The mechanic didn't finish with *Mathilde* until late afternoon."

"No. I'm not expecting anything. I'm calling because something's come up. I need to get back to New York as soon as possible."

"Oh," Wen said. "That's too bad."

"Yes, the timing is inopportune. At any rate, would it be too terribly inconvenient to give me a ride into town this morning? I'll pay you of course."

After a long pause, Wen replied, "I wish I could, but I can't. I'm sorry. My uncle passed away last night, and my dad and I are headed over to help his family—he left a wife and four kids."

Estelle gasped and her hand instinctively went to her heart. "Oh my gosh. I'm so sorry, Wen."

"I could try to come get you first thing tomorrow morning."

Estelle didn't even hesitate to respond. "No, no. You need to tend to your family. I can find another way off the island."

"It's okay, really," Wen said. "In fact, I could use the distraction."

"All right, if you insist. Tomorrow morning would be fine, if you're sure it's not too much of a bother." Claudia would pitch a fit when she found out Estelle wouldn't be back in New York until the following day, but so be it. She would relish having one more day on the river before she returned to the city.

After she got off the phone with Wen, she poured herself a cup of coffee and her mind drifted back to their brief conversation. What a strange coincidence that Ralph and Wen's uncle had died on the same night.

* * *

It was barely light out when Wen pulled her pickup truck into the marina the following morning. Thermos of coffee in hand, she crossed the gravel parking lot. The dense fog made it impossible to see *Mathilde* until she neared her berth. The gangway that led to the dock was slick with moisture and Wen shuffled her feet over its rough metal surface. She crossed her fingers and put the key in the boat's ignition. The engine fired up on the first turn. While she waited for it to warm up, she used an old towel to dry the captain's seat and the gauges on the dashboard.

Tears welled in her eyes as she thought about all the times she'd gone out on *Mathilde* with her uncle at the helm. The river was always his happy place. It still hadn't registered that he was gone. That she'd never hear his hearty laugh or see his warm smile again. And she and her family weren't the only ones who would miss him. The whole town would. He'd been such a fixture of Coopersville and his death would leave a big hole in the hearts of the community.

She wiped her eyes and steered *Mathilde* toward the channel, moving at a much slower pace than normal. The visibility was equivalent to driving through a vat of pea soup. Each time she passed a channel marker, she inched along in search of the next one, careful not to stray outside its boundary where the water quickly shallowed. When she reached the end of the channel, she put the boat in neutral and shot Estelle a text to let her know she'd be a little late due to the weather.

As she motored toward the Gage residence, it occurred to her that she had no idea how Estelle had gotten there in the first place. Although a handful of water taxi companies serviced the islands, few if any of them operated this early in the season, and now that the river had thawed, it was no longer possible to reach the islands via snowmobile. Perhaps Estelle had come in via helicopter? It certainly wasn't out of the question. She was a Gage after all.

By the time she reached Owl Island, the fog had burned off enough to make out its rocky shoreline from a hundred yards out. Estelle stood on the dock with two small leather duffel bags at her feet and Wen's pulse quickened at the sight of her. She pulled back on the boat's throttle and waved.

Estelle had traded in her paint-splattered jeans and work boots for snug wool slacks and low-heeled black boots. "Morning, Wen," she said as she picked the duffels up off the dock. "No need to tie up. I'll just hop onboard."

"Are you sure?" Wen asked. Estelle's outfit wasn't exactly conducive to jumping into a bobbing boat. Her pants probably cost more than Wen earned in a month, and heels, even low ones, generally weren't well suited to anything nautical in nature.

"Yes, I'm sure. I feel awful for making you come all the way out here to retrieve me, especially with your uncle's passing. The least I can do is be quick about it."

Wen extended a hand and Estelle latched onto it. The contrast between their hands was stark. One weathered and calloused with short, jagged nails, the other smooth with perfectly rounded nails, but if Estelle noticed she didn't give any indication. Her fingers remained curled around Wen's even once she was safely aboard.

Eventually Estelle unfurled her fingers and said, "I'm sorry. I guess I should give you your hand back."

Wen wanted to say, "no, please hold onto it as long as you like," but instead she slid behind the helm and busied herself maneuvering *Mathilde* away from the dock. Before she brought the boat up to full speed, she asked, "Do you want to join me on the captain's bench? It'll be much warmer if you're out of the wind."

Estelle rubbed her hands together and smiled. "Yes, thank you." The bench was barely wide enough for two people, and when she climbed up onto the worn, red leather cushion next to Wen, their thighs pressed together.

Wen guided the boat back toward the channel, occasionally stealing a glance at Estelle. A few wisps of hair had broken free from her ponytail and swirled next to her face. The suntanned skin around her eyes crinkled as she squinted in the morning sun. Estelle shifted on the bench and turned toward Wen. Their eyes locked briefly before Wen diverted her gaze. She tightened her grip on the steering wheel and glanced at the gauges on the dash.

The water was like glass and the boat cut through it effortlessly. Neither of them spoke until they reached the first *No Wake* buoy outside the marina. Wen slowed the boat and the roar of the engine lowered to a hum.

Estelle took Wen's hand and gave it a quick squeeze. "I'm sorry about your uncle. How old was he?"

"Only fifty. He had a lot of medical problems that we didn't know about…Until now, of course."

"His poor family. I can't imagine."

"Yeah, he was on his second marriage and his kids are super young. It's hard. But the Apollo clan looks out for each other. We'll do all we can to help them out."

"It's times like this that community is so important," Estelle said quietly. There was a wistfulness to her voice that made Wen wonder what kind of support network she had. Did the Gage family look out for each other too? Or were they all too busy being fabulous and rich?

"You mentioned that you had to go back to New York because something had come up," Wen said. "I hope everything is okay."

Estelle brushed a few strands of hair from her face. "Ironically, I'm going back for a funeral."

Now it was Wen's turn to take Estelle's hand and squeeze it. "Oh, no. I'm so sorry. I didn't know."

"How would you have? My ex-wife's business partner crashed his Ferrari."

"Were you close? You and the business partner, I mean?" Wen asked.

"We used to be, back when Claudia and I were married. He was a good guy, although I haven't seen him much over the last year."

When they reached the dock, Estelle stood and tossed her leather duffels to shore, seeming not to mind if they got scuffed. "I hope coming to get me was not too much of an inconvenience," she said.

"Not at all. Happy to do it."

"When is your uncle's funeral?"

"Day after tomorrow. His death was kinda sudden so we're scrambling to make arrangements." Wen's throat tightened.

"Losing someone close to you is hard." Estelle rubbed her back. "I'm always here if you want to talk."

"Thanks." Wen cleared her throat. "Um, how long will you be in New York?"

"Three days at the most," Estelle said.

"Sounds like you and I are both in for a rough couple of days."

"It certainly does."

CHAPTER SIX

"I hate to bring this up now," Wen's father said. "But we've got to make a decision about the mailboat."

Her mother rested a hand on his arm. "Arthur, do we need to talk about this now?"

"Yes, we do."

Wen fidgeted with the gold buttons on her navy blazer. They'd just gotten home from the reception after her uncle's funeral and she and her parents were gathered around the kitchen table. Her dad's eyes were puffy and bloodshot from crying and she knew he was struggling. Although he and Uncle Mark had not always seen eye to eye, they'd been close. Talking about *Mathilde* and the mailboat route was probably his way of coping. Presumably, it made him feel connected to his deceased brother. They'd grown up together on the water. And the truth was, they really did need to talk about the boat, sooner rather than later.

Although her uncle had taken over operation of *Mathilde*, her dad was the one who actually owned the boat, and now he needed a permanent replacement for Uncle Mark. That, and his contract with the US Postal Service would soon be up for renewal, and to secure it, he'd have to offer them assurances of reliable service.

Wen's father pushed the plate of chocolate chip cookies toward her. "I know you've got your heart set on going to Barcelona this summer..."

He didn't have to say it. The writing was on the wall. Wen was expected to put her plans on hold. The simple fact was, there was no one else to take over the mailboat. Her sisters certainly weren't going to do it, and her uncle's children were all too young.

"Coopersville is teeming with college kids in the summer," her mother said. "Maybe one of them could operate *Mathilde*. Cruising around in the boat has got to be infinitely more fun than serving tables at Miss Daisy's or scooping ice cream at Dusty's."

"Four generations of Apollos have run the boat," her father said. "It'd be a crying shame to hand it off to someone outside the family. And good luck finding a kid who knows the first thing about operating a boat like *Mathilde*, especially in these waters. Ben, down at the marina, makes a killing off all the idiots who run their boats aground."

"It's a nice thought, Mom, but Dad's right. It would be tough to find someone who's qualified, and even if we could, the college kids are only here for a couple of months. Who'd take over when they went back to school?"

"Your program in Barcelona is only six weeks long," her mother said. "You could come back and captain *Mathilde* in the fall."

Wen groaned internally. She knew her mother was trying to help, and it was true, she'd just be in Barcelona for a month and a half, but her mother forgot, or perhaps refused to accept a vital component. The Spanish immersion program was a stepping-stone toward volunteering for the Peace Corps. It would be pretty hard for Wen to run the mail route from a remote village halfway around the world. It was an either-or situation, and if she opted to take over the mailboat full time, it inevitably meant she'd operate it for the long term, at least in the eyes of her parents.

"Could I have a little more time to think about it?" she asked.

"Of course, kiddo," her dad said.

Wen's mom let out a big yawn.

Her dad did the same. "We should go to bed, Lucinda. It's been a long day." He snatched another cookie from the plate and held it in his teeth as he backed his wheelchair from the table.

"Night," her parents said in unison.

"Night," Wen said. She tugged her phone out of the pocket of her wool pants and was about to stab Ruby's number but paused. The pants itched liked crazy. She had to get them off before she did anything.

After she changed into sweatpants and her favorite hoodie, she snagged a beer from the fridge and plopped down on the couch in the living room. Its cushions were worn and faded, but it was the most comfortable seat in the house. She propped her slipper-clad feet on the wooden coffee table and took a long pull from the bottle of Corona.

She rested her head on the back of the couch and stared at the ceiling. The paint over the bay window was beginning to peel. "Paint living room" needed to be added to her ever-expanding list of to-dos. She sighed and pinched her eyes shut. *What the hell am I going to do?* Between family responsibilities and juggling multiple part-time jobs, it had taken her seven long years to earn her college degree, but she'd muddled through with one goal urging her along: Get out of Coopersville and see the world. And now that goal seemed as elusive as it ever had. After four generations, how could she allow the Apollos' reign as mailboat captains to come to an end?

No one had expected Uncle Mark to die so young. It had always been assumed, at least in Wen's mind, that one of his four kids would take over the boat eventually. But Mark's second wife was ten years his junior, their oldest was only nine, and right now he was way more interested in playing ice hockey than trolling the river in an unreliable rust bucket.

Ruby would know what to do. Wen pulled her phone out of the front pocket of her hoodie. A smile crossed her face as she eyed the last incoming call. Estelle. *I wonder what she's doing right now?* Probably hanging out with her ex-wife, whatever her name was. Wen tried to remember which day Estelle had left for New York. Had it been Thursday or Friday? The last few days, with her uncle's funeral and everything, had all blended together. All she knew was that today was Saturday, and Estelle had said she'd only be gone a few days. That meant she'd return soon and would need a lift back to the island. Would it be weird to text her? Wen's fingers hovered over her phone. They hardly knew each other, but inquiring whether Estelle needed transportation would be the courteous thing to do, wouldn't it? Before she could change her mind, she hammered off a text.

A response came back from Estelle a few minutes later. *You're so sweet to ask. Unfortunately, I'm going to be in New York longer than I anticipated.*

Wen slapped her forehead. Longer than anticipated? What the heck did that mean? A day longer, a week, a month? She tossed her phone on the coffee table. What if Estelle didn't come back to the islands until summer?

"Get a fucking grip, Apollo," she muttered. Estelle Gage was waaaay out of her league. She probably hadn't thought about Wen once since she'd left for New York.

She shot Ruby a text. *You up?*

Yes, but about to turn in.

Wen checked her watch. It was late and Ruby's mornings at the café started early. *Igloo tomorrow night? I need some career advice.*

Ruby responded with a thumbs-up.

* * *

Wen rested her elbows on the bar and covered her face with her hands. "I'm completely incapable of making a decision about the boat."

Ruby squeezed her shoulder. "Why don't we make a list of pros and cons?"

Wen sat up. "That's a great idea." She waved to the bartender. "Hey, Monique, you got a pen and a piece of paper?"

"Anything for you, sweetie," Monique said with a wink.

Wen scribbled *Take Over Mailboat* at the top of the paper, and then made columns for pros and cons. The first con was easy to come up with. Give up her dream of volunteering for the Peace Corps and exploring the world, at least for the foreseeable future. After that, she wrote, *Lose deposit.*

"Deposit on what?" Ruby asked.

"If I bail on the Spanish immersion program in Barcelona, I'll lose my deposit." Wen slapped her hand on the bar. "And shit, I bet my airline ticket is nonrefundable."

"That sorta sucks, but let's keep going. I think this is a useful exercise." Ruby snapped her fingers. "I've got one for the pro side of the list," she said. "Stay close to my BFF, Ruby."

Wen wrote that down and added, *Stay close to family.*

"Help your community," Ruby suggested.

Wen slumped forward on her stool. "How about 'be stuck in Coopersville for the rest of my life.'"

"Hey now, cheer up. That could be a positive. Staying in the town where you grew up and everyone knows and cares about you."

Wen added *Stay in Coopersville* to both the pro and con sides of the list and said, "Oooh, I can think of another good thing. Ever since I replaced the alternator, *Mathilde's* been running like a top."

"Add that to the pro list," Ruby said.

After Wen jotted it down, she said, "I still cannot get over the fact that Estelle Gage knows her way around a boat engine."

Ruby tossed back the last of her pint. "I know, me neither. You said she's got a degree in mechanical engineering, right?"

"Uh-huh, that's what she said." Wen's face cracked into a smile. "She's crazy smart."

"And she's got your heart in a flutter."

Wen groaned. "As much as I hate to admit it, you're right. Jeez, I'm pathetic. I'm literally counting the minutes until she gets back from New York."

Ruby snatched the pro/con list from Wen's hands and added something to it.

"What are you doing?" Wen leaned over to glance at the list. The name Estelle Gage was written in all caps under the pro list. She pulled the list out of Ruby's hand, crossed the name off and added it to the con list. "If I stay here to run the boat, I'll probably get even more obsessed with her and end up getting my heart broken."

"Come on, Wen. You have to beat back the women when you and I go down to Dela's. You're a total catch."

"Maybe for the ladies who like a butch in overalls, which I can assure you, Estelle Gage does not. And you're the one who said she was a little too rich for me. I believe your exact words were, 'I'm pretty sure you have to be born with a silver spoon in your mouth to hang out with someone like her.' You were right."

"No, I wasn't. That was a stupid thing to say. I'm sorry I said it."

"It wasn't stupid at all," Wen said. "*Our* people and *her* people don't mix. It's the way the world works." Wen lifted the piece of paper in her hand. "And talking about Estelle is not helping me get any closer to a decision about the boat. My father wants an answer before the end of the week. That gives me three days, maybe four."

"You know, one thing I don't understand," Ruby said. "Why is your dad so dead set on the mailboat staying in the family?"

"I don't know, but he is. I mean, I sort of get it. Four generations of Apollos have run it. My dad has always been big on family traditions and that sort of thing—he's a nostalgic guy—and I know it kills him not to be able to run the route himself. If someone in the family operates the boat, at least he still has a strong connection to it."

"I guess that makes sense."

"It just stinks that the burden is on me to keep it going," Wen said. "I know I shouldn't be bitter, but it pisses me off sometimes."

"Summer is insanely busy for me at the café," Ruby said, "but if you decide to take over the boat, I'll try to come out on the water with you as much as I can. And you know, as long as I own the café, you've got free food for the rest of your life."

Wen smiled at her. "You're the best, Rube. I love you, you know that."

CHAPTER SEVEN

Wen spent half the night staring at the ceiling in her bedroom and only fell asleep after she'd finally made up her mind. Her family would have to find someone else to take over the boat. She'd worked so hard to finish college, and she wasn't about to give up her dream. It was time she put her foot down.

When she woke up the next morning, the first words she uttered were, "Barcelona, *aquí vengo*."

She jumped out of bed and skipped to the bathroom. It was as if the weight of the world had been lifted off her shoulders. She whistled as she brushed her teeth and rummaged through her closet for a thermal shirt to wear out on the water. Temperatures were supposed to reach into the forties for the first time since last fall, which meant she'd only have to wear three layers today instead of her usual four. She stepped into her favorite Carhartt pants and pulled a hoodie from her dresser. Lavender-scented laundry detergent accosted her nostrils when she tugged it over her head.

"It's going to be choppy out there today," her father said when she wandered into the kitchen.

Wen nodded. Just as she did every morning, she'd checked the weather forecast before she got dressed—although a glance out the kitchen window would have sufficed. The neighbor's American flag snapped in the wind, threatening to splinter the flimsy wooden stick it was affixed to.

"I'm making you pancakes and eggs," her father announced. "You'll need the energy. The waves will toss you overboard if you aren't careful."

Wen debated whether to break the news about her decision now or wait until she got home that night. "Where's Mom?"

"She went to school early. Something about a burst pipe."

Well that settled that. No way Wen was telling her dad Barcelona had won out, not without her mother around to play interference. "Oh, that's too bad. Will they have to cancel school?"

"It doesn't sound like it. You know your mother. She'll figure something out."

When she finished eating, she put her plate in the dishwasher and filled her dented thermos with coffee.

"Time to head out." She leaned down to give her dad a one-armed hug. "See you tonight."

* * *

Her father had been right. There was a strong southwest wind whipping down the river. Even with the long stone breakwall protecting the marina, *Mathilde* bobbed in her slip, tugging at the lines that kept her tethered to the dock. Wen loaded the boat full of packages and set off to begin her deliveries. Beyond the breakwall, the river was angry. Whitecaps curled across the water and *Mathilde* rolled heavily from side to side. Thankfully, Wen wasn't one to get seasick. As she inched the boat through the channel, the wind howled outside the window sheltering the captain's chair. If her uncle were still alive, he'd have said the winds were "squealing"—a term the locals often used.

Once she reached the end of the channel, she turned *Mathilde* into the wind. The waves were relentless. Her bow crested each one, slapping down on the water before rising over the next. *Bang, bang, bang...* Wen braced herself between the captain's chair and the starboard rail to keep from getting tossed overboard. She didn't particularly enjoy being out on the river in weather like this, but it didn't make her anxious either. *Mathilde* was more than up to the task, and Wen trusted her skills as a captain.

Her first delivery took her to Yeti Island, a private island that was nearly as large as Owl Island. Apparently, its water pump was broken—most of the islands pumped their water directly from the river—and Wen had the parts the caretaker needed to fix it.

The clouds hung low over the river, and visibility was mediocre at best. Wen spotted something in the water just off her port side. From a distance, it appeared to be a log or a piece of wood from someone's dock. The water was high this time of year, and it wasn't that unusual to see debris floating in the river. She slowed the boat and eased toward the object. Best to retrieve it lest another boater hit it.

Holy shit! It wasn't a log. It was a fucking person. He... It looked like a he...

Oh, my, God. Is he dead?

She put the engine in neutral, yanked the safety ring off its hook, and flung it into the water. It splashed next to the man's head, and his eyes fluttered open, but he made no effort to grab onto it. Basketball-sized chunks of ice floated nearby. An ominous sign. Hypothermia would set in quickly, and she had no idea how long he'd been submerged. No other boats were in sight. Where the hell had he come from? And more importantly, what the hell should she do?

She jammed her hand into her coat pocket and pulled out her phone. Her hand shook as she dialed 911 and gave the dispatcher her current coordinates. It would take a rescue team at least twenty minutes to reach them, especially in this weather. The man might not last that long. She had to try to get him out of the water.

Between the current in the river and the unrelenting wind, she'd already drifted away from him. She maneuvered back beside him, returned the engine to neutral, and grabbed her telescoping boat hook. She extended it as long as it would go and braced herself against the side of the boat. The man had on a life vest with buckles—the kind you might wear to waterski or kayak—and she was able to hook onto one of its straps.

He was slender, which made him easy to pull, but his size would do him no favors in staving off hypothermia. Once she had him at the stern of the boat, she ditched the hook, secured a line around her waist—the last thing she needed was to end up in the drink with him—and stepped out onto the small platform off the back of *Mathilde*. She knelt, and with a hand around both shoulders of his life jacket, dragged him up out of the water and onto the transom. He was a grown man and his Carhartt jumpsuit was like a soggy sponge. There was no way she'd be able to get him all the way inside the boat. Instead, she worked to make sure all of his limbs were out of the water. He mumbled something incoherent, but his eyes remained closed, and his breath was slow and shallow. At least he was breathing.

"Can you sit up?" Wen asked.

No response.

She tried to prop him up against the stern, but a large wave rolled into the boat and nearly sent him back into the frothy water. She snatched up another one of her lines and, with one hand gripped tightly on the side of *Mathilde*, used the other to wind the line around the man's waist. Once he was secured, she climbed back into the boat, scrambled into its small cabin, and yanked the first-aid kit off the wall. Inside was a silver thermal insulation blanket. With that and an old wool blanket in hand, she clambered back to the stern and wrapped him up as best she could. There was still no sign of the rescue boat. If they didn't get here soon, this guy wasn't going to make it.

She considered trying to get him out of his wet clothes but thought better of it. It was windy as hell, and the air was only slightly warmer than the water.

"Think, Wen. Think."

It had been a few years, but she'd taken a first-aid class in college. *Warm fluids!* Her thermos might be old and dented, but it kept her coffee warm for hours. She scrambled back into the boat and snatched it from the cupholder. When she held it to the man's lips, his eyes drifted open, and he took a sip. That was an encouraging sign.

"Hang in there, buddy," she said. "Help will be here soon."

* * *

Wen followed the rescue boat back to town. They'd arrived in the nick of time. The man's body temperature had dropped precariously low. Once they'd moved him off *Mathilde*'s transom and into their boat, the paramedics had given him an IV with warm fluids and inserted a breathing tube to supply his lungs with warm air. His pulse was low, and he faded in and out of consciousness, but the rescue crew thought he'd pull through.

She'd quite possibly saved the man's life. That was pretty powerful. And remarkably, she hadn't panicked. A person never knew how'd they react in a situation like that. It had all happened so fast. She'd spotted the man in the water and the next thing she knew, the rescue boat was on the scene. Everything in between was a blur. The adrenaline from it all had begun to wear off and her brain was numb.

When they rounded the last island before the marina, red lights flashed across the water. An ambulance, waiting to take the man to the hospital. As they got closer to shore, Wen also spotted two police cars. She maneuvered *Mathilde* into her slip, tied her up, and walked over to greet the officers.

After she'd given them her statement, she called her father and told him what had happened.

"You should be proud of yourself, Wen," he said. "I know I am."

"Thanks, Dad."

"Like I've said a million times before, operating that mailboat is more important than simply delivering packages. As its captain, you're essential to this community, in so many ways."

The irony of his words was not lost on Wen. Although her dad didn't know it yet, she'd decided to walk away from the mailboat…walk away from her community. Was she really willing to do that? She tried to push the doubt out of her mind.

"Are you going to the hospital?" her father asked.

"Um, I thought I'd stop by later. I've still got a boatload of packages to deliver."

"After what happened, I hate the idea of you going back out on the water alone."

"I'll be okay. I'm going to go get some fresh coffee from Ruby at the café and then I'll deliver the most critical packages. Water pump parts for Yeti Island and a pharmacy delivery for Mrs. Grass. I'm not sure how desperate she is for the medications, but I know she gets lonely out on that island all alone and looks forward to my visits."

"You're a good egg," her father said.

Right after she finished visiting with Mrs. Grass on the tiny island of Zee, Wen's phone vibrated in her pocket. She smiled when she checked the screen. It was a message from Estelle. She'd be back in Coopersville tomorrow.

Wen pushed *Mathilde*'s throttle down almost as far as it would go. The river was still choppy, and the boat's bow pounded over the waves, but Wen didn't care. She pumped her hand in the air and let out a hoot and a holler.

CHAPTER EIGHT

Estelle's chest tightened when she saw *Mathilde* round the last channel marker outside the marina. She picked up her duffels and jogged toward the dock to meet the boat.

"Welcome back," Wen hollered as she eased *Mathilde* into the slip.

When their eyes met, Estelle tripped on one of the dock's cleats and nearly went headfirst into the water.

Wen scrambled to the bow of the boat. "You okay there?"

"Just a bit clumsy." Estelle lifted one of her feet. "And these are not really suitable for boating, I'm afraid."

"Ah, nothing wrong with cowboy boots."

"Apparently, when I got dressed this morning," Estelle said, "my head was not on straight. Or more aptly, I was in a New York City state of mind." She handed Wen her duffels and gestured toward shore. "I've got a cart full of groceries too."

Once they got everything loaded onto the boat, Estelle clasped onto a nearby pylon to brace herself before she stepped aboard. Wen placed a hand on her back and the gentle touch almost caused her to lose her footing again. Apparently, her attraction to Wen had not abated in the time she'd been away.

"Was the trip up here okay?" Wen asked as she took her place behind the wheel.

"Completely uneventful." Estelle tugged her hat lower on her head. "I'm just thankful to be here. For a while there, I thought I'd never escape New York." *Or more precisely, Claudia.*

As if reading her mind, Wen asked, "How did everything go down there? Is your ex-wife holding up okay?"

Estelle leaned up against the side of the boat and crossed her arms over her chest. "To be completely honest, it was an utter shit show."

"Oh, gosh, I'm sorry."

"I'll spare you the details, but my ex-wife is a mess. She caused a major scene at Ralph's—her business partner's—funeral and then had a meltdown about Illuminate, the business the two of them ran. Drama, drama, and more drama."

"Well, what do you say we get you back to Owl Island pronto," Wen said. "Sounds like a deserted island is exactly what you need right now."

"You can say that again." Estelle reached over and rested a hand on Wen's arm. "How about you, how are you holding up? I get the sense that you and your uncle were close."

Wen nodded. "It's been tough. And I just feel so sad for his kids. They're all so young. Too young to lose their father." She smiled. "Although, as far as funerals go, his was pretty drama free."

Estelle squeezed her arm and stepped back. "Well, that's good to hear."

Wen backed *Mathilde* out of the slip and pointed her toward the channel. As they sped across the water, Estelle sucked in the fresh air and let the stress from New York melt away. In the entire time she'd been away, she'd written exactly zero words, and she was eager to get back to her manuscript. Given the week she'd had, getting lost in her characters' world would be a welcome respite. Fingers crossed the creative juice gods would reappear as soon as she stepped back on the island. If they didn't, she'd be in a heap of trouble. She owed Harrison, her agent, a solid draft very soon.

When the Gage compound came into view, Estelle jumped to her feet and let out a "woot woot." It was an uncharacteristic reaction for her, but she couldn't help it. She felt like a bird who'd just been released from captivity. Before she'd left for New York, she'd cherished her time on the island, but now she'd be sure to fully relish it. Appreciate every sight and sound. Every bird singing, every sunset and every storm cloud overhead. Or perhaps more aptly, appreciate the lack of sound altogether. No honking horns, idling diesel engines, or beep-beep-beep of trucks backing up.

Estelle eyed Wen as she expertly brought *Mathilde* parallel to the dock. Although she wore a heavy coat, Estelle could visualize her taut muscles as they effortlessly spun the boat's wheel.

"Perfect landing," she said when Wen killed the engine.

"Ha, thanks," Wen said. "You get pretty good at it after you've done it a few thousand times."

Estelle picked her duffels up off the floor and tossed them ashore. Part of her wanted to spend a few quiet hours alone, but whether Wen had intended to or not, her calm, quiet demeanor had worked its magic on Estelle, and she didn't want her to leave.

After they carried everything up to the house, she said, "I picked up some homemade chicken noodle soup at the deli. Would you like to stay and have some? The least I can do is feed you after all your help."

Wen set the last grocery bag on the counter and then turned to face her. "Sure, but do you mind if I step outside to make a quick phone call first?"

"Of course not." No surprise Wen had more pressing matters than babysitting a brooding socialite. "Just come on back to the kitchen when you're done."

While she waited for Wen to make her call, Estelle busied herself with unpacking the groceries and heating the soup on the stove.

Wen stepped into the kitchen and eyed the cans and boxes of food piled on the counter. "Is there anything left at the grocery store?"

"Ha, ha. So maybe I went a little overboard, but it's not like I can run down to the corner market if I need something."

"Fair enough."

"Everything with your call go all right?" Estelle asked

Wen leaned up against the kitchen island and crossed her arms over her chest. "Yeah, I just needed to check on someone at the hospital."

"Oh, gosh, is someone in your family sick…That would be awful after your uncle just passed away."

"No, no, nobody in my family is sick. The person in the hospital is someone I just met. Well *met* probably isn't the right word. More like encountered. Suffice it to say I've had an eventful few days. Yesterday I rescued a fella who'd fallen in the water out near Yeti Island. He's still in the hospital and I called to check in on him."

Estelle covered her mouth with her hand. "That's awful. I mean, it's wonderful that you rescued him, but the water can't be much above freezing. Is he okay?"

"He was barely conscious when I found him, but yeah, it sounds like he'll make it."

"I certainly hope so," Estelle said. "Wow, you're so brave."

"I did what anyone would do."

"You're humble. I like that," Estelle said. She turned toward the stove and lifted the lid off the large stainless steel pot, sending a plume of steam rising above it. "Looks like the soup is warmed up," she said as she stirred the contents of the pot with a large ladle. She set two soup spoons on the counter, tugged two monogrammed paper napkins from a drawer, and nodded toward the kitchen table. "Would you mind setting these out… oh, and wait"—she pulled two tall glasses from the cupboard—"in case you want water."

* * *

The massive kitchen table occupied a nook under a broad bay window on the far side of the kitchen, and Wen counted twelve chairs sitting around it. She could almost hear the Gage family gathered on a warm summer night, laughing and talking.

"Do you want me to get placemats?" she asked.

"Um, sure," Estelle said. "There should be some in the hutch near the back staircase."

Once they settled at the table, Wen heard her mother's voice in her head, repeating the words she had uttered at least a thousand times. *Napkin in your lap. No slouching. No elbows on the table. No eating with your fingers. The silverware is there for a reason.* Since they were eating soup, Wen figured she wouldn't have trouble abiding by the last rule. She then watched Estelle dip her spoon into her bowl, lift it to her mouth, and consume it without even the slightest slurp. How the hell did she manage that?

Wen ladled a small amount of soup into her spoon, hoisted it to her lips, and tried to pour rather than suck the soup into her mouth. The method worked, sort of. She managed not to slurp, but warm broth trickled down her chin.

Estelle reached over and used her napkin to dab Wen's face. "Oh, no. Is it too hot?"

She wanted to crawl under the table. "No. I just apparently forgot how to eat."

Estelle set her napkin back in her lap, grabbed a hunk of bread from the basket on the table, and dunked it into her bowl. "If you ask me, this is the best way to enjoy soup."

Wen relaxed back in her chair. "I'm totally with you."

"So, aside from your daring rescue yesterday, how were things up here in the islands while I was gone?" Estelle asked.

"Fine, I guess." Wen paused before continuing, "But I did make a kind of major decision."

Estelle set down her spoon. "Oh really? What was that?"

"Do you remember me saying that I dreamed of leaving Coopersville to experience another culture?"

"Of course. And you said you were teaching yourself Spanish."

"Yes," Wen said. She told Estelle about the Spanish immersion program in Barcelona and her goal to volunteer in the Peace Corps. "Everything is lined up and I've decided to go ahead with my plans. You see, my uncle's passing put me in a bit of a bind. It forced me to make a decision I hadn't expected to have to make."

"What do you mean?"

"His death meant I had to decide between going off to Spain and staying here to run the mailboat. Until his heart attack, my uncle operated the boat. I was filling in for him while he recuperated. And now…"

"Your temporary gig has morphed into a full-time one?"

"Exactly. So now, my decision to leave Coopersville has more significant repercussions than it did before. It means the future of the mailboat is uncertain."

"Surely, there must be someone else who can run it," Estelle said.

"I wish it were that easy. I'll spare you all the details, but a gigantic amount of pressure was placed on me to put my plans on hold and take over the route. The boat's been run by a member of my family for generations, and let's just say there's a lot of resistance to passing the baton on to someone whose last name isn't Apollo."

"I thought you said your uncle had a few kids? And what about you? Do you have any siblings?"

Wen set her napkin on the table next to her bowl and leaned back in her chair. "Yes, my uncle had four children, and one of them may take over the boat one day, but right now they're all way too young. And, yes, I have two sisters. One younger and one older, but I'm the only one who lives locally and doesn't have a family."

"I see."

"My dad owns *Mathilde*, and he ran the route for years before my uncle took it over. He'd happily take it over again, but he can't. He lost both legs several years ago."

Estelle's hand flew to her mouth. "Oh my gosh. That's terrible. What happened?"

"A fluke ATV accident. He got pinned under a downed tree and help didn't arrive for hours. He was lucky that all he lost were his legs. The accident didn't break his spirit, though. He's as active as ever, zipping around town in his wheelchair. Still, as much as he loves the mailboat, there's no way he can handle it on his own."

"That must be hard on him."

"It is, or at least it was initially, but not long after the accident, he jumped into the role of Mr. Mom with both feet—his joke, not mine."

"I guess it's good he has a sense of humor about it," Estelle said. "What about your mom, what does she do?"

"She's principal of the school in town." Wen laughed. "My family is about as Coopersville as they come."

"Coopersville has a lot going for it," Estelle said. "It's beautiful up here, and the people are so welcoming. Hey, just look at me. I couldn't get out of New York fast enough to get back up to the islands."

"You must miss the city a little bit when you're up here. I mean, it's pretty sleepy in this neck of the woods, especially in the off-season."

"Sure, there are some things I miss, like being able to get delicious Indian food delivered to my door and all the art and culture, but if you're not careful, the city can hollow you out."

"I suppose that makes sense."

"So, how soon do you fly off to Barcelona?" Estelle asked.

"Not until mid-July."

"Well, I, for one, am excited for you. A great adventure awaits you." Estelle dabbed her mouth with her napkin and set it back down in her lap. "Although I bet you'll miss Coopersville more than you think you will."

"You might be right."

"The truth is, sometimes we have to leave a place to appreciate how much it means to us," Estelle said, almost wistfully.

Wen didn't doubt that was true, and for a moment she questioned her decision to leave. She glanced down at her empty soup bowl, and when she looked back up, Estelle's brown eyes were on her.

Wen gave her a soft smile. "Thanks for listening."

"It was my pleasure." Estelle gestured toward Wen's bowl. "Would you like more soup?"

"No, thanks. I'm stuffed, but it was yummy."

Estelle leaned forward in her chair and rested an elbow on the table. "I have a few friends in New York who volunteered for the Peace Corps. Let me know if you'd like to talk to them. I'm sure they'd be happy to tell you about their experiences."

"Thanks. I appreciate the offer, and I may take you up on it."

"My friend Trish didn't volunteer until she was almost forty. I don't think it's that unusual for people to join the Peace Corps later in life…" She paused as if contemplating whether she should say more. "I only mention that because, if for some reason you opt to put your plans on the back burner, it doesn't mean you can't pursue your dream at some point in the future."

"Huh," Wen said. "To be honest, I actually hadn't thought about that. I've always viewed it as a now or never type thing."

"I'm just pointing out that there are options, that's all." Estelle stood and began to clear the dishes.

In Wen's haste to help her, she jumped up and knocked her chair over backward. She scrambled to right it. "I'm so sorry. I'm such a klutz."

"Don't worry about it." Estelle smoothed a hand down Wen's back. "With all the kids running around here in the summer, it's not the first time something's been toppled over." She set the bowls by the sink and said, "I'll take care of these if you don't mind going out to stoke the fire."

"Of course. My pleasure."

"Given how cold it is this time of year, I've got to keep the stove going twenty-four-seven or else the house becomes an icebox. I'm petrified of running out of wood. Out of an abundance of caution, I had another cord delivered this morning."

"I noticed the pile of wood on the front lawn," Wen said.

"The caretaker offered to come by tomorrow to stack it, but I know he's got his hands full getting all of the cottages he oversees primped for the imminent arrival of their owners. I told him I'd do it. It'll be good exercise."

"I'd be happy to help you," Wen said. "Stacking an entire cord of wood isn't easy. Trust me, I've done it myself, many times."

"It's nice of you to offer, but I didn't ask you to stay for lunch so you could do manual labor."

"Come on, you know the old adage: many hands make light work." Wen flexed her arm. "And I am pretty strong."

"Oh, all right, if you insist."

Wen went to the living room to add a few logs to the fire and by the time she finished, Estelle was already bundled up and standing by the front door.

She handed Wen a pair of work gloves. "These will protect your hands from splinters."

"Thank you," Wen said as she accepted the gloves. "Although I can't say I've ever worn gloves to stack wood." She held up her rough, calloused hands to illustrate her point.

"I promise not to tell if you wear them. Don't want to hurt your big tough image."

Wen swatted Estelle's arm with the gloves. "I'd appreciate that. Can't have the townspeople think I'm going soft." She pulled on her jacket and followed Estelle outside.

Within ten minutes, they'd both shed their coats. Wen turned to grab a few more pieces of wood from the pile and caught Estelle staring at her.

"You weren't kidding when you said you were strong," Estelle said. "The muscles on your arms are, um, very toned." A smile crept across her face. "I was admiring them."

"Um, thanks."

"Are you blushing?" Estelle asked.

Wen's ears felt warm, so the answer was clearly yes. "Me, no, I must be flushed from stacking wood." She tried not to crack a smile but failed.

"What, nobody's ever complimented your arm muscles before?"

"Nobody as beautiful as you." Wen's mouth dropped open. It wasn't like her to be so bold. "I'm sorry, I didn't mean—"

"It's quite all right. I'm flattered."

"Uh, we should probably get back to work or we'll never get all this wood stacked."

They worked in silence, methodically gathering wood from the ground and adding it to the neat stacks they'd built. When they were almost finished, Estelle wrangled two thick logs off the pile and stumbled backward, tripping over a few pieces of wood that were scattered on the lawn. She landed with a thud on the ground and the two logs in her arms rolled away.

Wen dropped the logs in her hands and ran over to make sure she was okay.

"I'm fine," Estelle said with a laugh. "And you thought you were a klutz."

Wen squatted next to her and offered her a hand. "Sure you weren't just trying to impress me with your acrobatic moves?"

"I may have been," Estelle said as she got to her feet.

And suddenly, they were face-to-face. Neither of them moved. Wen blinked a few times and gazed into Estelle's eyes. They were as wide as saucers. The next thing she knew, her lips were on Estelle's, and it was the most wonderful thing in the world. She expected Estelle to pull back, but she didn't. Instead, her hands slid around Wen's waist and pulled her closer. They shared a few tender kisses, but neither of them moved to deepen them. Wen nearly melted right there on the grand lawn of Owl Island. The word soft did not come close to describing Estelle's lips. They were like silk. Warm and moist, but not too moist. Like everything else about Estelle, they were perfect.

She thought she heard footsteps approach, but she didn't care. It would take the jaws of life to tear her away from Estelle.

"Um, sorry to interrupt," a male voice said.

Wen whimpered when Estelle stepped back.

"Oh, hi, John." Estelle ran a hand through her hair and introduced Wen to the island's caretaker.

Wen recognized John but they'd never formally met. He was a large man with a twinkle in his eye.

"Just stopped by to make sure you were managing the wood okay." He winked. "But it appears you don't need my help after all. Looks like you've got things under control."

"Um, yes," Estelle said. "Wen was kind enough to help me."

"So I see," he said.

Estelle nodded toward the dock. "Where's your boat? I didn't hear you pull up."

"I kayaked over," he replied. "The wife's after me to get more exercise."

They said their goodbyes, and after John climbed in his kayak, Wen said, "Sorry. I shouldn't have…"

"Kissed me?"

"Yeah, that. I'm not sure what got into me."

"In case you didn't notice, I kissed you back."

"Yes, you did. Thank you."

Estelle laughed. "You're welcome."

Wen was mortified. She'd kissed Estelle Gage. Holy fucking shit. The chicken soup from the deli must have been laced with something. Nothing else could explain her bravery. It wasn't like her to go around kissing people, especially people who were way out of her league. She gathered up the last few logs on the lawn and set them on the stack nearest her. She couldn't even look at Estelle. There was no telling what she'd do if she did. *What if I try to kiss her again?*

With her gaze on the ground, she said, "I should probably get going."

Estelle touched her arm. "Are you sure?"

Eyes still fixed on the ground, Wen nodded. "Yes. I need to get back to town for something, something very important."

She mumbled a goodbye and trotted down to the dock. She wasn't one hundred percent sure she was fit to drive. It was possible she was in a state of shock.

CHAPTER NINE

Estelle sat at the wooden desk in the widow's watch and stared out over the river. The water glistened in the early afternoon sun and robins and chickadees fluttered between the barren branches of the maple trees dotting the island. Just as she was about to return to the chapter she'd been working on all morning, a boat appeared from behind an island in the distance. Could that be *Mathilde*? Estelle grabbed the binoculars off the window ledge and leapt to her feet. Her heart thumped in her chest when she brought the lenses to her eyes. It was Wen, and it looked like she was headed Estelle's way.

She ran her fingers over her lips and thought about their kiss. Wen's tender lips and the warmth of her body pressed against Estelle's own... The kiss had not been unwelcome, far from it, but it had been a bit of a surprise. There was no denying she was attracted to Wen. She'd be foolish not to be—Wen was beautiful and strong and smart and kind—but until the kiss, she hadn't known for sure if Wen was into women. Estelle had suspected she might be, but the kiss had removed all doubt. So, the next question was, where did they go from here? Did Wen want something more with her? Did she want something more with Wen?

Yes, definitely, yes.

But was she ready to get involved with someone new, someone who might be leaving for Barcelona in less than two months? A relationship with Wen, even if it was only a casual affair, would complicate things. It would be a distraction. And Estelle was here to focus on her writing, not on a sexy mailboat captain with sparkling blue eyes and soft, warm lips.

She took a deep breath and counted to ten before she ran down the narrow staircase to the kitchen. Even though the sun was out, the temperature outside hovered around forty degrees. She pulled her coat off the hook in the mudroom and tugged it on as she hurried toward the front of the house. She reached the dock just as Wen pulled up.

"Afternoon," Wen said, looking anywhere but at Estelle.

"Were you keeping an eye out for me?" she asked with a nervous laugh.

"Oh, no, I was up in the widow's watch, and I spotted you out on the water."

Wen lifted her head and smiled. She tossed Estelle her bow line and asked, "How's that working out as an office? Have you been able to get back into your writing?"

"It's working out beautifully. I've written over three thousand words today."

"That sounds like a lot."

"It is—for me, anyway. Before I left New York, I was lucky if I managed a thousand words a week."

"Is that a writer thing? To track progress based on how many words you write?"

"Among the writers that I know, yes, it's quite common."

"Huh, interesting." Wen snatched two medium-sized square boxes off the floor of the boat. "I have a couple more packages for you."

"Perhaps that's some of the hardware I ordered."

Wen flipped open a large cooler attached to the port side of the boat. "I've also got some things you ordered from the butcher."

"Fantastic, thank you." Estelle accepted the large paper bag of meat and set it on the dock. "If you don't mind waiting a moment, I've got a package to send back with you."

Wen jumped onto the dock and secured her stern line. "Don't mind at all."

"Okay, I'll run and grab it. It's just inside the boathouse."

"You need a hand?"

"Nope, but thank you." Estelle tucked a square box under each arm, trotted over to the boathouse, and emerged a few moments later with a different large, rectangular box slung over her shoulder.

Wen ran to Estelle's side. "Are you crazy? That thing is massive."

"But it's light as a feather."

Wen helped her slide the long box onto the boat. "You're right. It can't weigh more than fifteen pounds." Wen stood and faced her. "Okay, now you've got me curious. You're a writer…" Wen tapped her pointer finger against her lips. "This box is too light to be full of books, and it's too big to be a draft of your manuscript."

"Come here. I want to show you something." Estelle grabbed Wen's hand and led her over to the boathouse, stepped inside, and flicked on the light. "I'm working on that."

"Oh, my God. That's amazing." Wen walked over to the partially deconstructed woodie and ran her hand along its hull.

"It's a 1955 twenty-two-foot Chris-Craft Continental. My father spent years refurbishing it. He removed the entire interior—including the engine, fuel tank, and all the hardware and gauges—and stripped the boat down to the frame. After he rebuilt its bottom, he installed all-new mahogany planking to the rest of the boat. But unfortunately, he died before he was able to finish it." Estelle dabbed a tear from the corner of her eye and took a deep breath before she continued. "Anyway, I've picked up where he left off." She waved in the general direction of the dock. "That package I just gave you is full of the boat's cushions. They're being sent off to Maine to be re-covered."

"I had no idea restoring one of these boats was so involved," Wen said.

Estelle gave the woodie a loving pat. "Yes, it's a massive undertaking, that's for certain, and there's still a great deal of work to do, but my goal is to have it finished, or at least close to finished by the end of the summer…" Estelle almost added "before I head back to New York" but thought better of it. The last thing she wanted to do was think about leaving the island again, especially now that she and Wen had shared a kiss. A kiss she hoped would parlay into something more between the two of them. Just being in Wen's presence erased her earlier hesitancy.

Wen circled the boat and came back up beside Estelle. "Definitely let me know if you need help. Working on one of these would be really cool."

"You may regret that offer." Estelle nudged Wen with her hip. "I probably have ten more coats of varnish to apply before I get to any of the fun stuff."

"Did you say ten *more* coats?"

"I did," Estelle said. "Believe it or not, it'll probably take close to twenty coats to achieve that exquisite glossy mahogany hull woodies are known for. Once a boat has been stained, the secret is to get its surface perfectly flat, and the only way to achieve that is to apply varnish, and more varnish. With each layer, the gloss gets deeper and more uniform. When I'm finished, you'll be able to apply your makeup in front of it."

"Well, I would if I wore makeup."

Estelle ran the back of her fingers over Wen's cheek. "No need to with a face as naturally beautiful as yours."

Wen smiled her big, bright, delightful smile. "You certainly know how to make a girl blush."

Estelle was the one who was blushing. She stepped back and cleared her throat. "Um, anyway…The hardest part is going to be installing that." She pointed to a wide wooden crate in the corner of the boathouse.

"What's in there?"

"A new engine."

"Holy macaroni."

Estelle grabbed the stepladder that leaned against the wall. "You want to climb aboard?"

Wen gave her a wide-eyed stare. "Sure." She climbed up the ladder, swung her leg over the starboard side of the boat, and reached back to offer Estelle a hand.

Estelle was perfectly capable of getting into the boat on her own, but she wasn't about to pass up an opportunity to curl her hand around Wen's again. Their eyes met as Estelle stepped aboard, but Wen quickly looked away.

"I don't bite," Estelle said.

With her gaze still directed downward, Wen said, "I know, it's just, I'm sorry about the other day. About kissing you."

Estelle slipped a finger under Wen's chin and lifted it until their eyes met again. "There's no need to apologize. I'm glad you kissed me."

Wen shuffled her boots over the boat's unfinished floorboards.

"In fact," Estelle said. "I planned to ask you to go kayaking with me tomorrow. I know it's still a bit early in the season for it, but I love paddling around in the shallows of the tributary and I…"

"That sounds awesome," Wen said quietly. "I'd love to go."

Estelle's shoulders relaxed. "Great. And then maybe I can cook you dinner afterward, if you're amenable."

"Yes," Wen said with a smile. "I'm definitely amenable."

"Wonderful. It's a date then."

"I'll look forward to it."

"Me too." Estelle took Wen's hand again and squeezed it. What she really wanted to do was kiss her, but Wen still seemed a little skittish about their last kiss, and she didn't want to scare her off. Better to move back to a safe topic: the woodie. She released Wen's hand and gestured toward the grapefruit-sized holes on the boat's dashboard. "As I said, my father removed all the gauges." She looked absently around the boathouse. "A man in Michigan painstakingly refurbished them, and they're in a box around here somewhere. All I need to do is install them and get them wired."

"Oh, is that all?" Wen asked. "Guess that degree in mechanical engineering will come in handy."

"It might."

After they climbed back out of the boat, Wen pointed to two square boxes on the floor. "Are those the boxes I delivered today?"

"They are. They should contain some hardware I ordered for the Chris-Craft. When my father bought the boat, some components were missing, and if he ordered replacement parts, I haven't been able to locate them." She reached down and picked up one of the boxes but screeched and dropped it on the ground, her brain and mouth processing at the same time. "A snake!"

Wen stepped in front of her and eyed the striped snake coiled on the ground. "It's a garter snake. It won't hurt you."

Estelle wasn't so convinced. In her book, all snakes were bad. She cowered behind Wen.

"Poor little guy probably just came out of hibernation. I bet he's more scared of you than you are of him."

"I highly doubt that."

Wen grabbed a rake that leaned against the wall.

"Don't kill him."

"Don't worry, I won't hurt him. I'll scoop him up and put him outside."

"Good plan," Estelle said, stepping back to give Wen a wide berth.

After the snake had been repositioned and the rake returned to the boathouse, they both stepped outside, and Estelle squinted as her eyes adjusted to the light.

"I should probably be going," Wen said. "Your Chris-Craft is stunning. Thanks for showing it to me."

"Thank you for handling the snake." Estelle leaned forward and kissed her softly on the cheek. "You're so brave."

"Nah, there are lots of critters around here. I'm just used to them."

Estelle walked her down to the dock. "So does two o'clock sound good for kayaking? And then we can come back here for dinner."

"Perfect," Wen said.

"We've got a few kayaks in the boathouse, so no need to bring your own unless you want to."

"Okay." Wen turned to climb back aboard *Mathilde* but paused and looked back. "Oh, pardon my manners. I should have asked. Can I bring anything for dinner?"

"No need to bring anything, although, I may text you if I realize I'm missing a critical ingredient."

"Not a problem. Happy to pick up anything you need. Just let me know." Wen hopped aboard her boat and started the engine. She gave Estelle a wave goodbye as she motored out into the cove.

Estelle placed her hand on her heart as she watched her go. Yes, it was official. She had a colossal crush on Wen Apollo.

CHAPTER TEN

Wen still had to tell her parents about her decision not to take over the mailboat. It wasn't that she'd changed her mind, but she kept thinking about what Estelle had said. That volunteering for the Peace Corps was not something that was now or never, and that maybe she'd underestimated her bond to Coopersville and the people who lived there.

Ever since that conversation, she'd wavered between feeling certain and confident about her decision to go to Spain and second-guessing whether it was the right move for her right now. But she had to give her parents an answer soon. Like probably tonight. A lot hung in the balance, most critically the future of the mailboat.

When she walked into the house that evening, her mother jumped up from the kitchen table waving what looked like the Coopersville local newspaper in the air. "Have you seen the article?" she asked.

Wen kicked off her boots and set them on the mat by the back door. "What article?"

"This one." Her mother pushed the newspaper into her hand. "They're calling you heroic, a hometown hero."

"Oh, really?" She scanned the article. It identified the man she'd pulled from the water as Ray Ratchford and included a picture of her at the marina standing next to the rescue boat.

"Did you know he was one of the Ratchford boys?" her mother asked.

Wen shook her head. "No."

"You went to high school with his younger brother…What was his name?"

"Robert. He was a few years older than me. Everyone called him Robert Redford because of his striking good looks." Wen started to say something else but was interrupted by the ringing of the old chartreuse phone hanging on the kitchen wall. It was right next to her, and her mother nodded to indicate she should pick it up. "Hello. The Apollo residence."

"Wen?" a woman's voice on the other end asked.

"Yes."

"God bless you," the woman wailed into the phone. "You saved my Ray-Ray."

"Mrs. Ratchford?" Wen asked.

A man's voice echoed over the line. "Wen Apollo, you are a true hero."

"Mr. Ratchford, is that you?" He'd been Wen's peewee soccer coach, but the Ratchfords lived on the outskirts of town and she rarely saw them anymore. "How's Ray?"

A third voice spoke into the phone. "This is Robert Ratchford, Wen. We can't thank you enough. The doctor said you saved my brother's life."

"I was just in the right place at the right time," Wen said.

"You are an angel sent from heaven," Mrs. Ratchford said.

"Any idea how Ray ended up in the river?" Wen asked.

"He fell overboard," Mrs. Ratchford said. "He'd recently bought a new boat—new to him anyway—and he'd been itching to get it out on the water."

"It's a pretty small boat," Mr. Ratchford added, "and I warned him not to go out with the weather as it was, but of course he didn't listen to his old man. Sounds like the waves tossed him overboard and—"

"He's not a very good swimmer," Mrs. Ratchford cut in. "The darn boat drifted away."

"It was choppy out there that morning," Wen said.

"You're a tremendous asset to the community, young lady," Mr. Ratchford said. "Even as a little kid, I remember you were always watching out for your teammates. Always making sure everyone got a chance to play."

When Wen got off the phone, she turned to her mother. "That was the Ratchfords."

Her mother smiled. "I gathered."

"How's my hometown hero?" her father asked as he wheeled into the kitchen.

"I'm fine, Dad, thanks." She nodded toward the front of the house. "I'm going to go take a shower and get out of these clothes."

"You better be quick about it," her father called after her. "The lasagna will be ready in ten minutes, and I don't want it getting cold."

As soon as Wen climbed into the shower, tears rolled down her cheeks and the decision about the mailboat became crystal clear. She had to stay in Coopersville, at least for the time being. The outside world wasn't going anywhere. It would be there for her to explore when she was ready.

* * *

"I've made a decision about the boat," Wen announced after they sat down for dinner.

Her father looked up from the heap of lasagna on his plate. "And?"

"I'll take it over, at least through the fall," she said. "We can reassess come winter."

"That seems reasonable," her mother said.

Her father nodded. "Thank you, Wen. I know this means you'll have to drop out of that program in Barcelona."

"Yes, but that's okay," she said. "There'll be another one like it. Right now, it's more important for me to step up and take over the route." Although it wasn't the decision she'd settled on a few days earlier, she knew it was the right one.

Her father reached over and patted Wen's hand. "You're going to stay in Coopersville and captain *Mathilde*," he said with a smile.

"At least through the fall," she reminded him.

He nodded and dug his fork into his meal.

After dinner, the three of them assembled in her father's study to review all the paperwork and files associated with the boat.

Wen grabbed one of the towering stacks of paper from her father's desk and flipped through pages and pages with numbers and notes scribbled on them. A pile of gas receipts fluttered out and landed in her lap.

"As the newly crowned captain of *Mathilde*," she said, "my first order of business will be to get all of this into some sort of spreadsheet."

"I think that would be wise," her mother said. "It'll make it much easier to track everything."

Two hours into going through the records, her father pulled a manila folder out of the top drawer of his desk.

"I know you've only agreed to take over the boat on a temporary basis," he said as he flipped open the folder, "but I want to officially transfer ownership over to you." He pulled a thick piece of paper out of the folder and held it up. It had a raised seal in the center and the words *New York State* printed at the top. "This is the title for *Mathilde*. I've signed it over to you."

Wen scrunched her hands into tight balls and stared down at the document. "I, uh…maybe we should wait until…"

"Too late." He patted her on the shoulder. "If you decide not to take it over long term, we'll figure something out, don't worry. But going forward, you'll be responsible for all the decisions regarding *Mathilde*. Over the last few months, you've demonstrated that you're more than capable of running the operation."

"We hope this empowers you, Wen," her mother said. "That it makes you feel more invested in the boat and also freer to make the changes you deem necessary."

Wen shook her head. "But I only told you tonight that I wasn't going to Barcelona. How did you know that I—"

"We didn't know for sure," her father said. "But no matter what your future holds, we want the boat to be yours. You know how important it is to me that it stay in the Apollo family."

"I do," Wen said. She kneaded the base of her neck. "Um, thanks for trusting me."

"If necessary, we'll help you financially," her mother said.

Her father nodded in agreement and added, "Although hopefully the delivery route will generate sufficient income to cover all the boat's expenses and then some."

Based on Wen's experience thus far, he was right.

Her father yawned. "I think I'm going to hit the hay."

"Ditto," her mother said.

They left Wen alone in her father's office. She sat there for a long time and tried to absorb what had just transpired. Eventually, she picked up a big stack of papers, logged onto the computer, and opened a blank spreadsheet.

"Guess I better get busy," she muttered.

CHAPTER ELEVEN

Estelle paddled up alongside Wen once they reached the mouth of the tributary. The trees and shrubs along the bank were still bare but the shallow water teemed with tiny silver fish. She dipped her hand below the surface and tried to catch one, but they were too quick.

Wen dipped her hand into the water too. "Still a bit chilly for a swim."

"Ha," Estelle said. "Yeah, just a bit."

"It's so beautiful back in here though." Wen tapped one of the smooth green lily pads with her paddle. "Especially when all the white water lilies bloom."

"Oh, yes, aren't the flowers magical?"

"They sure are, although we've got a few more months to wait. They don't usually flower until late June or early July."

"A shame you'll miss them this year," Estelle said.

"What do you mean?"

"Won't you be off in Barcelona by then?"

"Um, actually, no. I had a change of heart. I plan to stay here this summer and operate the boat."

"Wow," Estelle said. "That's big."

"It is, but I feel good about the decision, and it certainly makes my parents happy, especially my father. The Peace Corps will just have to wait."

"For what it's worth, I think you made the right call," Estelle said.

"You do?"

"Yes. When we were talking the other day about your decision to stay or go, I sensed a reluctance to leave Coopersville, one that maybe you hadn't even acknowledged. And although you dream of seeing the world, my impression is that it's something you'd like to do, rather than something you long to do, if that makes sense."

"It does," Wen said. "Because the responsibility of the mailboat fell to me, I automatically viewed it as a burden, and I conjured resentment in response, resentment that I didn't really feel, at least not to the level I thought I did." She let out a big sigh and guided her kayak around a boulder in the middle of the tributary.

Estelle cringed internally. "I didn't mean to stick my nose in your personal business…"

Wen smiled over at her. "It helped to talk it through with you. Thank you." She glided through a dense patch of lily pads. "Anyway, enough about me. I want to hear more about your writing. What sort of things do you write?"

"Mostly mystery, high suspense."

"The other day, you said something about having an agent. Does that mean you've already published some stuff?"

"Yes, I've published two books thus far. The one currently working on will be my third."

"Are you writing a series?" Wen asked.

"No, each book is quite different from the others. The one I'm working on now is about a guy who hijacks a plane with millions of dollars in its cargo hold and crashes it in a dense forest."

"Oooh, that sounds fascinating. Does he survive the crash?"

"Yes. He crashes the plane intentionally. It's all part of his elaborate plan. Thing is, no one else knows whether he survives or not. Law enforcement surrounds the general area where he went down, but it's very remote, so tracking him down is far from easy."

"Does the robber guy get past them? Does he get out of the woods?"

Estelle smiled, delighted that Wen was taking an interest in her story. "Yes, he gets out. He has to, otherwise the rest of the plot goes down the tubes. Although, I must admit, I'm struggling a bit with how he pulls it off. I thought I had it worked out, but now I'm not so sure."

"How do you envision him sneaking out?"

"He builds a raft that looks like a big log, climbs inside, and floats down the river and out of the forest, right past the police perimeter."

"Huh, interesting…" Wen paddled around a bend before she responded. "I think that works, but how about this…What if he builds the raft, tosses in a little bit of the stolen money, maybe an article of his clothes, and sends it down the river?"

"You mean like a decoy?"

"Yes. To make law enforcement think he's no longer in the woods…make them think he drowned."

Estelle splashed water up with her paddle. "That's way better. You're brilliant, Wen. Figuring out the twists and turns is half the fun in writing a suspense, and it really helps to talk it all out with someone else."

* * *

Wen stripped off the layers she'd worn kayaking, dabbed herself with a warm washcloth, and pulled a clean long-sleeve T-shirt and a pair of jeans from her duffel bag. She had one leg in her pants when her phone rang, and she hopped over to snatch it off the corner of the sink.

"Hey, Rube. What's up?"

"Where are you?"

"At Estelle's house. We just got back from kayaking and I—"

"OMG, you know that hot woman who works at the hardware store in town?"

Wen laughed. "Of course. You're always inventing reasons to go there and see her…Last week it was a new staple gun, the week before…"

"She asked me out."

"What? That's awesome. When?"

"Tonight. Dinner at that new Italian place. I'm freaking out."

"Just be yourself. You got this."

"Oh, shit. I've gotta go. I need to leave soon, and I still have no idea what I'm going to wear."

"I can't wait to hear all about it. Have fun!"

Wen ended the call and finished getting dressed. She tidied up the bathroom, threw her duffel over her shoulder, and went in search of Estelle.

"All freshened up?" Estelle asked when she stepped into the kitchen.

"Yep. It's so warm in here. It feels wonderful." Wen rounded the kitchen island and saw why. A fire burned in the large cobblestone fireplace to the right of the pantry. Although the kitchen had obviously been updated recently, it was nice to see that the Gage family had left remnants of the original house intact.

"Spaghetti and meatballs okay for dinner?" Estelle asked.

"Yum. One of my all-time favorite meals."

"Thank goodness because I only know how to cook two things. Spaghetti and meatballs or grilled chicken and potatoes."

"So, what, you alternate between the two meals? Spaghetti Monday, Chicken Tuesday, Spaghetti Wednesday…"

"Very funny. I do eat other things. Occasionally, I have peanut butter and jelly sandwiches, and cheese and crackers."

Wen set her bag on a stool, unzipped it, and held up a brown paper bag. "For you. A baguette from my friend Ruby's café." She pulled a small glass bottle out of a pocket on the side of her duffel. "And this is some hot sauce my father made."

"That was sweet of you, thank you." Estelle took the bag of bread and set it on the counter and turned the glass bottle in her hand. "Apollo's Fiery Sauce."

"Apollo, that's my last name," Wen said.

Estelle peered up from the bottle and gave her a smile. "I know that." She put her hand on her hip. "What kind of woman do you think I am? Do you think I run around kissing people whose last names I don't even know?"

"I didn't mean to suggest…I just didn't want to assume—"

"You're cute when you get flustered."

Wen felt the blood rush to her face. "Uh, thanks, I guess."

Estelle set the bottle of hot sauce down. "I can't wait to try it. Please thank your father for me."

"I will. He was so excited when I asked if I could bring you a bottle. He takes great pride in his concoctions."

"So he makes more than hot sauce?"

"Oh, yeah, he makes and cans lots of things. Salsa, dill pickles, BBQ sauce, and all sorts of other stuff."

"Yum, I love pickles"—Estelle smacked her lips—"and BBQ." She tugged open the door to the fridge. "Would you like anything to drink? Beer, wine, a cocktail of some sort? Or perhaps a juice box? I noticed a few in the pantry, although I can't promise they aren't expired."

"I didn't think those things ever expired, but, um, a beer would be great, thanks."

Estelle popped a beer for Wen and poured herself a glass of red wine.

"What kind of wine is that?" Wen asked.

"Nebbiolo."

"That's Italian, right?"

"Yes. It's my favorite wine. Thankfully there are a few bottles in the wine cellar left over from last summer."

"Have you ever been to Italy?"

Estelle added a dash of something to the simmering pot of sauce on the stove and gave it a stir. "Yes, many times. It's a beautiful country."

"Lucky you."

"I'm very fortunate. My father traveled a great deal for business and often took me and one or two of my siblings along with him."

"How long ago did your dad pass away?"

"It'll be five years this summer." Estelle filled a large pot with water from the stainless steel faucet mounted over the stove.

"I bet you miss him. I can't even imagine what it would be like to lose my father."

Estelle put a lid on the pot and turned to face her. "Yes, I miss him terribly. He was kind and charming and funny. Everything my mother is not." She paused for a moment. "Although, I will give my mother credit for one thing. After my father died, she encouraged me to pursue my lifelong dream of becoming a writer. When my father was alive, my siblings and I were all expected to work for the foundation—my family has a foundation, the Gage Family Foundation."

"Yes, I've heard of it."

"The foundation meant everything to my father, and rightly so. It does phenomenal work, primarily working with communities in the US and across the globe to combat the impacts of climate change. Don't get me wrong, working for the foundation was immensely rewarding."

"It must have been. I've read about its support for grassroots efforts in Sub-Saharan Africa."

"Yes," Estelle said. "As I'm sure you are aware, Africa disproportionately feels the impacts of climate change despite contributing the least to global warming."

Wen nodded. "Did you get many opportunities to travel there?"

"Yes. I spent a lot of time in that region working alongside some of the most remarkable people I've ever encountered. People with incredible grit and spirit, a spirit that I cannot adequately describe with words."

"Wow, I can't even imagine how amazing that must have been."

"It was, which is why I'll come off as a spoiled brat when I tell you I partially walked away from the foundation after my father died. I'm still involved, but in a reduced capacity, to allow me time to do what I've always yearned to do: write. I've only been back to Africa once since he passed away, although I do plan to go again soon."

"I don't think you're a spoiled brat." Wen leaned on the counter and rested her chin on her hand. "It's a bit ironic, actually. In some ways, you and I are in the same boat—pardon the pun—because I was in a similar position with the mailboat. A family obligation prevented me from pursuing my dreams, or at least forced me to put them on hold."

Estelle took a long sip of wine. "The difference is, you opted to stay and do what people expected of you. I didn't."

"True, but I haven't committed to take the boat over for the long run. And if I didn't stick around to run it this summer, it might have left a lot of people high and dry. I don't mean to be harsh, but when you reduced your involvement with the foundation, I bet there were plenty of others who were able to step in. I mean, it's not like the people the foundation helped were directly impacted."

"I suppose you have a point. Still, what you're doing is admirable." Estelle turned back to the stove, added a fistful of pasta to the now boiling water, and set the timer on the stove. "Dinner should be ready soon. Do you mind grabbing the plates off the table?"

Wen shifted her gaze to the far end of the kitchen. Two places were set at one end of the long wooden dining table that lined the back wall. "Sure. No problem."

When she reached down to grab the blue pottery plates, she smiled at the care Estelle had taken in setting the table. A full set of shiny silverware sat upon crisply pressed dark green linen napkins. The round placemats were each adorned with a pair of cardinals, and a set of lighthouse-shaped salt and pepper shakers sat next to what looked like a crock of butter. Before moving back toward the stove, she once again eyed the twelve chairs around the table.

"This house is gigantic and all, but are there really twelve of you here all at one time?" she asked.

"Oftentimes, yes," Estelle said. "The whole Gage clan descends on this place at one point or another during the summer."

After dinner, Estelle wandered over to the mirrored bar in the wide hallway right outside the kitchen. "May I interest you in a splash of whiskey? I've been waiting for the opportunity to open the bottle of Redbreast, and tonight seems like the perfect time."

Wen hadn't the foggiest idea what Redbreast was, but she tried to play it cool. "Yes, please."

She watched as Estelle used little claw tongs to place ice cubes into two crystal rocks glasses and added a healthy pour to each. Estelle replaced the cork on the bottle and carefully set it back in its spot on the shelf.

She handed Wen one of the drinks. "Let's take this up to the widow's watch."

As they made their way toward the back stairs, Estelle snagged a thick wool blanket off the back of one of the kitchen chairs, and when they reached the glass-enclosed room at the top of the house, she wound a portion of it over her shoulders and tugged Wen in next to her.

Wen set her drink on the windowsill, pulled the blanket up over her own shoulders, and nestled closer to Estelle.

"This is nice," she whispered. "You're warm and you smell good."

Estelle snaked an arm around Wen's waist. "You are too."

Wen wanted to kiss her so badly, but she'd made the first move the last time, and she didn't want to come off as too aggressive. Instead, she stared out at the river. The light of the full moon reflected off the water, and a cargo ship crept through the channel in the distance. If not for the faint white light on its bow, she might not have noticed it.

Estelle picked up her glass and took a small sip. Wen did the same. The whiskey caused her to cough and she choked the liquid down.

"This Redbreast is great," she rasped.

"Are you sure?" Estelle asked with a laugh.

"Yes, it tastes pretty good. Just stronger than I expected. To be honest, I've never had whiskey before."

"I suppose it's an acquired taste. Don't feel like you have to finish it if you don't want to."

"I'll try a few more sips." She hoped the stuff wasn't like five hundred dollars a bottle.

Estelle used her glass to gesture toward the window. "It's a beautiful evening, isn't it?"

"It sure is."

"It must be difficult to crew on one of those cargo ships. Being away from home for such long stretches of time and living in such tight quarters."

Wen leaned into Estelle. "Tight quarters aren't always a bad thing."

"Good point." Estelle took one more slug of her whiskey, set it down, and reached for Wen's hand.

There was just enough light for Wen to make out the features of her face and the moon reflecting off her dark brown eyes.

Estelle turned and snaked her arms around Wen's waist, bringing their faces inches apart. "I really like you, Wen."

"I really like—" The words caught in Wen's throat. She tried again. "I really like you too, Estelle, a lot."

Estelle used her thumb to slowly trace Wen's lips. She cupped both cheeks, and when her hands slid into Wen's hair, Wen instinctively closed her eyes.

The first kiss was featherlight, teasing almost. Estelle brushed her lips over Wen's and then retreated. The peach fuzz of her cheek caressed Wen's face and her lips moved to nibble on Wen's neck, her collarbone, and that sensitive spot right below her ear before once again seeking out her mouth. With her eyes still closed, Wen parted her lips. This kiss was slow and tenuous. Estelle's tongue circled Wen's lips before dipping inside her mouth. Wen deepened the kiss and pressed Estelle back against the window. Estelle's hand scratched down her back and settled on her ass.

Estelle paused and whispered, "Will you stay?"

Wen stiffened. The bravado she'd had a moment before evaporated into thin air.

Apparently sensing her hesitation, Estelle took a step back. "I'm sorry. We can slow down and call it a night if you want. I didn't mean—"

"It's okay. I'm just feeling a little overwhelmed is all. Being here with you. Kissing you. Sorry, I'm a small-town dork."

Estelle kissed her softly on the lips. "You're charming, that's what you are. Being with you feels good."

Her words gave Wen a small boost of confidence. "I'd love to stay." She bowed her head slightly. "But, and this is super embarrassing, I have to text my parents to let them know. They'll worry if I don't come home."

"That's not embarrassing." Estelle ran a hand down Wen's arm. "It's endearing."

Wen tugged her phone from her back pocket and typed a message as quickly as she could. Spelling errors be damned. Her parents would get the gist. *Spwndimg nite on owl iland.*

When she finished, Estelle took her hand and led her back down the stairs. Only this time, instead of going all the way down to the kitchen, they stopped on the second floor. The wooden floorboards creaked as they crossed toward the front of the house and stepped into a large bedroom.

CHAPTER TWELVE

Estelle's urge to rip Wen's clothes off was very strong. But she wanted to respect Wen's feelings and take things slow, or as slow as two people who were about to fall into bed together could. And it wasn't only that. Although the two women had not known each other long, Estelle already had feelings that were probably stronger than they should be, and she wanted their first time together to be special.

The outside floodlight cast a soft glow over the room, and silhouettes of their bodies floated across the wall.

She ran her fingers over Wen's cheek, and down along the muscles of her neck. "Are you okay?"

Wen nodded and circled Estelle's waist with her strong arms.

Their eyes locked briefly, and Estelle's breath caught in her throat. She slid her hands up Wen's back and pulled their bodies tight together. *Slow*, she reminded herself.

Wen's lips crushed into hers. The heat built between Estelle's legs as their mouths moved together. She gasped when Wen's tongue sought out hers.

Wen pulled back. "I'm sorry."

"Don't apologize, that was a gasp of pleasure."

"Oh."

Estelle brought their lips back together and kissed Wen with a passion she had not known she possessed. Their bodies melted into one and they fell together onto the bed. She pushed a few strands of Wen's long blond hair from her face and said, "You are strikingly beautiful."

Wen's eyes fluttered shut. "Thank you."

Estelle sat up and straddled Wen. With as much patience as she could muster, she slipped the buttons on Wen's heavy flannel shirt from their holes. After she released the last one, she spread open the shirt and, with her nose hovering just above Wen's collarbone, took in her scent. Lavender with a trace of motor oil, an oddly intoxicating combination. Underneath her flannel, the butch boat captain was surprisingly feminine. A snug white cotton T-shirt hugged her full, round breasts and the curves of her waist.

Estelle drew her fingers over Wen's chest and inched toward the waistband of her pants. The muscles in Wen's stomach tautened under her touch. Estelle bent down to kiss her again. Without breaking the kiss, Wen rolled them over so that she was on top. They were both panting when they finally came up for air.

"I can say unequivocally, I have never ever been kissed like that," Wen said. "If that's any indication of what's to come, I may be in trouble." She shrugged out of her flannel shirt and tossed it aside. "Pardon my French, but I'm on fucking fire."

Estelle had to agree. The kiss had been pretty out of this world. She stroked one of Wen's strong arms. "You, Wen Apollo, are excellent inspiration." And if she wasn't careful, this woman would steal her heart.

"And you, Estelle Gage, are wearing entirely too many clothes."

Estelle pulled her sweater off. "Better?"

Wen shook her head. She reached down and plucked open the buttons on Estelle's blouse one by one, her movements deliberate and painstakingly slow.

"Faster," Estelle whispered. "I want to feel your hands on me."

Wen complied. She yanked the last button free and pushed Estelle's blouse open. Her fingers traced Estelle's collarbone, floated over the black silk of her bra, and moved down along her abdomen before making their way back up to cup her breasts. Estelle arched her back and Wen took the opportunity to reach back and unlatch her bra. Her finger circled each of Estelle's nipples before Wen bent down to caress them with her tongue.

The pulse in Estelle's clit grew more intense and she wriggled beneath Wen. A full-on three-alarm fire raged through her entire body.

Wen moved above her, breath warm on Estelle's neck. Their mouths came together for another searing kiss and Wen's hand slid down between Estelle's legs. It moved hard and slow, pausing briefly to fumble with the buttons on her jeans before gliding over her silk panties.

"My, my, aren't you wet," Wen whispered into her ear.

"I'm about to explode," she said through gritted teeth.

Wen gave her a wicked grin. She helped Estelle shimmy out of her pants and shed her panties before reaching up to peel off her own T-shirt and bra. Gentle fingers slipped between Estelle's folds and caressed her rhythmically.

"There," Estelle cried. "Oh, my, God. That feels so fucking good. Don't stop."

Wen took one of Estelle's nipples into her mouth while her fingers continued to work their magic.

Blood rushed to Estelle's core. She pinched her eyes shut and felt certain her body levitated over the bed. Every muscle tightened and her breathing slowed. She cried out as the orgasm crashed through her. It lingered, causing her body to tremble.

She opened her eyes and squinted up at Wen. "It's possible I just died and went to heaven."

"I sure hope not because I'm not done with you."

Estelle covered both of Wen's breasts with her hands. "Your boobs. They're big."

"I hope that's a good thing?"

"Oh, it's a very good thing indeed. Under your baggy flannel, it was hard to tell…" Estelle buried her face in the valley between Wen's breasts. "They're so warm and soft." She drew circles around Wen's nipples. "And now erect." She cupped Wen's breasts again. "They feel wonderful in my hands."

"Your hands feel wonderful on them."

"I bet they taste good too." Estelle rolled Wen over on her back and attacked her nipples with her mouth. "Hmmm," she mumbled. "I was right."

She moved down Wen's torso, kissing her warm, moist skin as she went. When she reached the top of Wen's jeans, she tore open the button and tugged down the zipper. Within an instant, the pants joined the heap of clothes at the end of the bed. Estelle swiped her fingers over Wen's wet mound, eliciting a moan. She followed with her tongue, riding Wen until she rose up toward her and collapsed back onto the bed.

"Feel free to invite me to dinner anytime," Wen said, her breathing labored. "I love what you serve for dessert."

* * *

A dazzling pink and purple sky greeted Wen the next morning, and a warm body was nestled up behind her. She let out a long, contented sigh and the warm body shifted slightly.

"Morning," Estelle whispered. She draped an arm over Wen and kissed the back of her head.

The night with Estelle had been amazing, beyond amazing. Still, as the two of them had drifted off to sleep in the wee hours of the morning, anxiety had niggled its way into Wen's brain. What if Estelle regretted taking her to bed? What if she regretted asking her to stay the night? The soft kisses currently being peppered on her bare shoulder did wonders to ease those concerns.

"Morning," she whispered back.

Estelle snuggled up even closer and nuzzled her face into Wen's neck. "Thank you for a wonderful evening."

"I'm the one who should be thanking you." Wen shifted to face Estelle, and they laid there, just staring into each other's eyes. Butterflies took flight in Wen's stomach. Uh-oh. It was way too soon for that. She broke eye contact and pulled Estelle into her arms.

They lay together silently for a long time until Estelle said, "Do you hear that?"

"I do. Loons."

"Yes." Estelle rolled back toward her pillow and propped her head on her hand. "It's the first I've heard them this season."

"Me too." Wen cupped a hand around her ear. "A lot of people think the loon's call is eerie, and I suppose it is, but I think it's the most beautiful sound on the river."

"I couldn't agree more, but isn't it a tad early for them to be in the islands?" Estelle slipped out of bed and padded over to the window. Her long brown hair was tousled as if, fittingly, she'd spent the night having passionate sex.

Wen struggled to recall what day it was, or shit, even what month. A serious post-incredible-sex haze hung over her brain, and the sight of Estelle's naked body in the early morning light only amped up her fog. Her small round butt cheeks and the suntanned skin on her long, lean back. Wonderful soft skin that Wen's hands had roamed for hours the night before…

"Um, I think the loons usually start to appear late April or early May…" She sat up in the bed and tugged the crisp white sheet around her. "Every year, it's so special to hear the first wail of a loon or to spot the first brilliant orange oriole of the season. It always puts a spring in my step."

"Good one. A spring in your step. Get it?"

"Ha, yeah. Those first signs of spring put a spring in my step." Wen slapped her forehead. "Someone kept me up way past my bedtime and I've apparently lost the ability to formulate a coherent sentence."

Estelle gave her a sympathetic smile and walked back toward the bed. She leaned down to kiss Wen on the lips, stood up, and turned toward the door.

"Where are you going?"

"I'm going to hit the loo—I've got this obsession about brushing my teeth—then I'll go down and make us some coffee."

"Ten-four." Wen watched her behind as she left the room. *Hot damn. What a beautiful day in the neighborhood.*

After she heard Estelle descend the creaky back staircase that led down to the kitchen, she climbed out of bed, slid on her T-shirt, and made her way to the bathroom. A tube of toothpaste sat on the edge of the sink, and she used her finger to brush her teeth. After she freshened up, she clambered back under the soft, high-thread count sheets.

Estelle came back a few moments later with two steaming mugs. Somewhere along the way she'd also acquired a fuzzy pink robe.

Wen pouted.

"What's wrong?" Estelle asked.

"When you left, you were naked, and I was kinda hoping you'd come back the same way."

"Sorry, I found this robe in the laundry room and I thought it prudent to put it on. I always worry John, the caretaker, is lurking around somewhere. Not in a creepy way. He's got a lot to do to get the house and the grounds primed for my mother's arrival next month."

They sat in bed sipping their coffee and staring out at the river. The sun crept higher and the birds sang in the trees and swooped in the sky. Wen pushed away thoughts of the mailboat and the mound of packages likely awaiting her at the marina. Sitting in bed with Estelle all day sounded way more appealing than motoring around the islands making deliveries.

"Penny for your thoughts," Estelle said.

"I was just thinking how nice this is, being here with you."

"Funny, I had the same thought."

Wen shook her head in disbelief. Was she really in Estelle Gage's bed? Had she really spent the night making love to the woman she'd lusted after for years? "I have to admit something."

"Oh, no. Don't tell me, you're married."

Wen laughed. "God no. Nothing like that." She set her coffee mug on the bedside table and turned to face Estelle. "I've had a crush on you for years."

Estelle's cheeks reddened. "You have?"

"Uh-huh. My friend Ruby has always kidded me about it. Whenever I saw you in town, I'd melt into a puddle."

"How come you never came up and said hello?"

"Are you freakin' kidding me?" she asked. "Just stroll up to Estelle Gage and introduce myself? Yeah, right. Even if I'd had the guts, which I most certainly did not, I never would have done it because I knew you were waaaay out of my league." Hell, she was still convinced of that.

"That's absolute rubbish, Wen." Estelle reached for her hand. "You're kind and thoughtful, not to mention extremely attractive. If anything, you're out of my league. These few weeks, spending time with you, have been incredible." She squeezed Wen's hand. "And I hope last night was the first of many, many nights we'll spend together. Not just in bed, although more time in bed would certainly be good, but talking and laughing together."

"I'm down with that," Wen said. "More time together both vertically and horizontally."

Estelle's phone vibrated on her nightstand. She peeked at it. "Shit, that's my agent."

"I can step out of the room if you need to take the call."

"No, no, I'll call him back, but I probably should get up and do some writing."

Wen scrambled to her feet, worried she'd overstayed her welcome. "I should probably be going anyway."

Estelle rounded the bed, circled her arms around Wen's waist, and kissed her softly on the lips. "When can I see you again?"

Soon, very soon. She shrugged. "Whenever."

"Would tomorrow night be too soon?"

Hell no. "Sure, that'll work."

CHAPTER THIRTEEN

Wen stared into her beer. "I'm, like, crazy into her...The night we spent together was, I don't know—"

"Magical?" Ruby asked with a smirk.

Wen rolled her eyes. Magical did pretty much describe the night she and Estelle had spent together, but Wen wasn't about to get all dreamy about it, especially not while she sat in the middle of a crowded bar. Earlier that day when she'd been out on the water making deliveries, she'd thought of little else aside from Estelle. The feel of tender lips against hers, the sensation of their bodies pressed together...

But now it was time to get real. "Ain't no way a woman like that will ever go for me. Not in a million years."

"Sounds to me like she already has," Ruby replied.

"Sure, up here in the remote islands, I'm probably handy to have around. Estelle's all alone in that big house, and she has needs...makes sense she'd jump my bones. It's not like she has a lot of other options, at least not until the rest of the summer folk start to arrive next month." In truth, Wen didn't fully believe what she'd said. She wasn't wholly convinced that their night together had just been a roll in the hay for Estelle, that she'd taken Wen to bed solely to scratch an itch. There'd been a tenderness between them, hadn't there? And that morning in bed, the way Estelle had nestled up against her and peppered Wen with kisses. Casual lovers didn't do that, did they?

"You're full of shit," Ruby said. She squeezed Wen's bicep. "You're the bomb. All tough and tomboy but gentle as a sheep."

Wen rolled her eyes again.

"I mean it, Wen. Not only do you have an amazing body, but you're a knockout. That golden blond hair and those piercing blue eyes. Half the boys in this town were heartbroken when you declared that you preferred the ladies."

Wen chuckled at the memory. She had in fact made such a declaration, Ellen DeGeneres style, on the band's mic, at her junior prom. Everyone kept asking her why she'd worn crisp black pants and a tuxedo shirt instead of a dress. Finally, she'd had enough. She climbed up on stage and stated that she had a public service announcement: "I hate dresses and wouldn't be caught dead in one." The crowd laughed and it gave her a boost of confidence. Before she handed the mic back to the lead singer, she added, "And while I have your attention, I'll confirm that the rumors are true. I prefer the ladies."

She still couldn't believe she'd done it. It was so not her style to do something so brazen and rash, but it had set the record straight, that was for sure, and it had also landed her a date with Lily, the captain of the girls' soccer team. Their relationship hadn't lasted long, but Lily was a fantastic kisser and she'd taught Wen a thing or two.

"When are you going to see her again?" Ruby asked.

"See who?"

Now it was Ruby's turn to roll her eyes. "Duh, Estelle Gage, you dumbass."

Wen bit back a smile when she responded. "Tomorrow night. For dinner at her place again."

"And maybe a little more sexy time?"

Wen felt the blood rush to her face. "Maybe, but like I said, I need to be careful. I can't let myself fall for her. A beautiful, wealthy, smart woman like Estelle can have any woman she wants. This thing with her is a temporary, friends with benefits type deal. If I can remember that, I'll be okay."

Ruby waved her off. "You said Estelle is an author, right?"

"Yeah, she writes mystery and suspense, stuff like that."

"Did you ask Ursula about her? Maybe she has one of Estelle's books in the store."

"No, not yet," Wen said. "But I did Google her. The search turned up a few short stories and two longer pieces that she wrote back in college, but that's it. She mentioned that she's published a couple of books already so she must have been referencing that older stuff? She's got an agent now though, so her current project might be her big breakout piece."

"I've got an idea." Ruby patted the bar. "Why don't you invite her here?"

"To the Igloo?"

"Yeah."

"Are you nuts? This is a townie bar."

"So what," Ruby said. "If you want my two cents, you need to stop making assumptions about Estelle. Just because she's a Gage doesn't mean she's stuck-up. Who knows, maybe she'll surprise you. From what you've told me so far, the woman has treated you with nothing but kindness and respect. She's welcomed you into her home"—Ruby snickered—"and her bed. We townies all complain that the summer folk stereotype us. Think we're a bunch of redneck idiots. But what you're doing, speculating that Estelle won't want to come here without even asking her, is just as bad."

Wen stared back down into her glass. "I suppose you have a point."

"I have a damn good point, and shit, it's obvious you like the woman."

Wen nodded. "I do, big time."

"All righty then. I can't wait to meet her." Ruby paused to take a sip of her beer. "Oh, and I meant to tell you, speaking of Ursula, I ran into her the other day. You know how she's got that little apartment over her bookstore?"

"Yeah."

"Apparently, the tenant she had lined up for the summer backed out at the last minute. Maybe you should see about renting the place."

"Huh, maybe I will. I've been dragging my feet about moving out of my parents' house, mostly because of money, and also because I thought I was going to Spain, but now that might be a good idea."

Ruby nudged Wen with her shoulder. "The apartment might be useful, you know, if you want to invite Estelle over."

* * *

Estelle added a fresh bag of peppermint tea to her mug and picked up the electric kettle from the window ledge in the widow's walk to pour herself more hot water. While she waited for the tea to steep, she stared out the window at the setting sun. It was nearly seven p.m. and her stomach growled with hunger, but she'd written a meager eight hundred words the entire day, and if she was ever going to get this manuscript done, she had to abide by her new pledge: no dinner, or wine for that matter, until she managed at least two thousand words for the day. But how the hell was she supposed to write when she couldn't get a certain strapping mailboat captain out of her head? Everything about Wen thrilled her and she wanted to be with her all the time.

They came from such different worlds. But did that really matter? They had a connection, one that differed so much from…from anything she'd ever experienced before. Wasn't that what was important? There was…she struggled for the word…an intimacy. Yes, an intimacy, an unspoken closeness, that she and Wen shared, one that was hard to put into words and one that Estelle had never quite had with another human being. Wen seemed to be able to read her thoughts. She knew just where to touch Estelle, and being around her made Estelle feel safe and, as cheesy as it sounded, special. One smile from Wen could brighten Estelle's whole day. Something glorious and unfamiliar had been roused inside of her, something akin to the wonder of a child, too often squashed by the cynicism of life, and rarely reignited. But that's how Estelle felt now. Full of wonder and excitement.

Of course, she'd come to Owl Island in the off-season not only to work on her book, but also to rediscover who she was, to get in touch with her inner being. With Claudia, she'd given up so much of what mattered to her. Her therapist's words ran through her mind. "Before you can give yourself over to another human being, it is essential you become reacquainted with who you are and remind yourself what makes you happy." He'd been right. That's why she paid him the big bucks, after all. But had she ever really known who she was? Was her journey of self-discovery more an unearthing as opposed to a reacquaintance?

Throughout her life, Estelle had rarely been single. She'd always been popular and had bounced from relationship to relationship. First with boys and then with girls, and as she grew older, eventually with women. Some relationships had lasted longer than others, and some had been better than others, but they all had one constant: Estelle let the relationship partially define who she was. With Claudia, however, it had reached a whole new stratosphere. As the years went by, Claudia became needier and more demanding, and Estelle became increasingly willing to meet her every need, even when it meant giving up things that were central to her. She'd given all she had to their marriage, and it had taken an emotional toll.

Estelle did not doubt she had the ability to love, she knew she did. She'd been deeply in love, or at least she thought she had been, with a woman or two along the way. She never would have married Claudia if she hadn't been in love with her. The question was, was it too soon to be falling into another relationship? Estelle had promised herself she'd try the single thing for a while. That's why coming up to the island had seemed like such a fantastic idea. Ah, the best laid plans...

Perhaps it was premature to call what was going on between her and Wen a relationship. Hell if Estelle knew. What she did know was, she needed to stop obsessing about the woman and get some writing done.

She curled her hands around her tea mug and breathed in the smell of the steaming liquid. Peppermint tea always calmed her. After she gave it a moment more to cool, she took a sip and forced herself to focus on the blank computer screen in front of her. The blinking cursor taunted her. Why was starting a new chapter always so hard?

She set down her mug, and her fingers went to work on the keyboard. Usually, once she got down a few sentences, the rest of the chapter flowed from there. She always developed a comprehensive outline before she began a story, and this time had been no different. What was different was that Estelle's brain fought to take a key portion of the story in a completely different direction. Ever since the kayak trip with Wen, when they'd discussed the protagonist's escape from the forest, other alternative twists and turns had wiggled their way into Estelle's head. Dutifully plotted story be damned. What would happen if she continued to stray from the outline? Would it be more tantalizing or become a scattered mess?

The answer to that question would have to wait. Estelle's phone buzzed on the windowsill with a text from Wen.

Do you like chicken pot pie?

I love it, why do you ask?

I thought I'd bring dinner tomorrow night, if that's okay.

Estelle was about to respond that that wasn't necessary, but her repertoire of recipes was sparse.

Sure, thank you.

How was your day? Get much writing done?

Not as much as I'd hoped… Estelle's fingers hovered over the phone. Should she admit she'd been daydreaming about Wen for approximately the entire day? Probably not. Might scare her away. *I had a hard time focusing.*

Funny, so did I. Almost backed Mathilde into the town pier.

Oh, gosh. I hope you're both okay?

Yeah, all good. I'm looking forward to dinner tomorrow.

Me too. Can't wait. Estelle set down her phone and closed her laptop. It was a lost cause. There was no way she'd get any more words down tonight. She stood and headed down the stairs in search of a glass of wine.

CHAPTER FOURTEEN

"How'd the writing go today?" Wen asked. She and Estelle were sipping wine in front of the fire while the chicken pot pie baked in the oven.

"Amazingly well. I managed almost five thousand words. I think that's a record for me and it's a good thing too because"—Estelle's lips curled into a smile and the skin around her eyes crinkled—"yesterday, my body hummed, and my head was in the clouds."

"I see. Why was that?"

"Because a certain mailboat captain brought me to the moon and back the night before."

"Well, I happen to know said boat captain would be happy to take you there again." Wen squirmed in her chair and held up her wineglass. What the hell had gotten into her? "Did you spike my drink? It's not like me to be so—"

"Forward?"

"The word bold came to mind, but yeah."

"It suddenly feels warm in here," Estelle said with a laugh. She stood and turned the damper on the stove to reduce the air flow.

Wen joined her in front of the stove and snaked her arms around Estelle's waist from behind, resting her chin on her shoulder. "My body was on fire all day yesterday too. Every time I thought about being with you…"

Estelle turned in her arms and kissed her on the lips. "I can't stop thinking about you."

"Same." Wen took a small step back. "Are we, you know…"

"Officially seeing each other?"

Wen nodded. "Yeah, that." She resisted the urge to slap her forehead. Estelle had definitely put something in her wine. Did she really just ask Estelle Gage if they were girlfriends? "I mean, it's totally cool if this is just a casual thing."

Estelle ran a hand down Wen's arm and squeezed her hand. "It's not just a casual thing, not for me anyway. As I said the other night, I like you, a lot, and yes, I would be interested in pursuing something with you."

Pursuing something? What the hell did that mean? "Um, okay, great."

Estelle picked up her wine and hoisted the glass into the air. "To us."

"I'll drink to that. To us."

The timer on Wen's phone went off, indicating that the chicken pot pie was done.

"This is fantastic," Estelle said once they sat down to dinner and dug in. "The crust is so flaky."

"Once again, I have my father to thank," Wen replied. "He made about twenty pies yesterday. He sells them at a little stand out in front of our house, and he's got a real following. When word gets out that he's made a fresh batch, they disappear like hotcakes."

"I can definitely see why."

After she took a few more bites of her dinner, Wen said, "So back to your book…How close are you to finishing it? And, oh gosh, I haven't even asked, does it have a title?"

Estelle rested her fork on the edge of her plate and dabbed her mouth with her cotton napkin. "Yes, it has a title. *In Plane Sight*. A play on words."

"Ooooh, I like it. Since the book is about a guy who disappears in a plane and slips past the police."

"Yes, and to answer your other question, the manuscript is not nearly as far along as it should be. To be honest, I've missed more than one deadline. Illuminate, Claudia's lighting design company—really started to take off."

"That's the business she ran with her partner who crashed his car, right?"

"Yes. Ralph ran the business side of things. Claudia is the *artiste*. Suffice it to say, she doesn't exactly have business acumen, and matters of accounting and business development are of no interest to her. When she struggled to get the business off the ground, I stepped in to help. Big mistake. Illuminate took over my life, and the larger it grew, the harder it became for me to step away. And well, not surprisingly, my writing got shoved to the back burner. In retrospect, I should have fought to bring Ralph onboard earlier than I did. He was a godsend. Not only did he know how to handle Claudia, but he took over the day-to-day management of the business."

"What will happen now that he's gone?" Wen asked.

"I honestly don't know," Estelle said. "Claudia has tried to lure me back into the business—she brought it up while I was in New York for the funeral and, since I've been back, she calls me at least once a day. Bottom line, I'm not interested. She needs to find a replacement for Ralph, and fast." She cringed slightly. "This is going to sound awful, but I've begun ignoring her phone calls."

"If you've made it clear you aren't interested and she keeps pestering you, then you have a good reason for avoiding her calls. I'd probably do the same thing."

"I know, it's just..." Estelle pushed her pot pie around on the plate with her fork. "I carry a lot of guilt when it comes to my ex-wife."

"How so?"

"I'm the one who ended our marriage." Estelle ran a hand through her long hair and her face scrunched like she was in pain. "Claudia cheated on me and continued to cheat even after I gave her a second chance."

Wen winced but didn't say anything in response.

"Eventually, I broke things off. Intellectually, I know Claudia is the one who bears the blame for breaking our marriage, but, emotionally, I get caught up by the fact that I'm the one who filed for divorce."

Wen reached out for Estelle's hand. "Not many people would have given her a second chance."

"I know." Estelle sat up straight in her chair and took a sip of wine. "Anyway, that's the sordid tale. As I told you before, Claudia's had a tougher time with the split than I have. Let's just say, she's struggled to let go. She was devastated when I ended things for good and claims she still is."

"People make no sense. Claudia sabotaged your marriage but plays victim when you told her it was over."

"Claudia has a lot of positive attributes, but she's not the most rational person. She knew cheating was wrong, but I don't think she fully grasped how it would impact our relationship. At any rate, the good news is, I'm back writing. Although admittedly, not at the pace I need to be. My new deadline is fast approaching." Estelle bit her bottom lip. "Fingers crossed I can make it. I don't like missing deadlines and, if I allow another one to slip, my publisher will punt me for sure."

"I have complete faith that you will."

"I wish I shared your confidence but thank you."

"Do you have the whole book plotted out or do you kind of make it up as you go along?" Wen asked.

Estelle relaxed back into her chair. "It's funny you ask. I always create elaborate outlines and timelines, even going as far as sketching out floorplans for the rooms where major scenes take place—when you're writing a mystery, the devil is in the details—but in the last few days my brain has been rebelling."

"How so?"

"It's got ideas of its own. Ideas about adding a twist that I hadn't originally envisioned. When you brought up the idea of a decoy while we were kayaking, I don't know, it had a domino effect, sparked all these other new ideas about other aspects of the story."

"I say, listen to your brain and go with it," Wen said.

Estelle placed her hands on her cheeks and gave Wen an expression of mock horror. "But that means straying from the plot I've carefully laid out."

"You said you were turning over a new leaf in your life. Throw caution to the wind."

"I tend to think you're right, but if I continue down this road, there's a strong possibility I'll break into hives."

"Don't worry, I'm a good nurse. Remember I recently saved a guy's life."

Estelle smiled. "I have no doubt you're an excellent nurse. It's just, if I make other changes, even small ones, it means I'll have to go back over everything to ensure all the elements still work. There are so many moving parts to keep in check and oftentimes, a minor change can have broad implications."

"My hunch is, you'll go back over everything regardless of whether you stray from your outline or not."

"You're right," Estelle said. She gave Wen a lopsided smile. "How is it that you already know me so well?"

"Just observant, that's all," Wen said. She scooped up the last bit of pot pie off her plate and slid it into her mouth. "And I suppose inquisitive. Which is why I have another question for you. The day when my engine wouldn't start and you fiddled with its alternator, you said you had a degree in mechanical engineering. Why not creative writing?"

Estelle tossed back her head and laughed. "Good question. Even though I've wanted to be a writer for as long as I can remember, I never believed I could actually become one, and I excelled at math. Mechanical engineering struck me as the more practical route, and my degree has been quite useful on occasion. For instance, much of the work the family foundation does takes place in remote areas. I've been called upon to set up generators, solar panel systems, you name it." She nudged Wen's leg. "And as you astutely noted the other day, a degree in mechanical engineering comes in handy when you've got a partially restored woodie sitting in your boathouse."

"Ha, I imagine it does. Given that I spend my days on a boat with a finicky motor, I wish I'd gotten a degree in that."

"What is your degree in?" Estelle held up her hand. "I'm sorry, I shouldn't automatically assume you went to college. Gah, that came out wrong. What I mean is—"

"Don't worry, it's okay. Took me seven long years to get it, but I did finally earn my bachelor's degree. It's in business administration."

"That's a degree you can definitely put to use running the mailboat business."

"Yep, like you, I went for something practical. I started out in anthropology but changed my major in my second year. Although, as useful as a business degree might be, it would do me good to learn more about how a boat engine works."

Estelle cupped her hand over Wen's. "Do you have to work tomorrow?"

"Nope, it's my day off."

"Maybe you could hang around in the morning and help me work on the woodie. I could give you some pointers on the mechanics of boat engines."

Wen traced a finger up Estelle's arm and brushed it over her cheek. "Are you presuming I'll spend the night?"

Estelle stood, swung a leg over Wen's lap, and straddled her waist. She ran both hands through Wen's hair and placed a gentle kiss on her lips. "I wouldn't be a very good hostess if I sent you out on the cold dark river all alone this time of night, now would I?"

Wen leaned in and whispered into Estelle's ear, "No, I suppose not."

* * *

Once again, Wen awoke to the feel of a warm body spooned up against her. *I could get used to this.* She rolled over, pulled Estelle into her arms, and whispered, "Morning."

Estelle smiled but didn't open her eyes. "Morning. You feel good."

"So do you. I may never let you go."

Estelle's eyes fluttered open, and she slid a hand through Wen's hair. "That would be fine with me." She held Wen's gaze, and a soft smile crossed her face.

"You've got the cutest little dimples," Wen said.

Estelle kissed her on the nose. "Thank you. One of them is deeper than the other."

Wen made a show of inspecting both her cheeks. "You're right, although just barely."

"When I was a kid, my grandfather said it was because I always propped my face on my hand when I read. I believed that for the longest time."

"Were you an avid reader as a kid?"

"Oh, yes. I devoured books. Everything from *Charlotte's Web* to *Little Women*, and I think I read all the Nancy Drew books like ten times."

"I loved Nancy Drew too. In the winter, whenever my mother had to work long hours at the school, she'd park me and my sisters at the library. It was the best, especially because I had a giant crush on the librarian, Ms. Allison, and she'd let me help her return books to the shelves."

Estelle stroked Wen's bare arm with her soft, delicate fingers. "I love that story."

Before Wen could reply, her stomach grumbled. It sounded like a bear waking from its winter's nap. She tugged the bedsheet over her face. "Sorry," she mumbled.

Estelle shimmied under the sheet next to her. "Don't be sorry. Given some of the acrobatics you demonstrated last night, it's no wonder you're starving."

Wen giggled. Acrobatics did accurately describe their activities of the previous evening. She'd first taken Estelle on her desk in the widow's watch and then again on the loveseat in her bedroom. Her groin pulsed at the thought of it. She reached up to smooth her hand over Estelle's breast, but her stupid stomach growled again.

"As much as I'd like to pick up where we left off last night," Estelle said. "It sounds like maybe we ought to get you some breakfast."

Wen flipped back the bedsheet. "You're probably right." She winked. "Rain check?"

Estelle planted a kiss on her lips and rolled out of bed. "You betcha."

After they each inhaled fried eggs, a mountain of bacon, and whole wheat toast, Wen followed Estelle outside to begin work on the woodie.

This time they entered the boathouse from the opposite side, crossed by three empty boat slips, and walked through a vast storage area. A musty smell mixed in with the scent of cedar, and the rafters overhead were laden with an assortment of paddle boards, kayaks, furled sails, and lumber. Two sunfish sailboats were overturned on top of sawhorses, and life jackets, coiled lines, bumpers, paddles, and partially deflated blow-up floaties hung from the hooks that sprouted from the walls. A door off the storage area led to the workshop where the woodie sat propped on wooden blocks.

"I'm afraid the work we have to do today is not terribly exciting," Estelle said. "We've got to apply another coat of varnish to the hull. But before we get to that, why don't I give you that boat engine tutorial I promised."

An old Evinrude outboard engine was fastened to a brightly painted plank of wood. Estelle removed its outer cover and said, "This is obviously a lot smaller than *Mathilde*'s engine, but it functions much the same way."

Wen took notes as Estelle walked her through the mechanics of the Evinrude, and once they'd covered the basics, they moved over to work on the woodie. Estelle showed Wen how to roll the varnish onto the hull of the boat and then "tip it"—sweep back over it—with a foam brush. It was harder than it looked, and even though the boathouse only had a small space heater, Wen broke a sweat. She paused to slip off her heavy flannel shirt and caught Estelle eyeing her.

"Whatcha staring at?"

Estelle shrugged. "Oh, nothing. Just the hot chick varnishing my boat."

Wen chased Estelle around the boat, causing her to squeal like a rabid bat. When she caught her near the bow, Wen pulled Estelle into her arms and kissed her. What was intended as a playful peck on the lips quickly turned into much more. Estelle teased her tongue over Wen's lips and coaxed her way into her mouth. Wen's legs quivered as their bodies melted into each other.

When they came up for air, Wen asked, "Holy mackerel, where did that come from?"

Estelle got a serious look on her face and cupped her hand over Wen's cheek. "You're a beautiful woman, and I find you utterly irresistible."

"Right back at you." Wen stared down at the cement floor and let out a low groan.

"What's wrong?"

"Sadly, I have to head back to the mainland. My sister's kid turns five today, and they're throwing him a big birthday bash."

Estelle pouted.

"You're cute when you pout."

"Thanks." Estelle kicked a small piece of scrap wood on the floor. "Will you come back soon?"

Wen paused before responding. Since they'd met, she and Estelle had spent nearly all their time together on Owl Island, but soon she'd have her own place. She'd talked to Ursula about the apartment over the bookstore and they'd agreed on a six-month lease. The apartment was sparsely furnished, but it did have a brand-new queen-size bed. Maybe she should take Ruby's advice and invite Estelle to hang out on the mainland. Obviously, the apartment wouldn't be nearly as grand as the Gage "cottage," but it was cozy, and if you leaned out the window you could see the water.

"I've lined up a new apartment," she said. "Maybe you could come over once I get moved in."

Estelle gave Wen one of her beautiful smiles. "I'd like that."

"You would?"

"Of course. I'd love to see your new place."

"It's nothing fancy."

"So what? As long as you're there, that's all that matters."

"Okay, cool. Maybe we could go for drinks at the Igloo. It's a bar in town near the—"

"I'm familiar with the Igloo."

Wen hid her surprise and reminded herself of what Ruby had said. She needed to stop making assumptions about Estelle. "Um, and if it's all right, maybe my friend Ruby could join us? She's my BFF and she'd love to meet you." Wen reached for her flannel. "I've told her about you"—she waved a hand between herself and Estelle—"about us."

"I'd love to meet her."

Estelle walked her down to where *Mathilde* was tied up and treated Wen to another searing kiss.

"I so don't want to leave."

"I so don't want you to go."

Wen gave Estelle one last kiss and reluctantly climbed aboard her boat. "Don't forget you owe me a rain check," she hollered over her shoulder as she steered the boat away from the dock.

CHAPTER FIFTEEN

Estelle tucked her arms behind her head and stretched out on the wicker lounge chair. She'd spent the morning cloistered in the widow's watch, hammering away at her keyboard, but it was a beautiful day, and she'd decided to call it quits to sit on the dock and get a little vitamin D.

The sun was high in the sky, the temperature had finally inched above sixty, and a few brave daffodils had poked their heads above ground. Spring was definitely in the air. Any day now, the landscape crew would arrive at the island on their barge to remove the burlap from the shrubs, tend to the flower beds, and treat the still dormant front lawn. Her mother would be in residence in just shy of a month—a fact Estelle didn't even want to contemplate right now—and an army of worker bees would be buzzing about to get the grounds and the house in ship shape before Catherine Gage arrived from New York.

In less than an hour, Wen would be by to pick her up for their big night in town. Estelle had only been to the Igloo once or twice before, but she recalled liking the place and was excited to go there with Wen and her friend. It represented a substantial step in their relationship, and Estelle hadn't stopped to consider the significance of it. They were bursting out of the cocoon that was Owl Island, and they were also "stepping out" as a couple in Wen's world. It was exciting, although…were things with them moving too fast?

She snatched her phone off the small table next to her deck chair and stabbed Fran's number.

"I'm having a minor freak-out," she said when Fran answered. "I have plans with Wen, to go out for drinks in town and meet up with one of her friends."

"That sounds like fun."

"I have no doubt it will be, it's just…things with us, they're moving quite quickly."

Fran laughed. "You've been enjoying each other's company for almost a month now…oh, shit, are you regretting having taken her to bed?"

"No, no, definitely not." A warmth moved through Estelle at the thought of Wen's strong body moving against her. "It's that, tonight we're doing a real couple thing. Not that having sex isn't a couple thing, but I don't know, going out in town, meeting her friends, it feels like a big step."

"It's not really," Fran said. "Maybe it feels that way because you two have been sequestered on that island of yours for the early part of your relationship. If you'd met the normal way, like at a bar or a dinner party in New York, you'd already be past the phase of going out together and meeting each other's friends."

"I suppose you're right. Still, for some reason I feel a bit skittish. Don't get me wrong, Wen has totally swept me off my feet, and I cherish every moment we have together, but…"

"But, what?"

"I'm only just learning how to let me be me. What if I lose sight of that again? You know how I am when I'm in a relationship…And what if my writing gets derailed again? It's been going so well and—"

Fran laughed again. "Take a deep breath, Estelle."

"I'm sorry," she said. "I suppose I'm overanalyzing everything."

"You need to push your past relationships aside. The way you behaved during them is not a determinant of how you will act in this budding relationship with Wen. You've worked so hard this past year…all those hours with the therapist have paid off. You're strong, Estelle. Trust yourself. And for what it's worth, remember, Wen is not Claudia. From what you've told me, she's sweet and kind and supportive. Maybe she'll enable you to see that you can give yourself to someone without losing yourself in the process."

"Perhaps," Estelle said. "But speaking of Claudia, ever since Ralph died, she's been hounding me about Illuminate, begging me to help her out."

Fran groaned into the phone. "Don't you dare let her claw her way back into your life again."

"I won't, don't worry." Estelle lifted her hand to shield her eyes and squinted out over the water. A black speck moved in her direction. "It looks like Wen is here."

"Great," Fran said. "Give her a big, messy kiss when you see her, and let loose tonight."

"Yes, ma'am." Estelle ended the call and waved at Wen as she got closer to the island.

* * *

Wen took Estelle's hand and led her through the front door of the Igloo. Once her eyes adjusted to the dim light inside, she scanned the bar.

"There she is," she said when she spotted Ruby's short, spiky black hair protruding above the back of a booth near the idle jukebox.

Estelle's shoulders visibly stiffened.

"Don't worry," Wen whispered, "she'll love you. How could she not."

Ruby jumped up when they approached, extended her hand, and introduced herself.

"It's a pleasure to meet you," Estelle said with a smile.

"Ditto," Ruby said. She nodded toward Wen. "This one has talked about you *a lot*."

Wen held her thumb and pointer finger a half an inch apart. "Only like this much." She placed a hand on the small of Estelle's back. "I'll go grab us a couple of beers." A glance at the table indicated Ruby's pint was nearly empty. "You ready for another one, Ruber?"

"Sure thing," Ruby replied. "I'm drinking the new Right Proper IPA. It's delish. You should try it."

"Okay," Wen said.

"I'll try one too," Estelle said.

Wen went off in search of beer.

Monique greeted her with a smile. "Hiya, Wen." She rested an elbow on the bar, leaned forward, and whispered, "Is that Estelle Gage in your booth?"

Wen peered over her shoulder, pleased to see that Ruby and Estelle were chatting. "Yep, it sure is."

"Huh, interesting. What the heck is she doing here?"

Wen ran a hand through her hair. "Um, we're kind of seeing each other."

Monique slapped the bar with her free hand. "No shit, you and Estelle Gage?"

"Yes."

Monique rested her other elbow on the bar and slowly shook her head. "Mmm, mmm, she sure is pretty to look at."

Before Wen could respond, Dana, a regular at the Igloo who was sitting on a nearby stool, mumbled, "What, the local girls aren't good enough for you?"

Dana always had a colossal chip on her shoulder. Wen ignored the comment and Monique rolled her eyes.

Wen ordered three IPAs and strode back to the booth with three pints triangled between her hands, careful not to let any of the cloudy brown liquid slosh over the rims of the glasses. She set the drinks on the table and slithered into the booth next to Estelle.

"Hmm, this is quite good," Estelle said after she'd taken a sip.

Wen peeked over at her, and when their eyes met, she felt warm all over. Estelle shifted on the booth's pleather cushion, and the light from the faux stained-glass lamp dangling overhead reflected off her thick silver bracelet.

Out on the island, Wen had never seen Estelle wear jewelry of any kind, aside from the diamond studs that always graced her ears. But tonight, she wore not one, but two bracelets, a funky silver braided ring, and—Wen slipped a finger under the neckline of Estelle's blouse and ran it over her collarbone—a delicate silver necklace. There was also a hint of makeup on Estelle's cheeks and around her eyes. Given that they were just hanging out at the hole-in-the-wall Igloo, she was touched Estelle had made an effort.

Estelle gestured toward Ruby. "I've had some of the baked goods from your café. They're out of this world."

Ruby sat up tall. "Thanks, Estelle. Kind of you to say."

"It's very impressive that you run your own business at your age," Estelle said. "You can't be more than, what, twenty-seven or twenty-eight?"

Ruby beamed. "I'm twenty-eight, just a few months older than Wen. I worked at Bella's all through high school, and when old Mrs. Ng decided to retire a few years ago, she offered to sell me the café. At that point I was practically running the place anyway, but I hadn't saved up much money, so she helped me finance it. It's a hefty note to carry, but knock on wood, business has been great so far. I made some changes to the menu when I took over—experimented with some new things—and it seems to be working. Sales have doubled in the last two years."

Wen couldn't help but smile. Ruby worked her ass off, and Wen knew she was extremely proud of the business she'd built, and rightfully so.

Estelle raised her pint. "Kudos to you."

Ruby nodded her thanks and took a sip of her beer. "So," she said. "Wen tells me you're living out on Owl Island all alone."

"Yes," Estelle said. "But I've been fortunate enough"—she nudged Wen with her shoulder and squeezed her thigh—"to have this one around to keep me company."

"So I hear," Ruby said with a wink.

Wen and Estelle locked eyes again, and Wen scooted closer so their legs touched.

Ruby cleared her throat and gave Wen a knowing look.

The blood rushed to Wen's face. Evidently they needed a little practice on how to cool the burners. Although she wasn't so sure any amount of practice would help matters. The urge to touch Estelle was simply too strong.

"Wen mentioned that you're working on a book," Ruby said.

Estelle nodded. "Yes, I am. Trying to anyway. Although I'm afraid the quiet days on the island will soon be coming to an end. My family is due to arrive in a few weeks."

Wen's shoulders slumped. She was so not ready for Estelle's family to raid Owl Island. The island belonged to the Gages, of course, and she had no right to think that way, but she couldn't help it. Being able to spend quiet nights there with Estelle had been out-of-this-world amazing.

Estelle patted Wen's thigh. "Would you mind sliding out for a moment? I've got to use the little girls' room."

Wen jumped up and reached out a hand to help Estelle extract herself from the tight space between the table and the back of the booth.

When Estelle got to her feet, she released Wen's hand and trailed a finger down her arm. "Be right back."

As soon as she was out of earshot, Ruby leaned across the table and whispered, "Dude, she's way into you."

Wen bounced in her seat. "You really think so?"

"I know so. The way she looks at you, the casual touches… oh yeah, she's whipped, whipped, whipped."

"I want to believe that, cuz, you know, I'm like totally into her, but God, what's going to happen when her family arrives? She might not want a scruffy mailboat captain hanging around anymore."

"Girl, you are not scruffy. You're a stud, and she's damn lucky to have you."

Wen reached across the table and squeezed Ruby's hand. "Thanks, friend."

Estelle was flushed when she returned from the ladies' room. She held up her phone. "Claudia just called. She's here in Coopersville. I'm afraid I need to go."

"I don't understand," Wen said.

"She's down at the marina. I need to go deal with her. I'll call you in a bit."

Wen watched Estelle walk out the front door of the Igloo and close the door behind her. "What the hell?" she muttered and slumped down in the booth.

* * *

Estelle suppressed a laugh when she spotted Claudia at the marina. She stood in the middle of the oil-stained gravel lot littered with boats in various stages of disrepair, donning a red wool Hermes shawl and snow-white slacks. And she looked fresh from a high-end salon. Her long blond hair draped her shoulders, the loose curls bouncing when she shifted her head.

"I thought you weren't supposed to wear white until after Memorial Day," Estelle said as she approached.

Claudia waved off the remark and leaned in to kiss her on the cheek. "Where's the water taxi that will take us to your island?" she asked when she pulled back.

"May I remind you that it's nine p.m. on a weekday in late April? There is no water taxi."

"You mean to tell me we're stuck in this miserable boatyard?"

Estelle gestured toward the streetlights in the distance. "There's a small hotel in town. We can talk there."

There were only two other patrons in the hotel's bar, and Estelle led Claudia to a table in the corner near the fireplace.

"Care to tell me what you're doing here?" she asked after they'd each ordered a glass of wine.

"I've come to get you and bring you back to New York," Claudia said, as if it were the most obvious thing in the world.

Estelle reached over, took her hand, and looked her straight in the eye. "I'm afraid you wasted your time coming up here. I am not going back with you."

Claudia yanked her hand free and crossed her arms over her chest. "I miss you, Stelle."

"Claudia, please don't—"

"What, I can't say I miss you?"

"I gave you a second chance," Estelle said, but stopped there. They'd been through this so many times, too many times.

"And I'm desperate. I need your help. With Ralph gone, there's no one to—"

"Claudia, I've made myself clear. You need to find someone to replace Ralph...someone who is not me. I've moved on to a new chapter in my life. You have to learn to accept that."

Estelle spent the next hour trying to talk some sense into Claudia but, like usual, most of what she said appeared to go in one ear and out the other.

Eventually she stood and said, "Come on, let's see if we can get you a room."

Claudia remained seated and twirled the last of the wine in her glass. "What about you?" she asked. "Where are you going to stay? I thought you said there were no boats back to the island tonight."

Estelle didn't hesitate before responding, "I'm staying with my girlfriend, Wen. In fact, I need to call her to let her know—"

The wineglass in Claudia's hand dropped onto the wood floor and shattered into a million pieces. "You didn't tell me you had a girlfriend."

"I'm sorry, I didn't realize that was information I was obliged to share with my ex-wife." Estelle pinched her eyes shut. "Gah, that came out more harshly than I intended."

Claudia balled her fists and looked as if she might launch at Estelle, but quickly regained her composure. Her eyes grew wide, and she got a curious look on her face, as if she'd just solved a riddle that she'd long muddled over.

The bartender ran over with a broom and dustpan.

"Sorry," Estelle whispered to him. She helped Claudia to her feet, took her arm, and walked her to the front desk of the hotel.

Once Claudia was settled in her room, Estelle called Wen to fill her in on the events of the evening.

"Jeez, Estelle, that sucks. I'm sorry," Wen said.

"Is it still okay if I spend the night with you?"

"Of course. Come on over. I'll make a pot of tea."

Estelle walked out of the hotel with a spring in her step. The look on Claudia's face right before they'd left the bar… something had clicked behind those rich brown eyes of hers. Had she finally accepted that their relationship was over, for good? Estelle could hope. Although this wouldn't be the first time she'd thought Claudia understood, only to be proven wrong.

CHAPTER SIXTEEN

Wen kissed Estelle's cheek and climbed out of bed. She got dressed in the dark and crept into her small galley kitchen to make coffee.

"Darling," Estelle called from the bedroom.

Wen nudged open the door and poked her head into the room. "Morning. I'm about to head out. Try to go back to sleep."

She had a few critical deliveries to make, and once she got them out of the way, Estelle had proposed they spend the afternoon in town to decorate Wen's apartment.

"I think I'll get up and do some writing while you're gone," Estelle said. She pushed back the covers and sat up in bed. The first hints of daylight streaked through the blinds and cast a glow over her face and her bare chest.

Wen sucked in a breath and fought the urge to climb back in bed with her. But duty called, and the sooner she made her deliveries, the sooner she'd be home. She blew Estelle a kiss and said, "See you in a few hours."

"Be safe out there," Estelle called after her.

A few hours turned into five hours out on the water, so it was almost noon by the time Wen got back to the marina. She trotted back to her apartment, and her jaw dropped when she opened the door. The sparse apartment she'd left that morning was now overflowing with furniture.

"Surprise," Estelle said.

"Oh, my God. I don't understand…how did you do all this?"

Estelle laughed. "I wish I could take credit, but I can't. About an hour after you left this morning, your father and two of his buddies showed up with a truck full of furniture. I helped them unload it, and then your father and I went to Target."

"I might need to get my hearing checked. It sounded like you said you went to Target with my father."

"I sure did." Estelle picked up a navy-blue throw pillow with little white anchors on it. "You should have seen him in the home goods department. He was like a kid in a candy store."

Wen scanned the apartment. "I like the nautical theme."

"I do too. It was your father's idea."

Wen eyed the kitchen table and smiled. "And you got me lighthouse salt and pepper shakers."

"Yes," Estelle said. "You seemed fond of the set we have on the island."

Wen was touched she'd remembered.

"Your dad is a real sweetheart, by the way. And super funny. We had the best time shopping together."

"I'm glad to hear that. But I'm dumbfounded by all that you accomplished while I was out on the water this morning."

"The place is coming together," Estelle said, "although there's still lots to do."

"There is?"

Estelle took her hand and led her toward the door. "Uh-huh. Come on, let's go. I want to get some nautical-themed prints to go over the couch, and I'm hoping we can find a glass coffee table for your living area. Your dad told me about a great secondhand furniture store on the edge of town."

"Um, okay," Wen replied. "You do realize I only have a six-month lease on this place, right?"

Estelle nodded. "Yes, but you might as well be comfortable while you're here."

"They have so much amazing stuff here," Estelle said as they roamed around Sofa So-good, the secondhand furniture store.

"Let me guess, you've never been to a place like this before?"

"Not exactly like this, no, but let me tell you, it will not be my last visit to this store. I see about fifty things I'd like to buy." Estelle picked up a straw hat and put it on her head. "Like this." She twirled around. "How do I look?"

"Like you belong in the middle of a cornfield."

"Very funny. Okay, how about this?" She replaced the straw hat with a giant cowboy hat that slid down over her eyes.

"You look like a goofball, that's what."

"A goofball, huh?" Estelle took off the cowboy hat and picked up the straw hat again. "Fine, then I'm getting this one. It'll keep my neck shaded when I'm out in the garden."

Wen pointed to a huge ornate desk and matching chair. With a straight face, she said, "I think that would be perfect for my apartment."

Estelle looked at the desk and chair and then back at Wen. "Oh, um, yes, it might work."

Wen gave her a soft punch in the arm. "I'm kidding. It's hideous, and it would take up half my living room."

Estelle smacked Wen's ass with the straw hat. "Phew, I was a little worried there for a second."

They finally settled on a small glass and metal coffee table plus three framed wildlife photos for above the couch.

Using a small toolkit that Wen's father had left behind, Estelle hung the pictures on the wall, but only after carefully measuring their placement. She stepped back, and together, they assessed her work.

"They look great, don't you think?" Estelle asked.

Wen nodded and waved her hand across the small apartment. "Now this place feels like home, thank you."

After they washed and dried all the sheets and towels Estelle and her father had bought that morning, they swung by the grocery store and hopped on *Mathilde* to head back to Owl Island.

Before dinner, Wen called her father to thank him for dropping off the furniture and accompanying Estelle on the Target shopping spree.

"No sweat," he said. "The furniture is all stuff my buddy Bob had sitting in his garage. He was more than happy to give it to you." He paused before adding. "I like your Estelle. Nice gal. Very classy."

Wen smiled into the phone. "I'm so glad you two met. I know Estelle enjoyed your excursion."

After they ended the call, she joined Estelle in the kitchen and helped her put away the groceries.

"Did you tell your dad I enjoyed meeting him?" Estelle asked.

"I did, and he said the same about you. Said you were a nice gal." Wen bit her bottom lip. "One thing has me worried though. When I thanked him for the furniture, he said his friend was happy to give it to me."

"What's wrong with that?"

"That he used the word *give* rather than *lend*. I haven't committed to staying in Coopersville beyond October. I just hope my father understands that. I don't want him to get the wrong idea. You know, get his hopes up about me staying long term."

"Maybe you need to have another chat with him," Estelle said. "Make that clear."

"Yeah, maybe."

CHAPTER SEVENTEEN

Estelle typed *THE END*, pumped her fist in the air, and leaned back in her chair. She still had some minor revisions to make to the manuscript, but she was almost there, almost ready to send it off to her editor. It was a miracle she'd finally finished it. Two months earlier, she never would have thought she'd get to this point, but she'd been on fire lately. In the last week alone she'd written ten thousand words and done some heavy revisions.

There'd been another aspect of the plot that hadn't sat right with her, but Wen had been kind enough to talk through it with her. And *bam!* Together they'd reached a most intriguing twist, one Estelle didn't think she would have ever devised on her own. Talking to Wen about her writing was, in a word, invigorating, and refreshing. When they'd been married, Claudia didn't even feign interest in her stories. Wen, on the other hand, seemed almost as engrossed in aspects of the plot as Estelle was.

Estelle loved the way the story had turned out, and she absolutely could not wait to release it into the world. She sent Wen a quick text and then called her agent.

"Fantastic," Harrison replied after she gave him an update on her status. "You had me a little worried there for a bit, Estelle."

"To be honest," she said, "I had myself a little worried there for a bit too, but it all came together in the end."

"As exciting as this is, it's going to be extremely tight."

"I know," Estelle replied. She'd used every inch of the latest extension her publisher had given her and, as a result, the turnaround on this manuscript would be significantly shorter than normal. The publisher had marketed the crap out of *In Plane Sight*, and there was no wiggle room on the release date.

"Eunice is dying to get her hands on it," he said, referring to Estelle's very stern but very talented editor.

"I'm certain she is."

When Estelle finished with Harrison, she dialed her publicist.

"I'm so glad you called, Estelle," Marianne said. "I was about to call you." After the perfunctory small talk—Marianne was from Georgia—she said, "I'm anxious to finalize a few high-profile stops on your book tour this fall."

Estelle ran a hand through her hair and tried not to audibly sigh through the phone. Book tours were a grind. Zigzagging the country on early morning flights and days packed with events. Still, she should be honored that her publisher even sent her on tour. It was no small expense, and these days most publishers, hers included, sent only a select few of their top-producing authors on tour.

"Okay," she said as she pulled her calendar up on her laptop.

"First on the list, the *Fresh Air* interview. You know they like the authors to be there in person, and while you're in DC, I've set up a few other things. Politics and Prose and probably Kramerbooks, because I know you have a soft spot for that place." Marianne was quiet for a moment and Estelle heard her tapping away on her keyboard. "Oh, and I need you in Seattle at the end of September…Denver…and then London…"

As Marianne went through a list of dates and events, Estelle made note of them on her calendar.

"The timing of the London trip should work nicely," she said. From there, she planned to hop over to Berlin to do some research for her next book and, if time permitted, take a trip to India for some business related to the Gage Family Foundation.

As Estelle was ending the call with Marianne, a text came in from Wen. *Leaving the marina now. Be there soon. xo*

Estelle smiled at the message. The "xo" was a new addition to Wen's messages. They'd begun to appear a few days earlier, and seeing them made Estelle all warm inside. She closed her laptop and went downstairs to freshen up before Wen arrived for dinner.

* * *

Wen killed *Mathilde*'s engine and jumped up on the dock just as Estelle emerged from the house. They'd finally gotten a string of nice warm days and Estelle wore a faded green Dartmouth T-shirt beneath a thin fleece jacket. Her hair was loose, and the light wind blew it back away from her face. As always, the sight of her sent Wen's heart into overdrive.

How the hell did I get so lucky?

"Hey, you," Estelle said as she trotted down the stone steps of the house. She greeted Wen with a lingering kiss.

Wen tugged the strap of her duffel bag up on her shoulder and held up a brown paper bag. "I brought a little something to celebrate you finishing the book."

Estelle treated her to a broad, dimpled smile. "That was very thoughtful of you."

"I remembered you like Nebbiolo, so I asked the guy at the liquor store for a recommendation." Wen laughed. "To be honest, I was surprised he even knew what it was—the folks in Coopersville tend toward box wine—but apparently, he's getting all stocked up for the onset of the summer folks." She handed the wine to Estelle. "I'm sure it's not as good as what you've got here in the cellar, but—"

Estelle placed a hand on her arm. "I'm sure it will be delicious, Wen, thank you."

Wen stopped walking. "Oh, shoot, hold on. I left the most important thing on the boat." She dropped her duffel on the grass and jogged back toward *Mathilde*. When she returned, she lifted the cardboard box in her hand. "Cupcakes from Ruby's café. She sends her congrats for finishing the book."

"What a sweetheart."

Once they got inside, Estelle put a frozen lasagna in the oven and poured them each a drink. "Given what a nice day it is, what do you say we sit out on the front porch while we wait for dinner to cook? There's a stash of wool blankets if we get cold."

Wen accepted a mug of beer and said, "Works for me."

There was only one rocking chair on the deck, but Estelle dragged another one from a storage shed and then pulled out two thick blankets. She tucked Wen into one chair and then did the same for herself.

"This is so cozy," Wen said.

The sun hung low on the horizon and cast a brilliant orange and pink hue over the water. A nighthawk swooped above the treetops on the island and then dove toward the ground, and Wen thought she detected the faint sound of an owl. The evening couldn't get any more perfect. The calm before the storm. Come summer, there'd be boats zipping across the water even at this time of evening, but right now, Wen didn't see or hear a single one. Only one thing was wrong with the otherwise ideal setting. Estelle wasn't snuggled next to her. Hopefully later.

"I love the silhouettes the trees cast on the water," Estelle said.

Wen nodded and drew her eyes along the line of oak and ash trees dotting the perimeter of the island. Here and there, small green buds sprouted from their limbs. "It's so beautiful on the river."

"It is, isn't it? I'm an idiot for not venturing up to the islands in the spring in years past. Being here before everyone else descends upon the place is simply heaven. So peaceful and quiet. Not to mention ideal for writing."

"On that note," Wen said, "when will your book come out?"

"Mid-September, which is utter insanity."

"Why so?"

"Because it's early May," Estelle said. "And in the wacky world of book publishing, that's an unbelievably tight timeline. My editor will pounce on the manuscript the second I submit it."

"I can't wait to read it."

"The story is much better because of you. Thank you again for working through portions of it with me."

"You give me too much credit. I just helped extract ideas from your head."

"Claudia never took much interest in my writing and…I'm sorry, I don't mean to bring her up again."

Wen pulled her hand out from under her blanket and stretched across to squeeze Estelle's arm. "It's okay. No sense pretending that she doesn't exist."

Estelle laughed. "Oftentimes I'd like to."

"How long were you two together?" Wen asked.

"Seven years, married for four. Things were good in the beginning. Claudia is smart and ambitious and charming. I was drawn to her the moment we met. It's hard to pinpoint the moment things began to unravel."

"When she started having an affair," Wen offered.

"That certainly didn't help matters," Estelle said flatly, "but we'd drifted apart even before then. After Ralph came onboard, we both got absorbed in our own thing—me with my writing and foundation work and her with Illuminate—and she and I almost never saw each other. Our relationship suffered. I pulled back from writing and reduced my travel to focus on our marriage. That was when I learned she was having an affair." Estelle shivered and tugged her blanket up around her neck. "When I confronted Claudia, she blamed me. Said if I hadn't been so MIA, she wouldn't have strayed."

"That's bullshit."

Estelle nodded. "I broke things off and Claudia went absolutely berserk. Begged me to give her a second chance, so I did. Things between us were okay for a brief time…Until I discovered she was still sneaking around, and I ended things for good." Estelle shivered again.

"Would you like my blanket?" Wen asked.

"You're sweet but no. Maybe we should head inside. The lasagna will be ready soon and I still need to make a salad."

After dinner, Wen opened the box of cupcakes from Ruby and set the beautiful chocolate creations out on a plate. Before she even had a chance to carry them to the table, Estelle snatched one and took a big bite out of it.

She groaned. "Damn, that Ruby is a genius."

Once Wen managed to swallow a massive bite of her own, she said, "I'll let her know you approve." She set down her cupcake, drew her finger through the thick mound of frosting swirled on top, and smeared it on Estelle's nose.

Estelle giggled and tried to swipe it with her tongue. She finally gave up, grabbed a dishtowel off the counter, and wiped it off. And then, in a lightning-fast move, she sunk her finger into her own cupcake and planted a long smudge of frosting on Wen's chin.

Wen grabbed another dishtowel off the counter and snapped Estelle's ass with it.

After snapping Wen back, Estelle took off across the kitchen shrieking like she'd seen a mouse.

By now, tears streamed down Wen's cheeks from laughing so hard. She let out a squeal of delight and chased after Estelle. When she caught her by the dining table, Wen pulled her into her arms and smothered her neck and face with gentle kisses and nibbles. Estelle stilled in her arms and her dark brown eyes sought out Wen's. They stood that way for a long time, holding each other's gaze. Wen's legs and arms tingled, and a warmth spread from her chest to her groin.

Estelle broke eye contact and the tip of her tongue traced Wen's lips before dipping inside her mouth. A groan escaped from the depth of Wen's chest. The heat between her legs was so intense, it threw her off balance and she was caught off guard when Estelle's hands slid over her hips and pressed her hard up against the wall. What started as a trail of light kisses down Wen's neck and over her collarbone turned to nibbles and finally to bites. They didn't hurt but they weren't gentle either. The air crackled with electricity.

Estelle paused to draw her tongue over Wen's chin and up behind her ear and then, without warning, she thrust them both toward the table and pinned Wen down on its hard wooden surface. Her hands grasped for Wen's shirt, yanked it from her pants and pushed it up and over her head to expose her red silk bra.

Cool air and warm fingers wafted over Wen's skin and her stomach muscles tightened under Estelle's touch.

"Can't reach," Estelle mumbled. She was still on her feet at the edge of the table, hovering over Wen. Her eyes were wild with hunger. She slowly drew her own shirt up over her head and her bra landed somewhere on the kitchen floor. Without a word, she crawled onto the table and straddled Wen.

"Will this thing hold us?" Wen asked.

"Guess we're about to find out," Estelle said with a laugh. She cupped a hand over one of Wen's breasts and then the other and kneaded her nipples through the silk.

Wen arched her back in response and Estelle capitalized on the opportunity to reach back for the clasp of her bra. When it clicked open and Wen's breasts spilled out, Estelle caressed them with the soft tips of her fingers, making lazy circles around Wen's nipples. Eventually, her tongue moved in to replace her fingers as Estelle's hands trailed down to claw at the buttons of Wen's jeans.

Estelle slid off the table to fully liberate Wen of her pants and spread her legs apart. "Hoping to get lucky tonight?" she whispered as she teased a finger over Wen's silk panties.

"Maybe," Wen said and ran a finger over the thin lace waistband of her thong. Normally, she stuck to boy shorts, but she'd gone online the week before to buy something sexy. Something special for Estelle. "You like?"

"Oh, I like." Estelle drew the thong down Wen's thighs, along her calves, and over her feet and twirled it on her finger before releasing it to sail to the kitchen floor. She kneeled before the table, pushed Wen's legs wider, and leaned in to swipe her tongue over Wen's clit.

It felt so good that, for a moment, Wen thought she might pass out. She closed her eyes and bit down hard on her bottom lip. Her body trembled and her breath caught in her chest as she approached the cliff. Estelle's fingernails dug into the soft skin inside her thighs and Wen cried out as she came. She'd never be able to look at the kitchen table the same again.

Estelle stood, tugged Wen to her feet, and pulled her into her arms. "I'm bound to snicker next time someone mentions eating at the kitchen table."

"A similar thought just ran through my mind," Wen said. She took Estelle's hand, led her into the living room, and laid a blanket out in front of the wood-burning stove. "My turn," she said as she lowered them to the floor.

CHAPTER EIGHTEEN

An incessant wailing forced Wen's eyes open. The early morning sun cast a glow over the room. *Right, alarm.* She snatched her phone off the nightstand to silence it.

Estelle snuggled up in the crux of Wen's arm. They lay together and listened to the chorus of birds singing and chirping outside.

Wen needed to return to the mainland to pick up the day's deliveries, but that would mean leaving Estelle's warm bed. Something she had no interest in doing. She scanned the room. Where were her clothes? Images of the previous evening floated through her mind and the kitchen table played a starring role. Good bet her clothes were somewhere in its vicinity. Lucky they were all alone on a remote island. She kicked off the covers, but Estelle clutched on to her.

"I don't want you to leave."

"Trust me. I'd give anything to stay in bed with you all day, but duty calls." She kissed Estelle on the forehead. "And don't you have some book revisions to finish?"

Estelle huffed and rolled over toward her side of the bed.

If the weather forecasters were right, another glorious spring day was in store and Wen got an idea. She followed Estelle into the bathroom and said, "Hey, assuming you have a productive morning, how about I kidnap you for a few hours this afternoon? You could join me out on the water while I make my last round of deliveries."

Estelle clapped her hands like a little kid. "That sounds wonderful. And it will undoubtedly motivate me to be extra focused on the manuscript this morning."

Estelle made them each a big bowl of oatmeal and sent Wen on her way with a lingering kiss and a tall travel mug of hot coffee.

As they cut across the water, Wen draped a hand over *Mathilde*'s steering wheel, leaned up against the side of the boat, and stared out over the bow, or more specifically, ogled the beautiful woman sitting up there. Estelle looked adorable in Wen's worn Coopersville baseball cap. A few strands of her long dark hair had escaped out the side of the hat, and her red slicker fluttered in the wind. A thick wool blanket was tucked around her legs, and she stared out across the shimmering water.

The sun sparkled high in the sky and there wasn't a cloud in sight, but the early spring air was crisp, especially with the boat at full throttle, which admittedly, for *Mathilde*, wasn't all that fast, but still fast enough to make it nippy. Or nippley. As if the scene spread before her wasn't perfect enough, a flock of double-crested cormorants coasted through the air in a V shape above the boat.

She was in deep—really deep. No question about it. She was falling in love with Estelle. It was as simple as that, and God did it feel good. Damn good… But what did the future hold for them?

Live in the moment, she reminded herself. *Stop obsessing about what might or might not be.*

Life had a funny way of working out sometimes. She should be busy preparing for her trip to Barcelona and buying things like power adapters, good walking shoes, and sunscreen. But instead, here she was, captaining *Mathilde* with a beautiful, kind, funny, smart woman as her copilot. At present, Wen was pretty darn pleased with her decision not to go abroad. In her mind, evenings alone on the island with Estelle were way better than anything she imagined Barcelona could offer. And not only was she falling in love, but business was booming. The summer season hadn't even kicked into gear yet and, due to some adjustments she'd made upon taking over the boat—tiering delivery charges based on distance, and plotting the most efficient route to take each day—she was already turning a tidy profit. She patted the boat's dashboard. And knock on wood, *Mathilde* had been running like a top.

Wen eased up on the throttle as they neared the rocky shores of Graf Island and Estelle jumped into action. She tossed back the blanket, sprang to her feet, and gathered the bow line. It sure would be handy to have her along every day. Maybe if business continued to be good, Wen would hire a local high school kid to help her out part time during the peak summer months. Of course, it wouldn't be the same as having Estelle aboard, but a second set of hands would mean even greater efficiency. Gas wasn't cheap, and every minute Wen shaved off running *Mathilde*'s engine meant money in the bank.

"Howdy, Mr. Green," Wen said once she'd maneuvered the boat parallel to the rickety dock jutting out from Graf Island. "We've got a load of stuff for you."

Mr. Green made a show of bringing his watch up toward his face. "'Bout time. I'd about given up on you for the day."

Wen bit her tongue and forced a smiled. She could arrive at six a.m. and Mr. Green would still grumble.

Estelle scooped up two big boxes, tucked one under each arm, and leapt ashore. She hopscotched over the broken boards on the dock and greeted Mr. Green with a broad smile.

"Where would you like these, sir?" she asked.

"On the front porch, if you don't mind."

Wen swore she detected a small smile creep across his face. *That would be a first.* She gathered up the rest of the items they had for him—a sack of groceries and a case of wine—and scrambled up the narrow dirt path to the house behind Estelle. The wine almost slipped from her arms at the sound of Mr. Green laughing. Apparently, Wen wasn't the only one who was enchanted with Estelle.

Over the course of the rest of the afternoon, Estelle continued to charm every one of Wen's customers, and on top of that, the two of them maneuvered cumbersome packages together as if they'd worked as a team for years.

"I sure could get used to having you as second mate," Wen said.

Estelle came up beside her at the helm and curled an arm around her waist. "I enjoyed it. Thanks for letting me tag along."

"You're welcome to come out anytime, although let me warn you, the fun factor dissipates quickly on a cold rainy day with gusts of thirty knots."

"I didn't mean to suggest your job was easy, I just—"

Wen kissed her on the cheek. "I know you didn't, and to be honest, perfect blue-sky days like today make all those frigid overcast ones worth it." She took both hands off the wheel and waved them in the air. "Sometimes I take the beauty of this place for granted. As far as offices go, it's not too shabby."

Estelle pointed to a large bird soaring overhead. "Oh my God, is that a bald eagle?"

Wen craned her neck toward the sky. "Wow, I think so."

Estelle watched the bird until it floated out of sight. "A perfect ending to a perfect day."

Wen nuzzled Estelle's neck and moved up to kiss her on the lips.

"Are you trying to seduce a member of your crew, captain?"

Wen held up a hand, gave Estelle a "who me?" look, and turned the boat back toward Owl Island. Life was damn good, no doubt about that.

CHAPTER NINETEEN

Wen and Estelle unloaded groceries from *Mathilde* and carried them up to the house. It was Friday night, and they planned to spend the entire weekend holed up on Owl Island. Their time alone at the house would soon come to an abrupt end. In seven short days, the rest of the Gage family would descend upon them. Estelle loved her family and looked forward to seeing them, but their arrival meant no more quiet evenings alone by the fire with Wen, evenings that more often than not led to long passionate nights in bed...or in the widow's watch, or on the kitchen table... Things would be very different once the house was full to the gills and there were children running around. And Estelle's mother was in residence.

As if reading her mind, Wen asked, "When exactly is everyone supposed to get here?"

"My mother and Pauline will arrive on the island next Friday afternoon."

"Pauline?"

"My mother's 'lady's maid,'" she said, making air quotes. "She doesn't go anywhere without Pauline."

"Kind of like on *Downton Abbey*?"

Estelle laughed. "Sort of, although Pauline does everything. Cooking, cleaning, you name it."

"Wow," Wen said. "She manages this whole big house on her own?"

"Yes and no. A cleaning crew comes in from the mainland once a week to do the heavy lifting, and when it comes to meals, Pauline's mostly tasked with keeping the fridge and freezer stocked with food—casseroles and soups, steaks for grilling, fruits and vegetables, yogurts and cereal for the kids—and we all help ourselves."

"What about the rest of your family, when will they start to appear?"

"People will start to trickle in after my mother has settled in, beginning with my sister, Whitney, on Saturday. As large as this house is, there isn't room for all six of us kids plus assorted significant others and grandkids. Me, my mom, and Whitney and her three boys will be here pretty much for the whole summer, but everyone else will kind of come and go. My brother Jimmy and his wife and daughter will probably be here for most of June and July, but my older brothers have their kids in a zillion different sports and they're always off at some tournament or another. It makes it hard for them to get up here for any length of time."

Wen set the last of the groceries on the counter. "Sure will be a lot different around here."

"Indeed," Estelle said, "which is why it's a darn good thing my manuscript is finally finished. Once everyone is here, it'll be impossible to find a quiet spot in the house."

"If you ever need to escape, you're more than welcome to crash at my apartment. It's small but—"

"I love your place, Wen, and I will definitely take you up on that offer." Estelle was quiet for a moment before she added, "It's going to be a lot more difficult for us to find time alone..."

Wen nodded and nibbled on her bottom lip. "I know...I've actually been thinking a lot about that. About what it'll be like once your family is here and whether..."

"Whether what?" Estelle asked.

"Whether I'll be invited ashore as a guest?"

"What do you mean? Of course you will."

Wen gave her a pained look. "I don't mean to make deliveries to the island, but like as your girlfriend?"

Wen was clearly more anxious about the arrival of the Gage clan than she'd let on. Estelle pulled her into a tight hug and rubbed her back. "Yes, as my girlfriend. I can't wait for everyone to meet you."

"Are you sure?"

Estelle stepped back and looked Wen in the eye. "I'm certain. It'll just be different. You and I are both going to have to get used to having people around."

Wen smiled. "You mean we can't have sex all over the house?"

"Not advisable." Estelle squeezed Wen's ass. "Which is why we need to make the most of this weekend." She nodded toward the bottle of wine on the counter and said, "Why don't I pour us some wine and we can adjourn to the living room."

They used cushions from the couch to make themselves a nest in front of the wood-burning stove. Estelle sat on the floor with her back up against the sofa and Wen wiggled in front of her and leaned back to nestle between her legs.

Estelle raked her fingers through Wen's hair and sighed. "It doesn't get much better than this, does it?"

"Sure doesn't."

Estelle curled her arms around Wen and hugged her tightly. A lump formed in her throat and her eyes moistened. It hit her then. She was in love with Wen, like full-on, one hundred percent in love with her. How on earth had that happened? She'd come up to the islands to focus on her writing and reconnect with herself, not to fall in love. But with Wen it had all been so easy and so different. Estelle had never lost sight of herself in their time together. Just the opposite. With Wen in her life, Estelle had never felt more connected to her own feelings and desires. Right now, she was more at peace with herself than she probably ever had been. She thought back to that first day, when *Mathilde* appeared off the shores on the island. How she'd gone out to help rescue Wen... The moment their eyes had met, Estelle was a goner.

She brushed Wen's hair back to expose her neck and nuzzled up against her warm soft skin. *I love you.* Should she say the words out loud? Or was it too soon to feel the way she did? Wen shifted in her arms and moved to sit next to her. Her eyes sought out Estelle's, and the look on her face told Estelle all she needed to know. Wen loved her too. The lump in her throat reappeared. She swallowed hard and ran her thumb over Wen's lips and cupped her cheek.

The words came out more easily than she expected. "I've fallen in love with you, Wen Apollo."

A smile slowly crept across Wen's face, but she didn't say anything in response. Instead, she turned her head and kissed Estelle's palm.

Estelle cringed. She was an idiot. Wen *didn't* feel the same way. She started to pull back, but strong arms wrapped tight around her and warm, soft lips crushed against hers.

Wen pulled back slightly, and her bright blue eyes were filled with tears. She reached down and took both of Estelle's hands in hers. "I'm madly in love with you, Estelle. Every time I look at you, my heart melts. You've reached in and touched something deep inside of me. Something I hadn't known was there..." Wen's bottom lip trembled, and her voice trailed away.

Estelle brought her hands to her heart. "The way I feel when I'm with you...it's not something I'm accustomed to. This will probably sound cheesy, but I feel in harmony with you."

"No, no, that doesn't sound cheesy at all," Wen said. "In harmony, that's a perfect way to describe how I feel. You put it into just the right words."

"The connection between us..." Estelle's voice cracked as she spoke. "It's not something I've ever experienced with another human being."

Wen nodded and stared down at her lap. "But we come from such different worlds..."

Estelle slid a finger under Wen's chin and lifted her head. "I know, but that only matters if we allow it to. I love you and I'm not going to let anything stand in the way of that."

Wen kissed her and whispered against her lips, "Will you take me to bed, please?"

They stood and walked silently toward the stairs, turning off lights as they went.

* * *

The next morning, Wen felt like a million bucks. Estelle snored softly in the bed next to her. She lay on her stomach, her long arms hugging the plump down pillow, and her breathing slow and shallow. Her lips were curled into a faint smile, as if she were having a pleasant dream. The sheet was bunched around her waist, leaving her strong, smooth back exposed. Even as relaxed as Estelle was, the muscles around her shoulder blades were well defined.

Wen kissed her bare shoulder, rolled out of bed, and tiptoed out of the room. Goose bumps instantly dotted her naked body, a clear indication that the fire needed tending. She started the coffeepot and snagged a wool blanket off one of the chairs at the kitchen table. The blanket itched her skin, but it was warm. She trailed a finger over the top of the table and an odd mix of emotions ran through her. Joy and arousal at the memory of being pinned beneath Estelle atop it, and anxiety and dread at the thought of the week to come. Soon—way too soon—the twelve chairs around the table would be occupied. She shook her head to try to erase the thought as she pulled two mugs from the cupboard.

Coffee in hand, she climbed the steps back to the bedroom. Estelle was exactly as she'd left her, but her eyes blinked open when Wen sat down on the edge of the bed.

"Morning, babe," Wen said, surprised that the word had just rolled off her tongue.

Estelle rolled over and sat up in bed, tugging the sheet up around her. "Morning, sweetheart."

Apparently, they'd both caught the term-of-endearment bug, although Wen supposed that was to be expected after declaring their love for one another.

She handed Estelle one of the steaming mugs of coffee and lifted the other to her lips, breathing in the aroma before she took a sip.

Estelle nodded toward the window. "Looks like it's going to be a beautiful day. Maybe we can take the woodie out this morning."

Wen bolted upright, nearly spilling her coffee. "Really? You think it's ready for the water?"

"There's still work to do on it, for sure, but I'm itching to take her for a spin." Estelle laughed. "You know, just to make sure she floats." She gave Wen a peck on the cheek. "If you're good, maybe I'll even let you drive."

"How good do I have to be exactly?" Wen's eyes raked Estelle's body. "If lascivious thoughts are on the naughty list, I'm screwed."

"Screwed," Estelle said with a wink. "Interesting word choice." She trailed a finger down Wen's bare chest. "Because I see some more naked gymnastics in your future."

Wen burst out laughing. "Naked gymnastics?"

"That's how a friend explained sex to me when I was a kid."

"In that case, please sign me up for multiple classes."

"Oh, I shall," Estelle replied. "And I'll make sure the instructor knows you need lots of special attention."

Wen set down her coffee, took the mug from Estelle's hand, and slipped under the covers next to her. She cupped her ass and rolled on top of her.

Estelle squealed. "Oh, my. You certainly are an eager student."

"It helps when you have the hots for the teacher."

* * *

Wen ran her hand along the sleek mahogany rail of the woodie after Estelle backed her out of the boathouse. "You've done an amazing job. This boat is exquisite."

"Thank you," Estelle said. "Like I said, she still needs more work. But I'm excited for my brother to see the progress I've made. Jimmy's equally as passionate about these old boats as I am."

Wen felt like a queen when Estelle relinquished the boat's three-spoke black steering wheel to her. She tugged off her baseball hat and let her hair flow behind her as the boat sliced through the water. Winds were light and the sun glimmered off the water's glass-like surface. She turned the wheel hard to port and then to starboard, leaving behind a zigzagging wake. After this, driving *Mathilde* would feel like maneuvering an eighteen-wheeler.

Once Wen started driving in a straight line again, Estelle bent down to pick something up off the wood floor and held it out for her to see. "Looks like one of the missing Yahtzee dice. Must have rolled out from under the seat."

Wen shrugged. "How'd it get on the boat?"

"My nephew Hunter, one of Whitney's kids, is always stealing the dice from board games. It's infuriating. Anyway, he probably hid this behind one of the open planks in the boat." She patted the rail. "This baby was on blocks in the boathouse all last summer and the kids are always playing hide-and-seek in there."

On Wen's first visit to Owl Island, when Estelle had invited her for tea, she recalled her boasting about being the residing Yahtzee champion.

"You won't believe this," Wen said. "But I've never actually played Yahtzee."

Estelle's eyes went wide. "That must be rectified immediately. I'll teach you after dinner tonight. Playing Yahtzee is a prerequisite for hanging out with the Gage family."

Wen smiled to herself. Hanging out with the Gage family. The thought semi-terrified her—correction, downright horrified her—but she took Estelle's comment as a good sign. It reinforced what she'd said the night before. That she envisioned Wen visiting the island even after her family arrived for the summer. Up until now, she'd been convinced that Estelle would try to keep the two sides of her life—Wen, and her family—segregated. But perhaps she'd been wrong about that.

She's in love with you, you goofball. Makes sense she'd want you to hobnob with her family.

CHAPTER TWENTY

Monday morning arrived way too quickly. Estelle and Wen moved sluggishly around the kitchen while they waited for the coffee to brew.

"Do you have time for pancakes?" Estelle asked.

"Sure," Wen said. She didn't need to check her watch; she knew it was late. Time to head to the mainland and begin her day, but deliveries be damned. A few extra minutes with Estelle proved irresistible.

Estelle held the yellow Bisquick box in the air. "They won't be from scratch, but I do have real Vermont maple syrup."

"If they're made by you, they'll be perfect," Wen said. She hugged Estelle from behind and buried her face in her hair. "Everything about you is perfect."

Estelle turned in her arms and slipped a finger under Wen's chin. "I love you," she whispered.

Wen kissed her on the lips. "I love you too, very much."

"Thank you for the most amazing weekend."

Wen groaned when Estelle pulled her into another kiss. Their hunger for each other never ceased to amaze her. She pushed Estelle up against the counter and deepened the kiss. Estelle's hand slid over her ass, but they jumped apart at the sound of a knock on the screen door off the kitchen.

"Shit," Estelle said under her breath.

"Um, hi. Sorry to interrupt," the man at the door called out. "I'm Chet Britty. I'm here to put up the net on the tennis court."

"Hi, Chet." Estelle smiled and went to greet him at the door.

"I'm just going to run upstairs and gather my stuff," Wen said.

Estelle glanced back over her shoulder. "Okay, sweetheart. I'll get the pancakes going."

They lingered over breakfast, but the intimacy from earlier had vanished. Wen chocked it up to *the intruder*, a.k.a Chet whatever his name was. With great reluctance, she stood from the table and cleared their plates.

"I've got to get going," she said.

Estelle walked her down to the dock and asked, "Are you sure you can't come back tonight?"

Wen jumped aboard *Mathilde* and shook her head. "I wish, but no. There's a fundraiser at the school, and I promised my mom I'd help sell baked goods. My dad did all the cooking, so it's the least I can do."

"Hey, I know," Estelle said. "How about I come into town and help you with the fundraiser?"

Wen smiled. "Really? You'd do that?"

"Of course. It'll be fun. Your dad's a hoot and it will be nice to meet your mom."

"Okay, cool." Wen blew Estelle a kiss.

"Hopefully you can come back out here for a night later in the week."

"I'll do my damnedest to make that work," Wen said. Her week was full of family commitments. Aside from the bake sale, there was her sister Bethany's birthday, and she'd promised to practice soccer with her cousin. Still, she'd find a way to make it out to the island at least one last time before Estelle's family began to arrive on Friday.

As she pulled away from the dock, tears welled up in her eyes. What the heck was wrong with her? Right now, everything was perfect. But would that all change with the arrival of the summer season? Sure, she and Estelle had professed their love for each other, but Estelle might change her mind once the outside world busted in on them. In her heart, Wen believed Estelle's love for her ran deep—she could see it in her eyes and feel it in her touch—but still, anxiety cloaked her.

"I LOVE YOU, ESTELLE GAGE," she yelled over the din of the engine. There was no one near enough to hear her, but it made her feel better anyway.

* * *

Estelle watched *Mathilde* make her way across the water, and only once the boat was a tiny speck on the horizon did she go to the tennis court to check on Chet. He assured her that everything was in good shape, so she made her way up to the widow's watch. By now, Wen had probably already arrived back at the marina, but Estelle still squinted out over the water in hopes of catching a glimpse of her. Given the warmer weather, boats were already out in droves. No longer could Estelle spot one in the distance and know with near certainty that it was *Mathilde*.

She leaned up against the window frame, crossed her arms over her chest, and mused over the weekend she and Wen had spent together. The word divine came to mind. The sex had been good, of course. It always was. Wen was a *very* attentive lover. At times hungry like a wild animal, and at others tender and sweet. But as much as Estelle enjoyed making love to Wen, she relished the hours they sat cuddled by the fire. Even the simple act of making dinner with her was special. And the expression on Wen's face as she drove the woodie around the islands. Pure joy. Joy that was infectious.

The fact that Wen loved boats and being out on the water as much as Estelle did was an added bonus. As much as she hated to keep comparing Wen to Claudia, it was difficult not to. The two women were polar opposites. Claudia hated it up in the islands. *"Too many bugs and those godforsaken birds, chirping before the sun was even up."* If ever there was a city girl, it was Claudia. Estelle pinched her eyes shut. She had to stop letting Claudia creep into her thoughts.

She pulled her phone from the back pocket of her jeans and called Fran.

"Hey, island girl," Fran said when she answered. "I texted you like twenty times over the weekend. Nothing but crickets in return."

"Sorry, my sweet. I was, uh, just busy."

"Busy *getting busy* with your mailboat captain."

Estelle smiled into the phone. "Maybe."

Fran cackled. "At least one of us is getting some action. Go figure it would be the one on a remote island in the middle of nowhere. Although…it sounds like your dreamy days as a recluse are about to come to an end. I ran into your mother the other night, at the gala for that new art center, and she told me she was headed north."

"Yes, she is. She's due to arrive here on Friday."

"Will that spell an end to your island love affair?"

"I certainly hope not," Estelle said. "Things will be different, of course…"

"Are you worried about how your mother will react?" Fran asked.

"To tell you the truth, I don't honestly give a shit what my mother thinks. I'm a grown woman and I can date whom I wish."

"You don't have to convince me, Estelle. You know I've been pro-Wen all along. In my opinion, she's the best thing to happen to you in a long time, but let's be honest, your mother isn't exactly the easiest person to be around and, how do I put this diplomatically…she can be a wee bit judgmental."

Estelle put a hand on her hip, her heart thudding in her chest. "Wen is extremely intelligent and confident, and I have no doubt she'll take my mother in stride."

"I hope you're right."

"I am right. Wen isn't easily ruffled, and she doesn't give two hoots what people think about her. It's one of the many things I love about her."

"Whoa," Fran said, "you mean *love*, love?"

"Yes," Estelle said softly. "I'm not exactly sure how it happened, but I've fallen in love with her."

"Are you sure it's not just the fresh island air getting to you?" Fran asked.

"I'm sure. What Wen and I have is real, more real than anything else I've ever experienced. I see myself with her long term."

"Okay, wow. That's great, Estelle, it really is, but, and I hate to point out the obvious, she lives there, and you live in New York. That is, presuming you don't plan to stay up in the islands forever."

"No, of course not. I'm fortunate that I was able to get away for this stretch of time, but the city is where my life is, and there are obligations there that I've already neglected for far too long."

"Are you anticipating that Wen will come here?"

"I don't know." Estelle tried to imagine Wen living in New York City. While she didn't doubt Wen could adapt to city living—she had, after all, planned to spend the summer in Barcelona—New York was about as different from Coopersville as you could get, and the stream of charity balls wore on even the most seasoned socialites. "My relationship with Wen is still relatively new," she said finally. "We'll cross that bridge when we get to it."

"Very well," Fran said. "I absolutely cannot wait to meet her."

CHAPTER TWENTY-ONE

"You did a great job with the hamburgers, Dad," Wen said. "They're cooked to perfection, and your special sauce is delish."

It was early afternoon on Memorial Day Monday. Wen and her family had spent the morning riding on a float in the Coopersville parade and were now hosting the twenty-fifth annual Apollo Memorial Day barbeque in their backyard.

Her dad patted her on the back. "Thanks, kiddo." He laughed. "I made a triple batch of my special 'Welcome Summer Sauce' this year and it still sold out in under an hour."

"No surprise there." Wen smiled to herself. It had been her idea to build the little farm stand in front of their house as a way for her father to sell a sampling of his culinary creations, although even she had not expected it to be such a roaring success. And the best part was, her father took such pride in it. He'd even painted a big sign that read *Arthur Apollo's Edibles* to put out near the sidewalk.

After her father's accident over a decade ago, he'd resisted taking on the role of Mr. Mom for about ten seconds before fully embracing it. Losing his legs had been an awful tragedy, of course, but ultimately it had almost been a blessing in disguise. Their house started to feel more like a *home* when her father took over all the domestic duties and her mother was able to give more of herself to the school. Two years after her dad's accident, Lucinda had been promoted to principal of Coopersville Central.

Wen popped the last of her hamburger into her mouth and instinctively reached for her phone.

"You've been checking that device an awful lot lately," her father said. "Waiting on something important?"

Wen shook her head. "Nah, it's just, I've barely heard from Estelle all weekend."

"Her family just arrived for the summer, right?"

"Uh-huh."

"I've heard that Catherine Gage is a real tyrant," he said. "Makes sense Estelle would be a little distracted while her mom gets settled in."

"I guess." Wen knew he was right. Estelle probably had a lot going on. Croquet, Yahtzee, tennis… She'd sent a brief *Hey, miss you* text yesterday, but otherwise it had been radio silence since her mother had arrived on Friday. Wen wasn't one to be all clingy, but the lack of communication made her super anxious. Why had Estelle dropped off the planet? *Does she really love me? Am I being unreasonable?*

Maybe it was the abrupt change. Going from cuddling by the fire every night and expressions of love for one another to practically no contact at all. Wen had had no delusions about the invasion of the Gage family being an adjustment, but perhaps she'd underestimated just how much of an adjustment.

* * *

Because of the three-day weekend and because Memorial Day marked the official start of the summer season, a mountain of packages greeted Wen when she arrived at the marina Tuesday morning. There were big boxes and little boxes, bundles of camp wood, an assortment of white paper bags from the pharmacy, and dozens of crates filled with groceries and booze.

She flicked on her GPS and consulted the map as she took an inventory of the packages and neatly stowed them on the boat. Although she was still irked that the flow of messages from Estelle had dropped to a trickle, her heart skipped a beat when she picked up a large box adorned with Amazon's smiling arrow. Destination: Owl Island. It made sense to deliver the box at the tail end of the day, but Wen made a small adjustment to her route so she'd hit the Gage residence closer to lunchtime.

The rain clouds that had hung around for much of Memorial Day weekend were now long gone and blue sky stretched for as far as the eye could see. She cranked her stereo and set out across the water, humming along to the music.

As planned, she headed for the Gage's just before noon. She approached the dock like she always did, but the island seemed like a totally different place. Children ran across the lawn and people occupied the now full set of rocking chairs on the deck to the house. With her shocking white hair and blue-striped blazer, it wasn't hard to spot the matriarch herself, Catherine Gage, among those gathered on the deck. Estelle was nowhere in sight, and as ridiculous as it was, Wen leered at the *interlopers*.

A tall, slightly heavyset woman stood on the grass flanked by two towheaded boys. She waved at Wen and walked toward the dock.

"I've got a package for Whitney Gage," Wen called out after she'd killed *Mathilde*'s gurgling diesel engine.

The woman gave her a weak smile. "That would be me." Her brown eyes weren't as dark or as expressive as Estelle's, but she was clearly a Gage.

Wen pulled the Amazon box from her neatly organized pile and handed it up to Estelle's sister.

"Thank you," Whitney muttered and turned back toward the house.

"Um," Wen said. "Is Estelle here by chance?"

Whitney glanced back over her shoulder, her face crinkled as if she'd caught a whiff of a rotting fish. "She's playing tennis," she said, as if it was the most obvious thing in the world.

"Would you please tell her Wen stopped by?"

Whitney turned back toward the boat, her face still contorted. "Wen?"

Wen's heart sunk. Estelle, a woman who days earlier had professed to love her, hadn't even mentioned her to her sister. Estelle had hinted that she and Whitney weren't close, but still... *You woulda thunk my name might have come up.* Surely, Estelle's family had asked her at least a few questions about the nearly two months she'd spent alone up in the islands.

"Never mind," Wen said. She turned the key in the boat's ignition and inched the throttle forward.

An hour later, her phone rang. Estelle. She considered letting it go to voice mail but decided that would be immature. She answered the call, trying to keep the irritation out of her voice.

"Hey, there."

"Hello, sweetheart. I heard you stopped by," Estelle said.

"Um, yeah. I had a package for Whitney." *You know, your sister, who has no idea who I am.*

"You should have come up to say hello."

Wen eased back on the throttle and clicked it into neutral. This conversation needed her full attention. "Let's just say your sister wasn't exactly warm and welcoming. That, and she didn't seem to know who the hell I was. When I asked after you, she looked at me like I had three heads. Call me crazy, but I thought maybe you would have mentioned—"

"Things between Whitney and I are tense with a capital T. We've barely spoken a word since she arrived yesterday."

"Yesterday? Wasn't she supposed to get here on Saturday?"

"Yes, but she came straight here from Brazil—she was there on Gage Foundation business—and there was an issue with her flight back to the US."

Wen pinched the bridge of her nose. She shouldn't have jumped down Estelle's throat without hearing her out. "Oh, that's too bad." She paused before adding, "You've never told me why you two don't get along."

"We're just two very different people. Even as kids, there was animosity between us, but our relationship has been especially rocky since Claudia and I split."

"How come?"

"Whitney warned me not to marry Claudia. She was emphatic but wouldn't tell me why. It wasn't until later that I learned she knew of past infidelities. At any rate, when Claudia and I separated, Whit wasted no time telling me 'I told you so.' And I didn't take hearing that very well."

"I don't blame you. I wouldn't have either. Your sister sounds like a real peach."

"She has her moments. Deep down I think she loves me and cares about my well-being. It's just, ever since her divorce, she's become a self-appointed expert on relationships. Suffice it to say, I didn't rush to call her up and tell her I'd fallen in love with you…"

Wen closed her eyes and smiled at those words.

"The entire time I was up on the island this spring," Estelle said, "Whit and I exchanged a grand total of two text messages, both focused entirely around the dates she and the boys would be in residence this summer. But enough about my sister, tell me about the Memorial Day parade? Did people like your family's float?"

"It was great, and yeah, the float was a colossal hit, although the gobs of candy we tossed to the crowd along the route probably helped."

"That's wonderful. I'd hoped to sneak away and catch a glimpse of the parade, but my brother is fixated on finishing the restoration of the woodie and he held me captive in the boathouse most of the weekend."

"Ah, that's okay," Wen said. "It wasn't exactly the Macy's Day Parade."

"Any parade you're in is worth seeing."

"I miss you like crazy."

"Same here," Estelle said. "When can I see you?"

"How about tonight? I can swing by and get you when I'm done for the day, and we can spend the night at my place."

"Tonight would be perfect. My mother is guaranteed to grumble when she realizes I've disappeared off the island, but she'll get over it."

"Cool. And, hey, sorry if I flew off the handle a little bit. I let my insecurities get the best of me."

"It's okay, but you have nothing to worry about when it comes to me. I meant it when I said I loved you. What you and I have is extremely important to me."

"It's important to me too," Wen croaked. It was then that she realized she was perilously close to the rocky tip of Gig Island. "I'll pick you up around five," she said quickly. "I have to go. I'm out on the water and I'm about to drift aground."

* * *

Estelle slipped back into bed with Wen and handed her a spoon and a container of ice cream. They'd briefly discussed going out to dinner but had abandoned that idea in favor of staying in and ordering pizza, and it was a darn good thing. Ever since they'd motored away from Owl Island, they hadn't been able to keep their hands off each other. When the pizza delivery guy had knocked at the door to Wen's apartment, their naked bodies had been entangled on the couch. Wen had scrambled to tug on her T-shirt and jeans before she'd opened the door and the smart-ass delivery boy had the gall to point out that her shirt was not only inside out but backward. As soon as Wen had closed the door behind him, she and Estelle had fallen into a fit of laughter.

"Yum, Rocky Road," Wen said as she dug into the round container of ice cream. "I'd actually forgotten I had this. My sister brought it over as a housewarming gift."

"I can't believe you let Rocky Road sit in your freezer that long without touching it," Estelle said. "You have a lot more willpower than I do."

"Um, may I remind you that I've hardly spent a minute here since I moved in."

Estelle scooped out a big spoonful of ice cream, slid it into Wen's mouth, and asked, "Oh, really, why is that?"

Wen swallowed her ice cream and licked her lips. "Because I've spent practically every night cloistered on a secluded island with my beautiful girlfriend."

"Oooh, that sounds heavenly."

"It was."

Estelle stabbed the spoon into the ice cream, set the container down on the nightstand, and reached for Wen's hands. "I'm sorry my family is here now."

"Um, it's kinda their island," Wen said.

"I know, and I love having them there, but quiet nights by the fire with you are infinitely more enjoyable."

"Are you sure?"

Estelle kissed Wen on the lips. "Uh-huh." She stared into Wen's eyes. "You know you're welcome on the island any time you like."

Wen shrugged. "If you say so."

"I do say so. In fact, why don't you come to dinner on Saturday?"

"I don't want to embarrass you."

Estelle sat up and cupped Wen's face in her hands. "You." Kiss. "Will." Kiss. "Never." Kiss. "Embarrass me."

"I wouldn't know what to wear."

"Any dinner jacket will do," Estelle said.

The expression on Wen's face was priceless.

Estelle burst out laughing. "I'm kidding."

"Oh."

"You can wear whatever you want. Except ripped jeans. My mother abhors ripped jeans."

"Okay."

"So you'll come?"

"Yes, I'll come. Just promise you won't leave me alone with your mother, or Whitney for that matter."

"I promise. I'll stay right by your side all night."

CHAPTER TWENTY-TWO

The following Saturday, Wen borrowed her friend's Boston Whaler motorboat. It had a few dings in it, but it was a heck of a lot better than the alternative: arriving in *Mathilde* for dinner with the Gages, especially because her engine had been acting up again. The diesel behemoth was even louder than normal, and it belched a nasty, thick black exhaust. Not exactly the first impression Wen was going for. With her calloused hands and scuffed shoes, she'd stand out enough. No need to draw any additional attention to the fact that she was working class.

On a typical day, she could dock a boat with her eyes closed. But today was not a typical day. It took her three tries before she properly landed the Boston Whaler at the dock on Owl Island. Way to wow the Gage family with her nautical prowess.

Wen's shoulders relaxed a tad when she spotted Estelle running down to meet her. As always, the sight of her caused Wen's lips to curl into a smile. *That beautiful woman is in love with you.* The thought gave her a slight burst of much-needed courage.

"Hi, sweetheart," Estelle said when she reached the dock. She pulled Wen into her arms and gave her a lingering kiss on the lips.

"Well that answers that question," Wen said.

"What question?" Estelle asked as they walked toward the house hand in hand.

"Whether you've told your family, you know"—she raised her eyebrows twice in quick succession—"that you and I are an item."

Estelle squeezed her hand. "I told them my girlfriend was coming to dinner."

Wen resisted the urge to skip like a child. "Gotcha. But don't forget your promise. Don't, under any circumstance, abandon me with *any* member of your family."

"They don't have fangs."

"I'll be the judge of that."

Catherine Gage greeted them at the front door, and although she was a few inches shorter than Estelle, she was an imposing figure. With her head held high, she peered down her nose at Wen. Massive diamond earrings poked out from her perfectly coiffed white hair, and bright red lipstick circled her stern lips.

Wen wiped a hand on her freshly ironed khakis and shook the hand Catherine extended. Damn, the old broad's grip was like a pit bull's locking jaw. She held on to Wen's hand and, with eyes that lacked even a glimmer of warmth, gave her a not so subtle up and down, like Wen was a piece of meat hanging from a hook at the butcher.

Mrs. Gage finally released Wen's hand and her lips pursed into what almost verged on a smile. "Welcome to Owl Island," she said. Her voice was raspy like a two-pack-a-day smoker, but her words were crisp.

Wen cleared her throat. "Thank you very much for having me, Mrs. Gage."

They stepped into the living room and although Wen had spent countless hours at the house, it felt unfamiliar. Not at all like the place she and Estelle had shared alone together. Upon quick inspection, she noted that nothing in the room had changed. All the furniture appeared to be in the same place.

When her eyes fell on the two leather chairs near the wood burning stove, her chest tightened and she reached for Estelle's hand, desperate to connect with her.

Estelle gave her a soft smile and mouthed, "I love you."

It was a fairly warm evening with a light breeze, and they sat for cocktails on the front porch. Pauline, Mrs. Gage's "lady's maid," made the matriarch a Manhattan, announced that a roast chicken was in the oven and would be ready in an hour, and excused herself for the evening. Estelle's brother Jimmy made vodka martinis for himself, his wife, and Whitney, but Estelle and Wen opted for white wine. Wen had really wanted a beer but feared it might be too proletariat for cocktail hour at the Gage residence.

She sipped her wine and slowly rocked back and forth in her rocking chair while she half listened to the conversation that took place around her, a conversation which, at present, centered on Catherine Gage's displeasure with the decorator they'd hired for the family compound in Boca Raton.

"So, Wen. Estelle tells us you run the delivery boat around the islands," a raspy voice said.

Wen nearly dropped her glass. She'd zoned out for a moment and hadn't realized the topic of conversation had shifted to her. She planted her loafers flat on the floor to slow her rocker and sat up straight.

"Um, yes, ma'am, I do." With a nod in the general direction of the Boston Whaler at the dock, she said, "Not in that boat. I've got a bigger one for deliveries. Her name's *Mathilde*." All eyes were on her as she spoke and a warmth crept up her neck, undoubtedly rendering her face beet red. Fantastic.

"That's quite an interesting line of work," Jimmy said. "How long have you been at it?" His eyes narrowed on Wen. "You can't be older than what, twenty-five?"

"I'm twenty-seven," she said, "and, I, um, just recently took over the route from my uncle." She almost added something about how she only planned to run the boat on a temporary basis and had plans to go off and see the world, but opted not to, lest she come off as a rambling idiot.

"Wen's uncle passed away this spring," Estelle said.

"Oh, what a shame," Mrs. Gage said.

"I'm sorry to hear that," Jimmy and Whitney said in unison.

"Was that always the plan?" Jimmy's wife asked. "For you to eventually take over the route from your uncle?"

Wen bit her lip while she decided how to respond. "Um, yes and no. It's kind of a long story. A member of my family has run the route for generations…" She hadn't really answered the question, but she opted to leave it at that.

"Very interesting," Mrs. Gage said.

Wen couldn't tell if she was being sincere or not, so she just smiled in response.

"What do you do in the wintertime?" Jimmy asked.

"I stay here in Coopersville," she replied, unsure if he was asking what she did work-wise, or if he was inquiring where she wintered.

"There can't be much of a population up on the islands in the colder months," Mrs. Gage said.

Wen shook her head. "No there isn't. Aside from a few hardy folks, most of the islands are un…habit…un…in…habited in the dead of winter." *Way to go, Wen. Now they think five syllable words are a stretch for you.*

Three boys and a girl ran across the lawn and up onto the deck. The oldest of the boys—Wen pegged him to be around ten—had a soccer ball tucked under one arm. He looked at Whitney and asked, "How long till dinner?"

"About forty-five minutes," she said, "but you need to come in before that and get washed up."

The kid cast a glance at Wen. "Who are you?"

"That's Wen," Estelle replied. "She's my girlfriend."

"Oh," the kid said.

Whitney turned toward Wen. "These are my boys"—she pointed to each one as she spoke their names—"Cob, Hunter, and Wyatt, and that's Jimmy's daughter, Olivia."

"Nice to meet you all," Wen said.

"Nice to meet you too," the four children replied in unison.

Wen pointed to the ball under Cob's arm. "I used to play soccer."

"Wen was the top scorer on her soccer team in high school," Estelle said.

"Cool," Cob replied. "Do you want to play with us?"

"Um…" Wen glimpsed over at Estelle. Playing soccer with the kids sounded like a whole lot more fun than sitting on the deck making small talk with the adults.

"Go ahead and play if you want, but don't feel obligated," Estelle said.

Wen stood from her chair so fast it rocked vigorously back and forth on the deck's wooden planks.

She spent the next thirty minutes running around the lawn with the kids. Estelle eventually came down and sat on the grass to watch them play. All the kids moaned when Whitney called them up for dinner.

"You're pretty good," Cob said to Wen as they walked back toward the house.

"Thanks, Cob. You're pretty good yourself."

He beamed and sprinted up the steps to the porch.

Before dinner, Wen popped into the powder room off the kitchen and used a damp towel to clean herself up. Soccer had rendered her hot and sticky. Wisps of hair flew this way and that and her hairline was moist with sweat.

The ten of them—the six adults and the four kids—took their seats around the long table in the kitchen. Thankfully, a red and white checkered tablecloth adorned it. *We had sex on this table, for Christ's sake.* Wen caught Estelle's eye and they shared a silent snicker.

Cob insisted on sitting next to Wen and they spent most of dinner talking about football and soccer. When Wen's hand hovered over the three forks laid out to the left of her plate, Cob made subtle gestures to guide her to the correct one. By the end of dinner, Wen wanted to hug the kid. He'd made what could have been an extremely awkward meal borderline enjoyable.

The kids were put on dish duty with Jimmy as their supervisor while the rest of the adults adjourned to the living room for what Catherine referred to as a digestif. Wen didn't know what the hell she was talking about until Estelle handed her a snifter of brandy. In an effort to pretend like she drank brandy after dinner every night, she swirled the brown liquid in its wide glass. Unfortunately, her act was quickly foiled. The digestif burned the crap out of her throat and her efforts to suppress a coughing fit made her eyes water. *Charming.*

Later that evening, Estelle and Wen grabbed a couple of beers from the fridge and escaped outside to the rocking chairs on the deck.

"Looks like you've got a little admirer," Estelle said. "Cob followed you around like a puppy dog all night."

"He's a great kid," Wen said.

Estelle nodded. "He is, which is nothing short of a miracle. His dad pushes him so hard, never lets up whether it's school or sports. Last year I went to see one of Cob's soccer games and he scored the winning goal with like two seconds left. His teammates hoisted him in the air, and you could see the pride on his face. His dad wiped it away in an instant, berating him for missing a shot earlier in the game."

Wen cringed and brought her hand to her mouth. "Jeez, that's horrible. How often does Cob see his dad?"

"Pretty often. He and Whit split custody of the boys."

Jimmy stepped outside. "We're all headed to bed. I came to say good night." He shifted his attention toward Wen. "It was nice to meet you."

Wen stood. "You too, Jimmy. Good night."

"Will you stay?" Estelle asked once he'd gone back inside.

Wen hugged her arms around her torso. "I'd love to, but, uh"—she nodded toward the house—"I'm not sure I should. I mean, won't it be awkward, you know, if I'm here in the morning?"

Estelle brushed a hand through the air. "Nah. My mother may be a lot of things, but she's not a prude, and God knows Jimmy and Whit won't care. They've each had their fair share of boyfriends and girlfriends traipsing through this house."

"Okay, then," Wen said. "That would be nice...as long as you don't think they'll mind."

CHAPTER TWENTY-THREE

Early the next morning, they crept out of Estelle's room. It was barely dawn and the floorboards in the old house creaked as they moved across them and descended the stairs to the kitchen. A noise that Estelle had barely noticed when it had only been the two of them on the island, but now, with a house full of sleeping people, it seemed on par with a jackhammer.

"Good morning, dear."

Estelle jumped back at the sound of her mother's voice and bumped into Wen on the staircase behind her. "Mother, what are you doing up?"

"The birds," her mother replied. "Every year when I come up here, it takes a spell before I grow accustomed to all their chirping and carrying on." She laughed. "I have the same reaction to the city when I return at the end of the season. All those honking horns and sirens. What a racket after the remoteness of this place."

"The birds are lovely, but they sure do like to sing." Estelle glanced back over her shoulder. Wen stood partway up the stairs frozen like a statue and Estelle gestured for her to come down into the kitchen.

Wen inched down the stairs, her jaw clenched and her eyes wide. Estelle tried to give her an encouraging smile.

"Sounds like someone else is awake," Estelle's mother said.

"Yes," Estelle replied. "It's Wen. She needs to return—"

Her mother's teacup rattled in its saucer. "Wen is still here, on the island?"

Wen poked her head into the kitchen. "Good morning, Mrs. Gage." She turned to Estelle. "I should get going."

"Don't you want some breakfast?" Estelle asked. She rested a hand on the small of Wen's back. "We still have some of that cinnamon oatmeal you like. It'll only take me a minute to make it."

"Um, no thank you. I can grab something at the marina." Wen stood tall and addressed Estelle's mother. "Thank you very much for dinner, Mrs. Gage."

Estelle's mother was stony-faced. "You're welcome," she said and turned her focus to the crossword puzzle on the table in front of her.

When she and Estelle reached the dock where the Boston Whaler was tied up, Wen said, "Your mother totally hates me."

"No, she doesn't. Admittedly, she's not the most effusive person, especially before her morning tea, but she'll warm up to you, I promise." Estelle kissed Wen on the lips. "When do I get to see you again?"

Wen kicked a pebble off the dock and it splashed in the water. "It's my dad's birthday on Wednesday and we're having a little party for him. Nothing fancy, just a barbecue. Would you like to come?"

"I'd love to," Estelle said. "Thank you for inviting me."

Wen gave her a broad smile. "Okay, great. I can come by and pick you up sometime that afternoon."

"You're busy enough without having to chauffeur me around. Now that our boats are in the water, I can come in on one of them."

"Are you sure?" Wen asked. "Because I don't mind."

"Yes, I'm sure." Estelle gave her one last kiss before she jumped aboard the boat.

Once Wen was out of sight, Estelle walked back up to the house. When she entered the kitchen, Pauline was pouring her mother another cup of tea.

"You're up mighty early, Estelle," Pauline said.

"Yes," Estelle replied. "My girlfriend, Wen, had to rush back to the mainland and I figured I might as well get up too. Never hurts to get a jump on the day."

Pauline shrugged and asked, "Can I make you some eggs?"

"No thank you. Coffee is good for now. I'll make myself something later."

"Suit yourself," Pauline said and busied herself tidying the kitchen.

Estelle poured herself a cup of coffee from the pot on the counter and started for the back stairs in hopes of getting some writing done before the rest of her family woke up.

"How long have you known this Wen person?" her mother asked when Estelle's foot hit the first step.

Estelle turned back to face her. "Nearly two months. She came by to deliver a package not long after I arrived in the islands this spring."

Her mother folded her hands in her lap and pursed her lips. "She seems like a lovely girl, but, Estelle dear, she's a townie."

Estelle tried to keep the anger from her voice but failed miserably. "What exactly are you implying?"

"You know darn well what I'm implying," her mother retorted. "I certainly don't begrudge you for wanting"—she wiggled her eyebrows—"a little company this spring when you were stowed away up here all alone, but the poor girl is clearly in love with you. You need to break things off with her before things get *messy*."

"Messy?" Estelle threw her hands in the air. "You are a piece of work. And for your information, I happen to be in love with her."

"Need I remind you, you're *a Gage*."

"Oh, so therefore I should stick to people of a certain pedigree, people like Claudia?" Estelle put her hands on her hips. "Need I remind you, dear mother, how *that* turned out?"

Her mother crossed her arms over her chest and leered at Estelle. "How can you be certain Wen doesn't look at you and see dollar signs?"

Estelle slammed her hand on the kitchen table, sending some of her mother's freshly poured tea sloshing over the rim of her teacup. In all her thirty-three years, she had never once, toddler tantrums aside, lost her temper in front of her mother, but this time she'd gone too far.

"How can you even say that? You met her. That's not who Wen is. She doesn't give a crap about money and social standing. That's one of the reasons I love her."

Estelle stormed out of the room, pushed through the screen door that led to the back porch, and let it slam behind her with a whack. A deep breath of the fresh morning air did nothing to calm her down. She stomped down to the far end of the island, just beyond the tennis court, and sat on a rock overlooking the small cove. A mist hung over the water and even though she couldn't see them, she could hear the loons in the distance. They made her think of Wen and the first night they'd spent together. Her mother be damned, Wen made her happy and she had absolutely no intention of breaking things off with her. Just the opposite. Estelle hoped she and Wen had a long, long future ahead of them.

She stood, walked down to the rocky shoreline, and picked up a flat round stone. It was cold but soft, and it slid easily between her thumb and pointer finger. She flicked her wrist and released the stone, sending it skipping, one, two, three, four times across the smooth surface of the water. It had been ages since she'd skipped stones and it was oddly soothing. She picked up another one and hurled it toward the water and it went even farther than the first one, hopping across the water seven times before disappearing into the mist.

"You're pretty good at that," a small voice said.

She scanned the shoreline and spotted Cob standing at the base of an oak tree, a fishing pole slung over his shoulder and a yellow bucket in his hand. "Morning, Cob."

"Morning, Aunt Estelle."

"Catch anything yet?"

He shook his head. "Nope, but Uncle Jimmy said he'd take me out in the boat later." He set down his bucket. "Is Wen still here?"

Estelle smiled. "No, she had to go home early this morning, but she'll be back soon."

A broad grin took over Cob's face. "I promised I'd teach her how to fish."

Given that Wen had grown up on the water, she was no doubt an adept fisher, but had obviously opted not to share this with Cob. Estelle made a mental note to thank her later. "That's nice of you, Cob. I bet she would appreciate that."

He turned to leave but paused and looked back over his shoulder. "Your girlfriend is really cool, Aunt Estelle."

Estelle's heart swelled. "Thanks, Cob. I think so too."

* * *

Wen rested her elbow on the bar and traced the rim of her pint glass with her finger. "Dude, Catherine Gage thinks I have no business being with her daughter. She didn't come right out and say it, but she didn't have to. This morning, when Estelle and I came downstairs, you should've seen the look she gave me. Utter disgust. Like how dare I spend the night in *her* house. I bet she's having the place fumigated as we speak."

"That bad, huh?" Ruby asked.

"Yes," Wen said. "That bad. Honestly, I wouldn't be surprised if she forbade me from ever stepping foot on their island again."

"Are you sure you aren't being a little melodramatic?" Ruby asked.

"Trust me, I'm not. Let's just say I won't be rushing back there anytime soon, at least as long as that snob of a woman is there."

"What about the night before, during dinner and stuff? What was Mrs. Gage like then?"

"Standoffish. I think she and I exchanged a grand total of three words the entire evening. She tolerated my presence, that's about it. Made like zero effort to make me feel welcome."

"She doesn't exactly have a reputation for being all warm and fuzzy. Maybe she's a cold fish to everyone."

"Maybe," Wen said, but she wasn't convinced. "I felt so out of place. If it hadn't been for Estelle's adorable nephew Cob, I'm not sure I would've survived the evening."

"What about Estelle?" Ruby asked. "Didn't she try to help matters?"

Wen's head bobbed up and down. "Oh, yeah, definitely. She stuck by me the whole night. The thing is, I don't think she fully gets it. What it's like for me to traipse into her world and be presented as her girlfriend. I mean, Estelle tried to make me feel comfortable, and I know she cares about me, but she comes from a world of such privilege. She can't begin to comprehend what it's like to walk in my shoes."

Ruby rubbed Wen's back. "It was just one dinner. Give it a little time. Who knows, maybe Catherine Gage will warm up to you."

Wen snorted out a laugh. "Fat chance." She lifted her pint and nodded toward Ruby. "I love how you're always so optimistic and like to see the best in people, but the truth is, Rube, I'm an idiot and I'm going to get my heart broken. Serves me right. I let myself fall for someone who's way out of my league. This spring, when she and I were out on the island alone, it was like a fairytale, but, duh, no way that was gonna last. Reality has reared its ugly head. I just wish I'd smartened up a little sooner…Like before I fell in love with her…"

"Promise me you won't do anything rash. Promise me you'll at least try to talk to Estelle about how you're feeling. I've seen you two together. You've got something special. Don't fuck it up."

"But—"

"No buts," Ruby said. "Remember this. Estelle's a grown woman and she can pick who she wants to date. And guess what? She picked you. Don't push her away just because her mother happens to be a bitch."

"A royal bitch," Wen muttered.

When Ruby excused herself to go to the bathroom, Wen pulled out her phone. There were a bunch of texts from Estelle. *Cob can't stop talking about you... Hope you're having a good time at the Igloo... Miss you.* She stuffed the phone back into her pocket and ordered another beer.

CHAPTER TWENTY-FOUR

What time is the barbecue for your dad?

Wen glanced at the text from Estelle while she brushed her teeth with one hand and brushed her hair with the other, not an easy feat. The barbecue was that night, and for reasons she hadn't fully unpacked, she'd been ignoring Estelle's texts and calls and had yet to share the details about the party with her. Was she worried Estelle wouldn't come? Maybe. Was she taking her anger at Catherine Gage out on Estelle? Possibly. Was that immature and stupid? Definitely.

There was also the fact that the week had been nuts and Wen hadn't had time to do much of anything except deliver packages. In all her years of helping her dad and uncle with the mailboat, she didn't ever remember it being this busy. Not even close. Perhaps it just seemed that way because this was the first summer the responsibility for the route rested on her shoulders alone. It would stand to reason that the burden of it felt much greater when it was hers alone to carry.

Between spoonfuls of Cheerios, she hammered off a text to Estelle. *The bbq is at six p.m. But I totally understand if you can't make it.*

I wouldn't miss it for the world.

Okay, great. Remember, it'll be nothing fancy. No need to get dressed up.

All she needed was for Estelle to show up wearing a linen suit and pearls.

She set her bowl in the sink and grabbed her backpack from the chair near the door. Before she left for the marina, she sent off one last text to Estelle.

I love you.

Ruby was right. Estelle had been nothing but kind, supportive, and loving to her. She'd done nothing to deserve the cold shoulder, and it wasn't her fault that her mother happened to be a stuck-up socialite.

"You need to woman up and stop acting like a brat," Wen mumbled to herself as she walked out the door. "You're in love with a beautiful woman who also happens to be in love with you."

Ruby's words echoed in her head. *Don't fuck it up.*

* * *

Wen jumped up from her lawn chair when Estelle walked into her parents' backyard at a quarter past six. She wore a casual, flowy floral dress with a thin sweater tied over her shoulders and her long brown hair was pulled back. Wen had never seen her wear a dress before but given that they had rarely ventured off Owl Island during their brief relationship, that wasn't all that surprising.

Wen's entire immediate family was there, including her sister Laura from DC, and friends and extended family had begun to trickle in.

She greeted Estelle with a kiss on the cheek and whispered, "You look beautiful. I'm so glad you made it." She stepped back and ran a hand down Estelle's arm. "Any problems finding the place?"

"Nope, not at all. I didn't even have to give Ken the taxi driver the address. As soon as I mentioned your name, he put the car in gear and off we went." Estelle gave her a gentle hip-check. "Apparently the Apollos are royalty in Coopersville."

"Ha, ha, I don't know about that. That's just small town living for you."

"Although Ken had to drop me at the end of the block."

"Why?" Wen asked.

"Because your dad's roadside stand is clogged with people. The line of cars wraps around the corner."

"He put out a fresh batch of pies this afternoon," Wen said. "He prepares a special edition every year on his birthday."

"The poor kid manning the till looked a bit exasperated."

"Grayson," Wen said, referring to the neighbor boy who sometimes helped her dad with the stand, "can handle it. He's dealt with the pie mob many times." She pointed across the small backyard. "Let's go say hello to my dad. He's looking forward to seeing you again and was excited when I told him you were coming."

They moved toward the grill where her dad and her sister Bethany stood. Wen's father gave Estelle a warm greeting but the smile on Bethany's face was far from genuine. When Estelle extended her hand, Bethany shook it limply and mumbled, "Nice to finally meet you." She wouldn't even make eye contact with Estelle, and the look on her face hovered somewhere between bored and annoyed, like a teenage boy forced to sit through his sister's flute recital.

Bethany resented the summer folks in a way that Wen never had, and apparently, she had no intention of hiding her disdain.

"Nice to see you again, Mr. Apollo," Estelle said. "Happy birthday."

"Thanks," he said.

Estelle laughed. "Half the town has flocked to your roadside stand."

Wen's dad beamed. "They show up in droves whenever I put out a new batch of something. Never ceases to amaze me." He patted Wen's back. "Thanks to this one, I now have my own Facebook page."

Bethany grunted and excused herself, apparently not interested in making small talk with one of the island people, even one who happened to be Wen's girlfriend.

Next, they moved on to Wen's mother, who chastised her for not offering her guest a beverage the moment she arrived.

"Gah, sorry," Wen said. "Estelle, may I offer you a cold beverage? Lemonade, beer, wine?"

"A beer would be wonderful, thanks, Wen."

When she returned with a Budweiser, Estelle and her mother were deep in conversation.

Estelle took the beer, uttered a thank-you to Wen, and said, "Your mom and I were just talking about her job at the school."

"She runs that place like a well-oiled machine," Wen said. "High school dropouts have decreased significantly since she took over the reins."

"Wow," Estelle said. "That's impressive, Mrs. Apollo."

An hour or so later, Ruby and Aunt Linda, Uncle Mark's widow, and her children arrived. Wen excused herself and left Estelle to continue chatting with her older sister Laura. Although Laura was a few years younger than Estelle, she apparently knew and worked with some of her Dartmouth classmates in DC, and they were busy playing the game of "do you know."

When it came time to eat dinner, everyone lined up at a table piled high with food. Hot dogs, hamburgers, barbecue chicken, potato and macaroni salad, coleslaw, and baked beans. The plate Estelle selected from the stack had a large chip on its edge. Wen cringed, tugged it from her hand, and handed her another one. They found a spot on the grass near Bethany and her family and devoured the mounds of food on their plates. Wen went up to the ice bin near the house to get them each another Bud, and by the time she got back, Estelle had taken on the role of human jungle gym. Bethany's two older boys giggled as they crawled all over her. Repeated warnings from Bethany to settle down because they'd just eaten went unheeded. She eventually gave up and sat back down on the grass next to her husband, who cradled their three-month-old in his arms. Estelle tickled the boys, intensifying their giggling and Wen could have sworn there was even a hint of a smile on her sister's face.

At the end of the night, Wen drove Estelle back to her apartment over the bookstore.

"Thank you for coming to the barbecue," she said as she closed the apartment door behind them. "It meant a lot to me to have you there."

Estelle pulled her into a hug. "I thoroughly enjoyed myself."

"Ah, you're only saying that to be nice. I'm sure spending the evening with my family was not high on your list. We're just simple folks."

Estelle kissed her forehead and stepped back to gaze into her eyes. "Spending the evening with your family *was*, in fact, high on my list, Wen. Very high. They are part of who you are, and it was nice to spend time with them. If by simple, you mean that they're humble and unpretentious, you're right, they are. That's extremely refreshing. Your parents, your sisters, and your friends are all good people."

"Even Bethany?" she asked with a smirk.

"Yes, even her. I think she thawed a little on me."

"She seemed to. I apologize for her behavior at the beginning of the night. She has a lot of preconceived notions about the summer folk."

Estelle laughed. "Some of them are probably spot-on." She wrapped her arms tight around Wen again. "Your family is wonderful and you're lucky to have them. And I'm lucky to have you."

"You're sweet," Wen said. She cupped Estelle's face in her hands and ran a thumb over her cheek. "But if it's okay, I don't want to talk about my family anymore. As amazing as you look in that dress, I'm dying to rip it off you and devour the luscious body beneath it."

CHAPTER TWENTY-FIVE

"This is heaven." Estelle let out a long, contented sigh.

She and Wen had taken a dip in the river and were now sprawled out on the wooden dock. The water was still fairly chilly—refreshing, as Estelle's father used to say—but her goose bumps had quickly melted away under the warm afternoon sun. They were on Logan Island, a small island whose owners were on an Alaskan cruise with their children and grandchildren and had enlisted Wen to caretake in their absence.

"It is, isn't it?" Wen's eyes slipped closed. "I might doze off."

Estelle raked Wen's body with her eyes. As cute as her board shorts were, Estelle bemoaned the fact that bathing suits were advisable, at least until that evening when a skinny dip might be in order. Right now, though, weekend boat traffic zipped around everywhere.

Estelle rolled toward Wen and drew a finger up one of her arms and down the other. If only they could freeze this moment. Blue skies, glistening water as far as the eye could see, birds soaring overhead, and their own little island paradise. Logan

Island was small, but it was situated off on its own, away from the nearby cluster of islands, so it felt more isolated than it actually was. All that was missing were the umbrella drinks.

Although she was reluctant to ruin their perfect afternoon, Estelle had no choice; she had to break the news to Wen. News that she'd held back, partially because she herself didn't want to think about it. She propped her head up on her hand and sucked in a breath.

"I have to go back to New York on Monday," she blurted.

Wen bolted upright and squinted in the sunlight. "What? Why?"

"I have to meet with my editor. She's gone through my manuscript and she's ready to talk it through with me."

"Can't you just Zoom or whatever?"

"I wish, but no," Estelle said. "Eunice is quite old school, and she prefers to mull over plot points in person, preferably while enjoying a cup of Earl Grey. And while I'm in New York, I also need to meet with my publicist—she's hounding me to finalize a number of book tour dates—and I have to record a podcast. The producer insists I do it in their sound studio."

"Well, that sucks…"

"I know, sweetheart. Trust me, I don't want to go." Estelle rested a hand on Wen's bare stomach. "I'd invite you to come along, but I know that's not possible because—"

"I've got to stay here and run the boat."

"Yes, because of the boat. It's peak season, and I realize you can't leave town. I should only be gone for a week."

* * *

The day after Estelle left for New York, Wen moped around her apartment as she readied herself for the day on the water. It was only a week. She'd live. Although she wasn't sure she would. In the short time they'd known each other, Estelle had become the center of her universe, and now, with five hundred miles between them, Wen was off-kilter. She'd dated a few women here and there over the years, and she'd been in a love before, but never like this. It was scary. To care so strongly about someone that you wanted to be with them every minute of every day and it ached to be apart.

As she tied her work boots, she thought back to the conversation they'd had on the dock while sunning themselves on Logan Island. Wen slapped her forehead. *Wake up and smell the coffee, you nitwit.* Estelle had come to the islands to finish her book, and she had... That probably meant she'd soon return to New York, for good. And then there was the matter of the book tour, which might involve traveling all over the country, and maybe the world. *All while I'm stuck here in Coopersville.* Wen had promised her father she'd run the boat through the fall, and although she wanted to, she could not renege on that promise, especially because she was now the legal owner of *Mathilde*. Even if Estelle was able to stay on the river through much of the rest of the summer, the two of them would likely face months apart soon.

By the time Wen reached the marina, her spirits were about as low as they'd ever been, and the mountain of packages awaiting her did nothing to help matters. She loaded the boat like a robot and cursed as she struggled to lift two large boxes aboard. What the fuck was in those things? Rocks? A set of dumbbells? She checked the address. Owl Island. Fucking fantastic. With Estelle off in New York, the Gage residence was the absolute last place she wanted to go. It would remind her of how much she missed Estelle, and it probably meant another encounter with Whitney or steely Catherine. She kicked one of the heavy boxes with her boot. Could this day get any shittier?

The answer to that question was "yes." Not long after she'd delivered the bulky packages to Owl Island, *Mathilde's* engine conked out in the middle of the river and Wen couldn't get it restarted. She stomped around the boat, waving her arms in the air and yelling out every curse word she could think of. Her tirade attracted the attention of a nearby boater, a middle-aged guy and his family out enjoying a nice summer day in what looked like a brand-new Grady White with two gigantic outboard motors hanging off the back. They were kind enough to tow her to the marina, and while the mechanic checked out *Mathilde*, Wen borrowed her friend's Boston Whaler to finish the day's deliveries.

Right after she dropped off her last package, the mechanic called.

"I'm afraid the news isn't good, Wen."

She put the Boston Whaler in neutral and gripped the side of the boat. "Please, please don't tell me she needs a new engine."

"I'm sorry, but yes, *Mathilde* needs a new engine," he said. "I could try to fix it, but it should have been replaced years ago, and if you ask me, you'd be throwing money down the drain."

Wen sighed into the phone.

"There's a good chance," he continued, "that I can find a refurbished engine on eBay—it's amazing what you can find online these days—but still, it ain't gonna be cheap."

Wen pinched her eyes shut. "How much do you think?"

"Twenty grand at least, plus labor," he said. "Of course, I'll give you the special Wen Apollo labor rate and I…"

Wen didn't hear the rest of what he said. Business had been great lately, but coughing up twenty grand would push her deep into the red. When she ended the call with the mechanic, she put her face in her hands and began to sob. It wasn't until she was nearly on top of a shoal of rocks that her brain clicked back into gear. *Right. Adrift in the river.* She reversed away from the shoal, shifted the Boston Whaler's throttle forward, and made a beeline for Logan Island. She needed somewhere quiet to think, and since she'd been hired as the island's caretaker, it would probably behoove her to check on the place.

Once she checked the house and watered the plants, she lay down on the dock and pulled out her phone to call Estelle, desperate to hear her voice.

"Please answer, please answer," she whispered into the phone as it rang.

"Hey, sweetheart." Estelle sounded out of breath.

"Hey, baby," Wen replied. "I'm sorry to bother you. Do you have a minute?"

"Actually, your timing is perfect. Eunice and I just finished for the day and I'm not meeting with my publicist until—"

Without warning, Wen broke down again. With heaving breaths, she blubbered into the phone.

"Wen, honey, what's wrong?"

"Eb...rey...fing." She took a few gulps of air in an effort to dampen her sobs. "Every...fing."

"I wish I was there with you," Estelle said. "I miss you terribly. Talk to me. Tell me what's the matter."

Wen sniffed into the phone and wiped the back of her hand across her nose. She opted not to delve into her anxieties about Estelle returning to New York at the end of the summer, and about the book tour, and instead told her about *Mathilde*'s engine. "It'll cost at least twenty grand to fix. Money I so don't have right now."

Without missing a beat, Estelle said, "I'll wire you twenty grand this afternoon. Might even be in your bank account before you get home."

Wen sat up and moved her phone from one ear to the other, although what she really wanted to do was throw it in the water. "I wasn't asking you for money, Estelle."

"Wen, please, I just want to help."

"I don't want or need your charity!"

There was a long pause before Estelle responded. "Fine. But let me know if you change your mind."

"I need to go," Wen said. She stabbed her phone to end the call and scrambled to her feet.

Clay pots full of little purple and yellow flowers lined the dock. Normally, Wen would have considered them pretty, but right now they just pissed her off. She punted one of the pots off the dock and it landed in the water with a plunk.

"Ouch!" she hollered.

Her toe throbbed inside her work boot. She hopped on one foot and cursed her stupidity. Now she had to get the damn thing out of the water. She stripped down to her underwear and sports bra, jumped into the river, and scooped it up. Borrowing dirt and flowers from the other pots, she did her best to make the one she'd kicked look presentable. She got dressed and climbed back aboard the Boston Whaler, but before she set off, she sent Ruby an SOS text.

I need a beer, bad. Igloo in an hour?

* * *

"Dude, that totally sucks," Ruby said once Wen had filled her in on the events of the day and the status of *Mathilde's* engine. "I'm sorry, pal."

"And I haven't even told you the worst part yet." She swiveled on her stool to face Ruby. "I called Estelle—she's in New York for the whole freakin' week—and told her about the engine, and you know what she said?" Wen didn't even give Ruby a chance to respond. She just rattled on. "She said she'd wire me twenty grand. Like it was nothing. It'd take me half a summer season of busting my ass to make that much money. I bet she'd drop that on a designer handbag and not even bat an eye. And, anyway, I basically hung up on her."

"That was super mature."

"Bite me," Wen said. "I was pissed. You remember the other night, when I said Estelle doesn't have a clue what it's like to walk in my shoes?"

Ruby nodded.

"Well, it's true. Having to work for a living is a foreign concept to her. She doesn't respect how hard I work, and offering to wire me money…it was insulting."

"You're being a little harsh, don't you think?" Ruby asked. "She loves you and she's only trying to help."

Wen slapped her hand on the bar. "I don't want her help and honestly, right now, I've got enough shit to deal with. I don't have time for a socialite princess. *Mathilde* is out of commission until I can come up with a pile of cash for her new engine, and in the meantime, I'll have to do the route with the Boston Whaler, which is way too small to carry all the packages I'll probably have to deliver, which means I'll have to loop back to the marina two or three times each day and—"

Ruby held up her hand. "Whoa. Hit the pause button for a sec. Take a sip of beer."

Wen did as she was told and then slumped against the bar and propped her head in her hand. "Sorry," she mumbled. "I'm just super overwhelmed and so goddam angry at Estelle."

"Let's start there," Ruby said. "I think you need to call her back and apologize for hanging up on her."

"To hell I will. She's the one who should call me to apologize."

"Listen, Wen, you have a valid point. Estelle probably doesn't fully appreciate what it's like to be a working stiff or what it's like to stress about money, but I know one thing, she definitely respects how hard you work. I talked to her at your dad's birthday party, and she commented on how impressive it was that both you and I ran our own *successful* businesses at such a young age."

"She did?"

"Uh-huh. She may have gobs of money, but as you've said yourself, she's down-to-earth. And I'm certain she's well aware of how fortunate she is to have grown up rich and privileged. Which is probably partially why she wants to help you."

Wen shrugged. "All right, all right, maybe I'm being a tiny bit unfair." She threw back the rest of her beer and set the pint on the bar. "And while I absolutely will not accept a dime from her, I suppose I do owe her an apology."

Ruby gestured toward the front door of the Igloo. "Well, what the hell are you waiting for. Go call her."

Wen wandered outside and pulled out her phone.

"Hello," Estelle said when she picked up.

Wen melted into the side of the building at the sound of her voice. "Hey, listen, I'm sorry about earlier. I was frustrated and anxious about the boat and everything and I took it out on you. That wasn't fair."

"No, it wasn't, but thank you for calling to apologize."

"I know you were just trying to help."

"I was," Estelle said.

Wen took a deep breath. "I love you, Estelle."

"I love you too, very much."

"So do you forgive me for being an idiot?"

There was another long pause. "Yes, I do. But I hope next time you're upset, you'll talk to me rather than fly off the handle."

Wen pinched her eyes shut. She was such a schmuck. "Okay, I will. I promise."

"Good," Estelle said.

"How was the meeting with your publicist?"

"It went well, very well. In fact, I have some good news."

"What's that?"

"Things here in New York are going more smoothly than I anticipated and it looks like I'll be able to get back up there a few days earlier than I planned."

Wen slapped her thigh. "That's by far the best news I've had all day."

"So, we're good?" Estelle asked.

"Yeah, we're good."

CHAPTER TWENTY-SIX

A few days after Estelle got back from New York, a massive storm blew in. The little Boston Whaler was no match for the whitecaps curling across the river. Wen had managed to scrounge up the money to repair *Mathilde*, but the sturdy boat was still out of the water awaiting its new engine. So there she was, with a mound of packages to deliver, and no way to get them to their destination. She'd have to scramble once the storm blew over, but it wasn't the end of the world. Most of the deliveries could wait. Their contents, while important, were not essential. Except for one. It contained insulin for one of Wen's year-round customers, Mrs. Grass on Zee Island. According to the pharmacist in Coopersville, the old woman's supply was nearly depleted.

Estelle's woodie could handle the choppy waters, but no one in their right mind would bring a meticulously refurbished boat like that out in this weather. The rain was torrential and there was nothing to protect the woodie's lavish interior, or its occupants, from the elements.

Think, Wen, think. She took off running for the city pier with Mrs. Grass's insulin tucked inside her slicker. As she'd hoped, the *River Rat* bobbed wildly under a large rectangular sign that read: *River Tours. Seven days a week. June–Aug.* Under normal circumstances, the *River Rat* would be carting selfie-stick-toting tourists around the islands, but not today. Any tourist brave enough to venture out on the water would likely be rewarded with a serious bout of sea sickness for their efforts.

Wen went up to the small shack next to the *River Rat* and knocked on the door.

Roger McRae, *River Rat's* captain and owner, peered up from his book and gestured for her to step inside and out of the rain. "Howdy, Wen. What brings you by on such a god-awful day?"

Wen pulled the bag of insulin out from inside her coat. "I've got to get this to Zee Island. It's insulin for Mrs. Grass. My boat is out of commission and—"

Roger was on his feet before she could finish explaining. "I'll take you on the *River Rat.*" He chuckled. "But it's pretty rough out there. You might lose your lunch."

Wen patted him on the back. "Thank you, Roger. You're a lifesaver, literally. And don't worry, luckily I don't get seasick."

"No surprise there," he said as he reached for his foul weather gear hanging on the hook near the door. "You and me, we both got river water in our blood."

If possible, it was raining even harder by the time Roger and Wen got back to the pier after delivering the insulin to a very thankful Mrs. Grass. The wind howled down Main Street in Coopersville and whipped across the water as Wen stood under the awning at Ruby's café and studied the weather app on her phone. The inclement weather was in no hurry to clear out. According to the forecast, the sun wouldn't make an appearance for another twenty-four hours.

She and Estelle had planned to have dinner at the new Indian restaurant in town that evening, but given the weather, there was like zero chance Estelle would be able to get to the mainland. Island life could be a real drag sometimes.

Wen pulled her hood up over her head, stepped out from under the awning, and sloshed through the puddles in her rubber boots as she made her way back to her apartment. Much to her surprise, the lights were on at Ursula's Books. If ever there was a night made for curling up with a good book, it was tonight. The door to the bookstore jangled when she tugged it open and stepped inside. The shop was warm and smelled faintly of cinnamon. She slipped off her jacket, draped it over the umbrella stand near the door, and brushed a few wet strands of hair off her face.

Her jaw dropped open. A massive banner stood right in front of her. At the top, in big bold letters, were the words, *A new mystery from* New York Times *best-selling author Greta Crabb*. An image of the cover for *In Plane Sight* encompassed most of the rest of the banner. Scrawled at the bottom, next to a small headshot of Estelle, was the date for an author reading.

Ursula appeared from the back storeroom. "Hiya, Wen."

"Hey, Urse." Wen pointed at the banner. "What's that?"

"Oh, isn't it exciting? Greta Crabb is going to come *here*, to my little shop in the middle of nowhere, to give a reading. Can you imagine? It'll be standing room only, that's for sure. Maybe we can overflow into the empty space next door and—"

"I don't understand," Wen said.

"I know, I was floored too. Out of the blue, a gentleman from New York City called me and said Ms. Crabb had specifically requested to do a reading here. FedEx delivered this snazzy banner this morning and I put it up right away even though the reading isn't until September."

Wen pointed to the banner again and said, "That's Estelle."

Ursula eyed the banner and then looked back at Wen. "Your Estelle?"

"Uh-huh."

Ursula tapped on the small headshot. "You know, when I unfurled the banner, I thought the woman in the picture looked familiar, but I figured it was just because I'd probably seen her in a magazine or on TV. Estelle's hair is a little different, shorter maybe, but now that you mention it, it does look a lot like her. I recall you mentioning she was a writer, but I had no idea she and Greta Crabb were one in the same. Of course, now it all makes sense, I mean why she chose to do a reading here, of all places." Ursula laughed. "Her girlfriend lives over the shop!"

Wen was glad it made sense to Ursula because it certainly didn't make any sense to her. How come Estelle had never divulged that she wrote under a pen name? How come she'd never mentioned that she was a mega big-time author? Admittedly, Wen should have put two and two together. All the signs had been there. Estelle had a publicist, for God's sake. And the book tour.

"I've never heard the name Greta Crabb before," Wen said.

"No surprise, I suppose," Ursula said. "After all, I know you don't read much fiction these days, and unless you monitor the *New York Times* Best Seller list, it makes sense that you don't know the name." She leaned in to inspect Estelle's photo again. "It seems this little banner has brought us both a bit of unexpected news."

"Yes, it has." Wen hung her head. She couldn't wait to get upstairs to her apartment to call Estelle. She had some 'splainin' to do. Although Wen also felt like a jerk for not knowing how famous Estelle was. *Rich and famous.* Would that put even more strain on their relationship?

"So, what is it you were looking for?" Ursula asked.

Wen looked up. "I'm sorry, what?"

"I presume you came into the store for something. A new book perhaps?"

"Yes, I mean, no. I'm good. I should go up and get out of my wet clothes."

Wen slogged up the stairs to her apartment, changed into sweats and a hoodie, and picked up her phone. There were three missed calls and a slew of text messages from Estelle. Rather than read them, Wen called.

"Sweetheart." Estelle gasped when she answered. "Is everything okay? I've been worried sick about you with the weather and all."

"Yes, I'm fine. I didn't go out on the water today, well except to deliver some medication to…never mind. I just popped into Ursula's bookstore…How come you didn't tell me you were a rock star author? A freakin' *New York Times* Best Seller."

"I thought you knew."

"How would I know?" Wen asked. "You never once mentioned that you wrote under a pen name."

"I didn't think it was important."

"Not important. How can you say that?"

"I didn't want to scare you away," Estelle admitted. "But I should have told you. I'm sorry. Very few people know I write under a pen name. Although it shouldn't matter. It doesn't change anything."

"It matters to me," Wen said. "I just wish I'd known. I've struggled enough with the fact that we come from such different worlds, and this makes the gap between them even wider. Before, you were like a billion times out of my league, but now, it's like we don't even live on the same planet."

"Don't be ridiculous, Wen. I love you and I want to be with you."

"Yeah, but for how long?"

"Please, don't do this, Wen." Estelle's voice remained even, but her tone grew colder. "I think we should talk this through in person."

"Um, kinda hard to do that in the middle of a freaking monsoon."

"The worst of the storm will blow out by morning. Why don't you come out to the island when you finish up tomorrow? I'll have Pauline make us a picnic dinner and we can eat it in the boathouse. It'll give us a little privacy to talk this out."

"Okay, fine." Wen dropped down on the couch. "You're right. Talking it out is a good idea."

"It's a date then."

"Yeah, it's a date, and I'm sorry I bit your head off. I love you and I don't want to lose you and sometimes I freak out."

"You're not going to lose me," Estelle said. "I wish I was there with you now. Stupid weather."

"Stupid weather is right. And heads up, I might not get there until late tomorrow. I wasn't able to make any deliveries today, so I'll be on double duty when the weather clears."

"Come whenever you can," Estelle said. "Just text me when you're on the way. Oh, and I can't wait for you to see the progress I've made on the woodie."

"I can't wait to see it, and you," Wen said. She picked at the threads on her couch. "And again, I'm sorry if I overreacted. It was such a shock to see your face on the banner in the bookstore. I had no doubt that you were an amazing writer, I just had no clue how amazing. I should be proud of you rather than acting like a brat."

"It's okay, sweetheart. Perhaps I should have been more forthright."

When they ended the call, Wen paced around her apartment. Being in love was making her crazy. Stupid anxiety. Why couldn't she just enjoy what she and Estelle had? Estelle wasn't fixated on the fact that they came from different worlds, so why was she? *Because I'm common folk and she's not.* She batted the thought out of her mind and tried to think positive. Talking things through with Estelle would be good. Hopefully she didn't have any more surprises.

CHAPTER TWENTY-SEVEN

The wind rattled the windows of the boathouse and rain pelted its metal roof, but inside it was warm and dry.

"Talk about good timing," Estelle said. The sky had opened up not two minutes after she and Wen stepped inside.

"You can say that again," Wen replied. She pointed to the picnic basket on the floor. "I'm beyond starving. What did Pauline pack us for dinner?"

"I'm not sure." Estelle picked up the large wicker basket and set it on a stool. "Let's look."

She pushed the handles aside, opened the lid, and ceremoniously began to pull out its contents. First, she withdrew a red and white checkered tablecloth. She shook it out and draped it over the small wooden table she'd positioned in the center of the boathouse's workshop. Next up, two silver candlesticks, salt and pepper shakers, an assortment of forks and spoons, two cloth napkins and a set of steak knives.

"Steak knives? That's a promising sign," Wen said, "but please tell me there's some actual food in there."

Estelle held up a finger and dug back into the basket. This time she came out with a plate covered in aluminum foil. A sticky note was affixed to the top of it with the letter "E" scrawled on it in black marker.

Estelle gave Wen a wicked grin. "Well, looks like there's a meal for me anyway."

Wen came up beside her and peeked in the basket. Inside was a second plate, this one with the letter "W" on it.

"Why the letters?" she asked.

"Knowing Pauline, she cooked my steak medium and yours medium-rare."

"Wow, she's good."

"The best," Estelle said. "Although it's no surprise. Working for my mother for all these years cannot have been easy."

"I'll reserve judgment."

"Oh, and I almost forgot the best part." Estelle walked over to the metal shelving lining the wall and returned with a bottle of red wine in one hand and a bottle opener in the other. "Wine?"

"Twist my arm."

She opened the bottle, pulled two stemless wineglasses from the picnic basket, and poured them each a healthy portion. When she was done, she gestured toward the table and said, "Shall we?"

They sat across from one another, and Estelle lifted her wineglass. "To us."

Wen hoisted her glass and tapped it against Estelle's. "To us."

In unison, they removed the foil from their plates to reveal the feast beneath. Ribeye steaks surrounded by a bundle of long green beans and a heap of french fries.

Wen licked her lips and picked up her fork and knife. "My mouth is literally watering."

After she ate every morsel off her plate, Estelle picked up her wineglass and leaned back in her chair. The rain had eased some but still pitter-patted on the roof. Otherwise, it was utter silence. The inclement weather meant the rest of the Gage clan was inside. When she'd left the house to meet Wen at the dock, all the kids were either working on a puzzle or playing cards. The rain drowned out any other sound, even the persistent lapping of water up against the boathouse and the rocky shoreline.

"It's so quiet, it almost feels like we're alone on the island again," she said.

Wen bit down on her bottom lip and nodded. "Yeah, it does."

"Can we talk about us?"

"I guess."

Estelle set down her glass and reached across the table to take Wen's hands in hers. "Our relationship is the most important thing in the world to me, and I'm going to do everything in my power to make it work."

Wen's lips formed a small smile. "Okay."

"I'll be here for a few more weeks, and I say we do our best to make the most of the time we have together."

"Okay," Wen said again, her eyes as wide as saucers. "But what happens after you leave?"

"We should probably talk about that," Estelle said.

"I want to be with you, that's all I know."

"And I want to be with you. I see you in my life long term."

Wen took her hand and squeezed it. "Same."

"We just need to figure out what that looks like. Presumably, we'll both be in the islands during the summer months, so…"

"It's the rest of the year we need to worry about," Wen said.

Estelle nodded. "Yeah." She blew out a breath. "I can try and sneak up to Coopersville for a long weekend here and there when I'm not off promoting my book or busy with the foundation."

"I want more than that."

"Maybe you could join me in New York?" Estelle asked quietly.

"You know I would if I could. I just don't see how…" Wen stared at the floor. "As I see it, when it comes to the mail route, I have three options, and none of them are very good, or very feasible, for that matter."

"What's option number one?" Estelle asked.

"I try and find someone to take over the route during the winter months, say November through March."

"That sounds like a pretty good plan to me."

Wen shrugged. "Yeah, in theory. But good luck finding someone to do it. You've never spent a winter up here. It's brutally cold and dark. Most of the people who work in the restaurants and stuff during the summer hightail it out of here before the first flurry. When the tourists disappear, so do they. Among the scant number of year-round residents, only half are able-bodied and of working age and of those remaining, most have good paying, full-time jobs at the school or the police department. Plus, it's a special breed who's willing to zip over the ice-covered river in a snowmobile in subzero temperatures to deliver provisions and get paid peanuts for their efforts."

"Fair enough. Okay, how about option number two?"

"I sell *Mathilde* and completely wash my hands of the mailboat route. It would free me to do whatever I wanted but at what cost? Like option one, it would require me to find someone to take over the route, but on a year-round basis. However, in option number two a person with the last name Apollo would no longer be affiliated with the route. My father would be devastated if I completely passed it on to an *outsider* after it had been operated by a member of my family for so many generations. And if I couldn't find someone to take it over, it would leave a lot of people in this community high and dry, people who rely on me to deliver medications and other necessities."

"Why don't we take option two off the table for now," Estelle said. "What's the last option?"

"I stay here and run the route year-round. Which would suck because it would mean you and I would be apart more time than we're together."

Estelle agreed, it would be far from an ideal solution, but they needed to be realistic. "I think for now, we need to assume you'll stay up here and run the boat. Being apart for long stretches of time will be hard, but no matter what, I'm not giving up on you, on us. What we have is extremely special, and if we truly love each other, we'll find a way to make things work."

Wen dabbed her eyes. "I love you, Estelle, with every bone in my body, but I won't lie, I'm scared."

"I'm scared too, Wen. If I ever lost you, I don't know what I'd do." Estelle reached out and brushed a finger over Wen's cheek. "Just give me your word that you'll talk to me, tell me when you're anxious or afraid."

"I'll try. I know I need to be better about communicating. My instinct is to curl up into a ball when I feel vulnerable, when I'm convinced you'll forget about me when you go back to New York. But, yes, I'll talk to you instead of pushing you away. I'll listen to you instead of the voice inside my head that tells me I'm not good enough for you."

Estelle stood, walked over to a small radio on the metal shelves, and clicked it on. Ella Fitzgerald's low, fiery voice competed with the rain on the roof. Estelle pulled Wen to her feet and snaked her hands around her waist. With their bodies pressed tight together, they swayed to the music.

When the song ended, Estelle whispered, "Everything is going to be okay. You have to believe me." She kissed Wen softly on the lips.

"Can I ask you a question?" Wen said when they broke apart.

"Of course. You can ask me anything."

"How'd you come up with the name Greta Crabb? Did you just make it up?"

Estelle chuckled. "Pretty much. Crabb was my grandmother's maiden name and"—Estelle bowed her head and covered her eyes with her right hand—"I can't believe I'm going to admit this, but Greta was the name of the girl I had a crush on in the seventh grade."

Wen burst out laughing. "That's classic."

"I thought Greta Crabb had a nice ring to it and, if nothing else, it's a unique name which makes me more Googleable, or so I'm told."

"Gotcha," Wen said. "Probably wouldn't make too much sense to pick a pen name like Jane Smith, although I guess you'd also want to stay away from names that are impossible to spell." Wen took a sip of her wine and set down the glass. "Okay, next question. Why'd you decide to write under a pen name? Estelle

Gage is a solid name, and I'd imagine it's pretty Googleable too."

"The truth is, there was no one real reason," Estelle said. "I was attracted to the idea of creating a new identity, an alter ego, if you like—I am a mystery writer, after all—and writing as Greta Crabb allows me to compartmentalize my writing life and my personal life. As I told you, it's not top secret that Greta Crabb and Estelle Gage are one in the same, but it's also not something I go out of my way to advertise. As a writer, I've got to maintain a social media presence, at least according to my agent, and it's refreshing to have that persona be separate from me as Estelle Gage. Does that make sense?"

"It makes perfect sense. In fact, if I ever write a book, I'm totally making up a pen name."

"What would it be?"

Wen swept an errant strand of hair from her face and tucked it behind her ear. "Hmmm, well, off the top of my head, I'd say *Mathilde*, perhaps Mattie for short, after my boat of course. Maybe Mattie Barcelona because I've always wanted to visit Spain."

"Mattie Barcelona! Talk about a fantastic pen name. I'd buy a book written by her for sure." Estelle pulled Wen back into her arms and whispered, "Will you stay the night?"

Wen nodded. "I'd like that."

* * *

The next morning, Wen crept down the stairs behind Estelle, praying that Mrs. Gage wasn't up yet.

"Good morning," a raspy voice called out.

Dammit. Wen plastered a smile on her face. "Good morning, Mrs. Gage."

Estelle went to pour them each a cup of coffee, leaving Wen alone with her mother.

There was an awkward silence until Mrs. Gage said, "Why don't you help yourself to a biscuit. Pauline made them fresh this morning."

"Oh, thank you. They smell delicious," Wen said, reaching into the basket to get a biscuit. It was still warm, and had she been anywhere else, she would have stuffed it into her mouth and taken a big bite. Instead, she set it on a plate, took a seat, and placed her napkin in her lap.

After she and Estelle had coffee and breakfast, Wen climbed aboard the Boston Whaler and reluctantly made her way back to the mainland to begin her day. As she cut across the water, she replayed the conversation they'd had the night before in the boathouse.

Had Estelle meant what she'd said? That their relationship was the most important thing in the world to her. Wen wanted to believe it, she really did.

Estelle had been right. Being apart would be hard, at times, and it would put a lot of strain on their relationship. Wen needed to be strong. She owed it to herself and to Estelle. Not to let her insecurities fuck things up. If their relationship fell apart because she was weak, she'd never forgive herself. Now that Estelle was part of her life, she couldn't imagine it without her. Even though it was a warm, muggy morning, the thought sent a shiver through her. Wen loved Estelle and Estelle loved her. That was all that mattered. Together, they'd work the other stuff out.

CHAPTER TWENTY-EIGHT

The remaining weeks of summer passed way too quickly, and before Estelle knew it, it was nearly time to return to New York. In her final days up in the islands, she and Jimmy finally finished the woodie their father had begun to refinish years before, and in his honor, they christened her *Alastair*. Although her father had always gone by Chip, Alastair was his legal name.

After they smashed a bottle of champagne over *Alastair*'s bow, Estelle fired up the engine and backed her away from the dock. Moments later, Jimmy emerged from the boathouse behind the wheel of the *TeeBoo*, the other woodie they owned, the one her father had finished before he died, and together she and her brother raced across the water. Estelle knew her father would be proud of the work she and Jimmy had done to return *Alastair* to her original beauty. In fact, if Estelle were honest, *Alastair* was even more exquisitely refurbished than the *TeeBoo*.

When she and Jimmy returned to the island, Wen was there waiting for them.

Estelle eased *Alastair* up alongside the dock.

"Wow, what a beauty," Wen said.

"Care to go for a spin?" Estelle asked.

Without responding, Wen leapt aboard, and they took off back down the river, zigzagging around the islands.

This is one of life's perfect moments, Estelle thought. The wind in her hair, the sun on her face, and the woman of her dreams by her side. If only she could bottle this snippet of time. If only she didn't have to go back to New York. Her heart clenched in her chest at the thought that she'd leave in a few short days. If only she could stay. Stay here with Wen, and the river, and the birds, and the peace and quiet. But it just wasn't possible, at least not at the moment. She had a multitude of foundation and other obligations in New York, not to mention her impending book tour and an obligatory trip to India.

After they returned *Alastair* to the boathouse, she and Wen climbed aboard *Mathilde* and headed for the mainland. Later that afternoon, there was a soccer game to raise money for the local foodbank. Alumnae of Coopersville HS, women ranging in age from eighteen to fifty-three, would play against the current roster of girls on the team. The annual event always drew a big crowd and Wen was playing forward on the alumnae team for the eighth year in a row. Estelle was excited to watch the game, and Jimmy and Cob planned to come into town to catch the second half.

She chose a seat high up in the bleachers and watched the two squads warm up. Wen looked sexy as hell in her uniform. Her strong legs carried her up and down the field as she dribbled the ball and passed it back and forth with her teammates. The temperature hung in the low seventies and, even though it was only mid-August, a hint of orange and yellow tinged the leaves on the trees surrounding the ball fields.

The whistle blew to indicate the start of the first half and Estelle jumped up to cheer when the alumnae team goalie dove to save an early shot on goal. But the crowd let out a collective gasp when the goalie rolled over on her back and writhed in pain as she clutched her left leg. The ref called a time out and the alumnae coach and the school's athletic trainer raced from the sideline and crouched beside the goalie. After they escorted the injured player off the field, Wen ran up into the bleachers.

When she reached Estelle, she asked, "Do you feel like playing soccer?"

Estelle rested a hand on Wen's arm. "What are you talking about?"

"Only twelve alumnae players suited up. Looks like our goalie might be out for the remainder of the game and"—Wen waved toward the field—"Kristie, one of the other forwards, is our backup goalie. Our only sub is Marylyn and she's not in the best shape. It's questionable whether she can even make it to halftime."

"I'm not exactly dressed for the occasion," Estelle replied.

"You can run to my apartment, change, and be back in time for the second half."

Estelle stood. "Okay. Why the heck not." Like Wen, she'd played forward on her high school team.

Wen returned to the field and Estelle took off for the parking lot. She made it back in time to join the alumnae team in their halftime huddle and took Marylyn's place on the front line at the start of the second half.

Wen and Estelle had kicked the soccer ball around together a few times on the lawn at Owl Island, but they'd never played a real game together. It didn't seem to matter. After the star forward on the HS team scored a goal, Wen and Estelle drifted down the field passing the ball in moves that looked choreographed by Megan Rapinoe. Estelle tapped the ball off her left foot to tie the game. The crowd went wild, whistling and stomping their feet on the metal bleachers, sending a deafening thunder across the field.

The game was tied at two and less than three minutes remained on the clock. Estelle carried the ball down the right side of the field, maneuvered past two defenders, and crossed the ball in front of the goal. Wen jumped into the air and headed the ball, sending it into the top right corner of the net. It was a textbook play. The HS goalie never stood a chance.

Wen's hands went up in the air and she tore across the field toward Estelle and leapt into her arms.

"You're amazing, baby," she said. "That cross was perfect."

"I'd say *we're* amazing," Estelle whispered into her ear. "My cross may have been perfect but so was your header."

The rest of the alumnae players surrounded them for a big group hug.

The HS team took one final shot on goal right before the ref blew her whistle to signal the end of the game, but Kristie, the backup goalie, knocked it away with her fist. The alumnae team had won the game for only the second time since the first fundraiser game a decade earlier.

The "old-timers" poured the orange cooler of water over their coach's head and posed for photos. Cob ran down from the bleachers and gave both Estelle and Wen fist bumps.

"You two looked pretty good out there," Jimmy said. He lay his arm across Estelle's shoulders. "Not bad for an old lady."

"Hey, now," Estelle said. "I'm only thirty-three." She poked Jimmy in the stomach. "I'd like to see you out there."

After the game, the alumnae crew went to the Igloo to celebrate their win. Kristie bought Wen and Estelle their first round and raised her beer to them. "You two are quite the dynamic duo."

Estelle had to agree, but the comment sent a wave of melancholy through her. She stole a glance at Wen. It was going to be so hard to leave her. She'd be back in Coopersville for the author reading at Ursula's in September, but right now that seemed so far away, and what about after that? When would she and Wen be able to see each other again?

That night, she lay wide awake in bed. Tears slid down her cheeks and onto her pillowcase. Wen was sprawled beside her, sound asleep. Estelle rolled over on her side, propped her head in her hand, and watched Wen's chest rise and fall. She ached to reach out and touch her but didn't want to wake her. The clock on the bedside table read 3:17 a.m. The streetlight outside the window cast a soft glow over the room. Through her tears, Estelle studied the details of Wen's beautiful face. Her smooth, suntanned skin, high round cheeks, full lips, and the small scar on her angular chin. Although Wen's bright blue eyes were hidden behind her eyelids, they were forever etched in Estelle's mind.

"I'm going to miss you so much," she whispered.

She'd asked Wen to believe that everything with them would be okay, but did she believe it herself? Their relationship felt solid and fragile at the same time. Could it withstand them being apart for weeks at a time? Or maybe even months at a time? How would they cope if Estelle's travel schedule was especially demanding, or if Wen's obligations tethered her to Coopersville long term? She sighed into the dark room. They needed to have another heart-to-heart conversation about their future soon. At this point, there were still a lot of question marks.

She wiped a hand over her nose, rolled back onto her pillow, and stared at the ceiling. The alarm would go off early and she needed to get some sleep. Meditation had never been her thing, but she decided to give it a shot. A deep breath in, count to five, a deep breath out, count to five…

Her muscles began to relax, but sleep still evaded her. Starting with her toes, she tried to imagine each part of her body falling asleep. When that failed, she pictured a remote tropical island. Warm sand funneling between her toes, waves curling across the water and collapsing on the shoreline, wind rustling through the palm trees, and she and Wen walking hand in hand…

Her eyes flew open. That was it. When her book tour was over, she'd take Wen on vacation somewhere. Perhaps to the beach…or maybe the mountains. Estelle didn't much care. She'd let Wen choose. It would help to have a trip like that to look forward to. She couldn't wait to share the idea with Wen in the morning. Hopefully she'd be able to get away, even if it was only for a few days.

CHAPTER TWENTY-NINE

Wen's phone vibrated in her back pocket. She reached for it with her left hand while using her right to steer *Mathilde* into her slip at the marina. The boat bumped into the dock, causing her to drop the phone. She muttered a few profanities under her breath and focused on getting the boat secured before reaching down to snatch her phone off the floor.

It was too late. The call had gone to voice mail. More profanities escaped from her mouth. Once again, she'd missed a call from Estelle. This long-distance thing sucked. In the two weeks since she'd left for New York, they'd spent more time playing phone tag than actually talking. Sure, they texted back and forth, but Wen missed hearing Estelle's voice and seeing her face. Not to mention the feel of their bodies pressed together, the sensation of Estelle's lips grazing hers...

She ran a hand along the weathered rail of the boat. "What am I going to do, old gal?"

Mathilde creaked when the wake of a passing boat rolled beneath her hull.

"I feel the same way," Wen said, as if the old boat were talking to her. Part of her believed it was.

Although it hadn't even been six months since she'd taken over the mail route on a full-time basis, she'd probably spent a quarter of her life aboard the old boat. Her father had bought a gently used *Mathilde* when Wen was ten, and she'd spent every summer helping him, and eventually her uncle, on the route. *Mathilde* was like an old friend, and Wen adored captaining her around the islands, she really did. But right now, with Estelle off in New York, the boat was an encumbrance.

After all, it *was Mathilde* that tethered Wen to Coopersville and prevented her from joining Estelle in New York and on her book tour. And not only that. The boat had cost Wen a small fortune over the last few months. Between her new engine and various other mechanical problems, Wen's mailboat business was barely breaking even. Any dream she had of buying a new, more reliable boat was pretty much that, a dream. It was ridiculous, actually. The more money she threw at *Mathilde*, the more remote the possibility of replacing her became.

Of course, there was always the option to sell the boat and walk away, but as far as she was concerned, that was still off the table for all the reasons she'd discussed with Estelle.

The reality was, back in the spring, when she'd told her parents she'd take over the boat at least until the fall, all she'd done was kick the can down the road. As a result, now she faced the same dilemma she had back then. Except now the stakes were even higher. Now she wasn't deciding between the boat and jetting off to Barcelona. Now she had to choose between the boat and being with the woman she loved.

Lunch pail and thermos in hand, she climbed out onto the dock and trudged across the parking lot to her truck. Labor Day weekend had been glorious. Sunny and warm. But now, only three days later, it was as if Mother Nature had flipped a switch. The blue skies had turned gray. Heavy clouds hung over the river and a persistent drizzle made it especially raw.

She fired up her truck and cranked the heat. The wipers intermittently swished across the windshield as she made her way into town. The weather punctuated a dismal fact. Summer was over, and the short, brutally cold days of winter would fast be upon them. As if Wen wasn't depressed enough.

She closed the door of her apartment and tossed her keys in the bowl. While she stripped off her damp clothes, she put her phone on speaker and called Estelle.

"Surprise, surprise," she muttered when it went to voice mail. Seconds later, a text came in.

Just landed in LA. Okay if I call you when I get to the hotel?

Wen responded with a *yeah, sure* and set down her phone. She reached in to turn on the shower, peeled off her socks and boy shorts, tossed them in the hamper, and stepped under the hot stream of water.

Once she was dressed, she padded into the kitchen, pulled a beer from the fridge, and plopped down on the couch. For the next hour, she aimlessly flipped between the Weather Channel and a tournament on the Golf Channel. She'd never even held a golf club, but for some odd reason, watching the game on TV relaxed her. Eventually, her grumbling stomach motivated her to look for something to eat. Her phone rang while she assembled the ingredients for a salad. Wen dove onto the couch and wrestled her phone from between the cushions.

"Hey, babe. How's LA?"

"Hello, sweetheart. It's wonderful to hear your voice. LA is LA."

Wen had never been to LA, or to California for that matter. Her image of it was based on what she'd seen on TV, and so she pictured Estelle sitting by a pool with beautiful people roaming around in the background.

"You're three hours behind me, right?" she asked.

"Yes, it's five p.m. here. I've got an hour to get showered and dressed before I get whisked off to a cocktail reception. Marianne, my publicist, went a little overboard. The schedule she's arranged is brutal. I'm exhausted and I'm only three days into the book tour. And get this, not only do I have to fly to London next week for an event, but it now looks like I may have to go straight from there to India. I'd hoped for a few days of downtime in between trips, but it doesn't appear I'll get my wish."

Wen listened to her rattle on about her hectic itinerary. Could their lives be any different? Estelle was off hopping continents. Compare that to Wen's travel plans for the week: driving to the neighboring town to get new tires for her truck. Still, she could hear the exhaustion in Estelle's voice and although she got to jet off to cool places, it was for work, and it sounded far from pleasurable.

"I wish I was there. It sounds like you could use a hug and a back massage."

"I wish you were here too, although honestly, I barely have time to eat, let alone do anything else. You'd probably be bored if you'd tagged along."

"I doubt that."

"I've got to run," Estelle said. "You'll be asleep by the time I get home, but I'll call you tomorrow."

After Estelle ended the call, Wen tossed her phone back on the couch and returned to making her salad. She knew she had to remain positive about things with Estelle, but it was getting increasingly difficult.

There had to be a solution, a way for them to be together during the nine months of the year that were not summer in the islands. As she ate her dinner, she once again racked her brain for a solution.

One option she'd briefly discussed with her father, back when Uncle Mark was sick, was having him captain the boat and hiring someone to run the packages. This might work in the warmer months, but not once it got colder. Even after a light snowfall, the marina and the docks were inhospitable to anyone in a wheelchair. And once winter settled in and the river froze over, it would put her back at square one. No one would be around to help her father even if he could drive a snowmobile, which he couldn't.

* * *

The next morning, Wen scrolled through the Twitter feed on her phone while she waited for the woman behind the counter to make her breakfast sandwich. She'd gotten an account at Estelle's urging, and since Wen only followed a handful of people, tweets from Greta Crabb—a.k.a Estelle—dominated her feed. An abundance of glitzy photos of her at glamorous parties and giving readings. According to Estelle, Marianne managed all her Greta Crabb social media accounts because she had neither the inclination nor the capacity to do it on her own. Even though Estelle's books were at the top of the *New York Times* Best Seller list, she was a reluctant celebrity and had admitted to Wen that she shied from the spotlight.

Breakfast sandwich in hand, Wen sat at a table and mindlessly stuffed the warm bacon, egg, and cheese deliciousness into her mouth with one hand while she continued to scroll Twitter with the other. Her fingers dug into the flaky biscuit when she came across a photo of Estelle walking out of what looked like a swanky LA restaurant with a drop-dead gorgeous blond woman. Who the hell was that? And why was the mystery woman clinging to Estelle's arm?

Wen didn't want to jump to conclusions, but the evidence was pretty damning. The two women's eyes were locked on each other...like they couldn't wait to get home and rip each other's clothes off. A pang of jealousy coursed through her. She zoomed in and glared at the photo. The woman had high cheekbones, and a chic-looking suit hugged her exquisite curves. *I bet she's European.*

She jammed her phone in her pocket, balled her unfinished breakfast sandwich in its foil wrapper, and went outside to get some fresh air.

It was only six a.m. in LA, but Wen needed answers, pronto. She pulled her phone back out to call Estelle. Surely there was an explanation. There had to be.

A groggy Estelle answered the phone. "Sweetheart? Is everything okay?"

Wen tried to keep her voice even. "Um, I don't know. You tell me."

"I don't understand."

"I was scrolling through Twitter this morning and couldn't help but notice the stunning woman hanging on your arm last night. Is there something you need to tell me?"

Estelle sighed into the phone. "You must be speaking of Annika, my escort."

Escort? WTF? "Come again?"

"Annika is my escort here in LA. I have one in every city on the book tour." Estelle snorted into the phone. "That came out wrong. Annika is my *media* escort. Marianne has arranged for me to have one at each stop of my tour. They pick me up at the airport, ferry me to my hotels, and accompany me to all the events on my schedule."

"Okay," Wen said.

"The escort's role is to make sure everything runs smoothly. To ensure I'm where I need to be on time. That's it. Please believe me."

"Okay," Wen said again. "I do believe you." Or at least, she wanted to.

"Well, good," Estelle replied, the frustration evident in her voice, "because it's the truth. And, honestly, the last person I need shit from right now is you."

"Whoa," Wen said. "Give me a break. You're traipsing around LA with a hot woman on your arm. The optics aren't exactly great. What am I supposed to think?"

"You're supposed to trust me. Trust my love for you."

"I do."

"You certainly have a funny way of showing it."

"I'm sorry," Wen said. "I shouldn't have automatically assumed…"

"I'm sorry too," Estelle said, her voice barely above a whisper. "I'm exhausted, and I have a shorter fuse than normal."

Wen's hand tightened around her phone. "I miss you."

"I miss you too, like crazy."

"If I could, I'd be on a plane in an instant." Wen pinched the bridge of her nose. "I can't just up and leave. You understand that, right?"

"Yes, of course I do, sweetheart."

"Even though summer is over, and things have quieted down some, there are still loads of people around, and I've got heaps of packages to deliver."

"When I get back from India, my mother has wrangled me into a slew of speaking engagements related to the foundation, but I'll be up there at the end of the month for the reading at Ursula's. After that, we can hide away on the island for a few days. Just the two of us."

Wen sucked in a breath. "God, that cannot come soon enough. How long do you think you can stay?"

"I hope almost a full week. I may have to bribe Marianne to cancel or postpone one of my book events, but I don't care. Spending a few days with you is way more important to me."

"It is?" Wen asked quietly.

"Yes."

"I can't wait to see you," Wen said. "And I'm sorry I called so early."

"It's okay, my alarm was about to go off anyway. I want to sneak in a workout before the insane day Marianne has planned for me."

When they ended the call, Wen walked to her truck and made her way to the marina to begin her workday. The next few weeks would be tough, really tough, but she had to try harder not to let her insecurities get the best of her. She had to do everything in her power to make sure her relationship with Estelle endured.

That night when she got in from the water, she went straight to her parents' house.

"Hey, kiddo," her dad said when she walked in the back door. "What brings you by?"

"Do you mind if I use your woodshop?" Wen asked. "I've got a quick project I want to work on."

"Not at all. Anything I can help with?"

"Nope, but thanks."

Her dad held up the plate in his hand. "Let me finish the dishes and I'll come out to keep you company."

"Sounds good," she said and turned and headed out to the shop in the garage.

Her dad kept a big crate full of scrap wood and she rummaged through it to find the perfect piece. When she spotted a small block of what she thought was cherry, she pulled it out, set in on the counter, and scanned the array of knives and other tools her father had hanging around the shop. She selected a few and sat on a stool to get to work. The first knife she selected barely pierced the wood, so she picked up a slightly bigger one. It slipped across the block of wood and nearly took her finger off.

"Cherry is a difficult wood to whittle," her father said as he wheeled beside her. "What is it you're trying to make?"

"I want to carve a little boat for Estelle." In Wen's mind, the piece she'd create would be a miniature replica of *Alastair*, the woodie Estelle had just finished refurbishing.

Her dad went over to the crate of wood and pulled out a different piece. "Here, try this. It's pine. It'll be a little more forgiving."

Wen spent the next two hours carving the piece of wood into something that sort of resembled a boat. The end product wasn't exactly what she'd envisioned, far from it, but it was the thought that counted, right? She filled the shop sink with water to test her little boat. It floated!

Tomorrow, she'd mail her wooden creation to Estelle in New York so it would be there waiting for her when she returned from her whirlwind book tour and the jaunt to India. Only one problem, though. She didn't know Estelle's address in New York, but a quick phone call would solve that.

Estelle picked up on the first ring. "Hey, babe."

"Question for you," Wen said. "Where exactly is your apartment in New York? I have something I want to mail to you."

"It's on Fifth Avenue." Estelle rattled off the address and then added, "It's on the Upper East Side, right near Central Park."

Wen let out a whistle. "I may not know much about New York, but even I've heard of Fifth Avenue. It's like the premier address, right?"

"It's a very nice area, yes."

Very nice area, my ass. The street was probably paved with gold.

CHAPTER THIRTY

Estelle's flight from India landed in Dubai right on time. Only one more flight and she'd be home, at last. In the past month, she'd spent a grand total of three nights in her own bed. The book tour had been a smashing success, at least as far as her publisher was concerned. Standing room only at most of the dozen or so events. She was thrilled her book had been so well received—the reviews had been utterly glowing—but her schedule over the last month had taken a toll on her, especially with the side trip for the foundation tossed in.

She showed her boarding pass to the agent at the business class lounge, ventured over to the bar to order a glass of sauvignon blanc, and settled into a seat overlooking the tarmac. While she sipped her wine, she stared out at the flurry of activity around the massive Airbus A380 parked just outside. Luggage carts zipped this way and that, pallets of cargo were being hoisted into the belly of the plane, and a catering truck rose toward the forward door of the aircraft.

Her phone buzzed in her blazer pocket, and she pulled it out. It was a text from Fran. *Have you RSVP'd for Grace's wedding?*

Estelle sighed. Her friend's wedding invite had arrived the day she'd left New York two weeks earlier. She'd opened it, but she'd only been in town for the night and hadn't had time to formally respond. The wedding promised to be quite an affair. Rumor had it that more than three hundred people were on the guest list—the who's who of New York society—and Elton John was scheduled to perform. She hoped Wen would be her "plus one" but hadn't yet had a chance to ask her. It was possible she'd be mildly overwhelmed by the elaborate affair, but Estelle was confident she could handle it, and nothing would make her happier than to walk into the wedding with Wen on her arm.

Instead of responding to Fran's text, she fired one off to Wen, inviting her to the wedding.

A response came back a few minutes later. *I'd love to but I have to be in Coopersville that weekend. It's my cousin's first communion and I'm substitute coaching the girls pee-wee basketball team.*

Estelle stuffed her phone back in her pocket, crossed her arms over her chest, and let out a huff. "Well, that sucks," she mumbled. She took a few calming breaths. Why was she so upset? It wasn't the end of the world. It wasn't like she'd never gone to a wedding solo before. It was just, she wanted to go with the woman she loved. Was that too much to ask?

A female voice came over the loudspeaker in the lounge. "Due to a mechanical issue, Emirates flight 201 with service to New York's JFK is delayed. It will now depart at 19:59."

The man sitting behind Estelle slapped his hand on the armrest of his chair. "That's a goddam two-hour delay!"

Estelle was equally frustrated but kept her thoughts to herself.

In the end, it took more than twenty-four hours to get home from India. Her connection in Dubai had been delayed for an additional hour, and it was nearly midnight when she landed at JFK. By the time she finally pulled up in front of her building in New York, she was hungry and tired and in desperate need of a shower. The doorman on night duty helped her upstairs with her luggage and wished her a good evening.

She closed the door behind him and gazed around her empty apartment. The faint noise of a car honking its horn echoed from the street many floors below, but otherwise it was quiet. Too quiet. No one was there to welcome her home. The woman she loved was hundreds of miles away. Would it always be that way?

She collapsed in a wingback chair, covered her face with her hands, and began to cry. What was she doing? What were she and Wen doing? Spending more of their lives apart than together with no alternative in sight. If her relationship with Claudia had taught her one thing, it was that absence did *not* make the heart grow fonder. Whoever had said that was full of shit. She pulled her knees up to her chest and hugged them.

It was late, but she had to call Wen. Hearing her voice would help console her. She rummaged through her briefcase for her phone.

"Hey, baby," a groggy voice answered. "You make it home?"

Estelle leaned back in the chair and closed her eyes. "Yes, I just got it in. I'm sorry to call so late, but I…"

"It's okay. I tracked your flight online, and I tried to stay awake, but I must have fallen asleep."

"I wish you were here."

"I do too."

"Coming home to an empty apartment…sucked. Being apart sucks. I need someone who—"

"Who what?" Wen asked.

"Forget it. Never mind."

"You said if our love was strong enough…we'd figure out a way to make it work. I believed that. I believed you."

"Well, maybe I was wrong."

"How can you say that?" Wen asked.

Estelle didn't respond. She curled into a ball again and moved the phone to her other ear.

"I sent you something," Wen said, her voice barely above a whisper. "A small gift. Did you get it?"

Estelle glanced over at the pile of mail her housekeeper had neatly piled on the kitchen island. "I don't know. I just got home. I haven't had a chance to look through the mail yet." She unfurled herself and stood. "I need to go. I'm sorry. I shouldn't have called so late."

She ended the call and wiped a tear from her cheek.

* * *

The next morning while Wen loaded packages on *Mathilde*, a text came in from Estelle.

I love the little boat.

She put her hand on her heart and whispered, "And I love you." Last night, after she'd gotten off the phone with Estelle, she'd tossed and turned until dawn, constantly replaying their conversation in her mind. As time went on, would the strain of being apart be too much to bear? Would it spell the end of their relationship? The thought made her shudder. She needed to figure something out, and fast. Rather than reply to Estelle's text, she called.

Estelle picked up right away, but it was nearly impossible to hear her over the noise in the background.

"Where are you?" Wen asked.

"At home," Estelle yelled. "Apparently they're doing work on the roof. I've been gone for most of the last month and they decided to start work this morning."

"That bites."

"Yes, it's unfortunate. Can I call you later?"

"Um, sure, no sweat."

Estelle said something else before she ended the call, but Wen couldn't make it out over the racket in the background.

That evening, Wen had another fundraiser. This time the Igloo was hosting an event for the local theater and people had paid good money to dunk her and a handful of others in a tank. Estelle called back a few minutes before it was Wen's turn on the hot seat. She stepped outside to take the call.

"I'm afraid I have some bad news," Estelle said. "My mother was just taken to the hospital."

"Oh, no," Wen said. "Is it serious?"

"I don't know yet. Apparently, she took a fall as she walked into the club. She didn't lose consciousness but appeared confused and disoriented. We're waiting for some test results."

"That's so scary. I hope she's okay."

"Me too." Estelle paused before adding, "I may need to postpone the reading at Ursula's. If my mother is still in the hospital, I don't feel like I can leave."

Wen's heart sunk. She'd been counting the days until Estelle's visit, but had the situation been reversed, she'd want to stay put until she knew her mother was okay too. "That's too bad, but I totally understand, and I know Ursula will too."

"I'll call the bookstore myself to reschedule. I know she's gone to so much effort."

"She'll be disappointed, but you have a very valid reason for canceling."

Ruby stepped outside to let Wen know it was her turn in the tank. She held up her finger to signal that she'd be right there.

"Will you call me as soon as you hear more about your mother?" she asked Estelle.

"Of course."

"I'm sorry, I have to go." She explained about the fundraiser and ended the call, shaking her head as she walked back inside. It felt as though their schedules were conspiring against them. She was desperate to connect with Estelle. Desperate to find a way for them to be together.

CHAPTER THIRTY-ONE

Wen nursed a cup of coffee while she waited for Ruby to finish tending to the morning rush at Bella's. She alternated between staring out at the water and flipping through the local paper someone had left behind. When a hand squeezed her shoulder, she bolted up right, sloshing coffee on the table.

"Golly, Wen, I'm sorry. I didn't mean to startle you."

Wen turned in the direction of the voice. Roger McRae, *River Rat*'s captain, stood before her. "Hey, Roger. No worries. I was in my own little world."

"Do you have a minute? I've got something I'd like to discuss with you."

Wen gestured toward the empty chair across the table from her. "Sure. I'm just waiting on Ruby." She nodded toward the line of people snaked around the display case of baked goods. "And from the looks of it, she might be a while."

Roger took a seat and said, "Ruby's done a fine job with this place."

"She sure has." Wen took a sip of her coffee and waited for Roger to bring up whatever it was he wanted to discuss, but he just sat there and played with the sugar packets in the dish on the table. To break the silence, she asked, "Have you put the *River Rat* away for the season?"

There were still oodles of tourists milling around Coopersville, but in addition to operating the tour boat, Roger taught high school chemistry. Once the school year started, he didn't have time to run the boat. As a result, Labor Day weekend typically marked the end of the *River Rat*'s season.

"Yep, she's tucked away for her long winter's nap." Roger pushed aside the dish of sugar packets and folded his hands on the table. "Actually, that's what I wanted to talk to you about. The *River Rat*."

"What about it?"

"Well, I'm not getting any younger, and Martha is angling for us to buy an RV. 'Bout time for me to retire from teaching... And, I um, wondered if you might be interested in taking over the *River Rat*?"

Wen's jaw dropped. She hadn't seen that coming. "Wow, uh, I don't know what to say. I've got my hands pretty full with the mailboat, and even if I could manage the tour boat on top of that, I've got a little bit of a cash flow problem right now."

"I understand," he said, "but will you at least think it over? I've got a small note on the boat. If you're able to pay that off, the *River Rat* is all yours. Martha and I can live off my teacher's pension. I'm more interested in the *River Rat* going to someone I know and trust than selling the business to some out-of-towner." He winked. "And if you took over running the boat, maybe you'd let me take out a tour every now and again, just for old times' sake."

"Yes, yes, of course," Wen replied. "But, like I said, I'm not really in a position to take the business over. I'm very flattered that you—"

"Why don't you run it by your father?" Roger asked. "He's a resourceful guy. I bet you two will figure something out." He gave her a few more details about the tour boat and stood to leave.

Wen agreed to chat with her dad about it but kindly suggested that Roger consider other options. As it was, she struggled to keep up with the mailboat in the peak summer months. There was no way in the world she could take on the *River Rat* too. And even if she could, why would she want to? It would only tie her more firmly to Coopersville. That, and if she assumed the note on the tour boat, it would mean more debt, which was the last thing she needed, especially right now with *Mathilde*'s recurring mechanical problems.

Because she'd promised Roger she would, Wen stopped by her parents' house at the end of the day to discuss the *River Rat* with her father. "I just don't think it's in the cards," she said after she relayed the conversation with Roger.

"You're going to think I'm crazy," her father said, "but I think it would be a great opportunity."

"Yeah, maybe for somebody else."

Her father patted her hand. "Please, hear me out."

Wen leaned back in her chair and crossed her legs. "Okay, fine, but you're not going to change my mind."

"First," her father said, "there's tremendous potential to expand *River Rat*'s business. Think about it. Roger runs the tour boat three months a year—June, July, and August—because of his job at the school. Tourists start pouring into Coopersville in early May, and the town will teem with them at least through the end of September. There's plenty of demand to operate the boat at least five months a year."

"I don't disagree, but…"

Her father held up his hand. "Let me finish. Roger's a great guy, don't get me wrong, but there are so many revenue opportunities he hasn't tapped."

"Oh, yeah, like what?" she asked.

"Like offering wine and cheese tours, or sunrise coffee and muffin cruises."

"That would be cool, I'll admit, but again, it ain't gonna happen. I'm overwhelmed as it is. And I don't know shit about wine."

"You'd have to hire people to help you, of course." Her dad tapped his lips with his pointer finger. "And I think I may have just the people you need."

Wen sat up straighter in her chair and waited for him to continue.

"Last week, Lew Webster stopped by my roadside stand. His daughter, Tina, and her husband, Asher, recently moved back to Coopersville after backpacking around Europe for two years and neither one of them has the foggiest idea what they're going to do for work. The only reason they came home is because they ran out of money. As you can imagine, Lew is anxious for them to get full-time jobs and move out of his house.

Wen had babysat for Tina Webster when she was in junior high but otherwise knew little about her, and she'd never met her husband. "What makes you think they have what it takes to run a tour boat?" she asked.

"For one, they both speak multiple languages. That sure would come in handy with all the foreign tourists we've been getting in the islands lately."

"That's all well and good," Wen said, "but do either Tina or Asher know the first thing about operating a big boat like the *River Rat*?"

"Well, Lew mentioned that Asher grew up on Cape Cod and helped run his family's fishing charter company. I guess he and Tina have even talked about starting a charter company here on the river, but they don't have the money to do it right now."

"Even if they were willing to help, which is a big if, you're forgetting one thing," Wen said.

"What's that?"

"*No tengo dinero.*"

"English, please."

"Money. I don't have any, at least not enough to pay off Roger's note."

"Did he tell you how much it was?" he asked.

"Thirty-seven grand."

Her father was quiet for a minute but then he got a sparkle in his eye. "Your mom and I have a little money saved up. Maybe we could help you out."

Wen smiled at him. "That's super sweet of you, Dad, but I've never asked you and Mom for money and I'm not about to start."

"Look at it this way," her father said. "We wouldn't be giving you money, we'd be investing in your business. A business I know will flourish."

Wen opened her mouth to tell him it wouldn't work, but an idea popped into her head. She jumped out of her chair and cracked her knuckles as her brain churned. Maybe, just maybe, during the summer, she could run the mailboat while Tina and Asher operated the tour boat, just as her dad had suggested. Then…Wen made laps around the kitchen…maybe, come fall, when the flow of tourist slowed to a trickle, the husband-and-wife duo could shift to running the mailboat. *Which would free me up to be with Estelle during the off-season.* And, for all intents and purposes, the mailboat would remain in the Apollo family.

If it all came together, this plan would enable Wen to continue to serve her community during the high season but would also mean she could leave Coopersville for a large portion of the year…*to see the world with my girlfriend.*

She turned toward her father. "You know what, this might work after all." She sat back down at the table and told him her idea.

"Wen, that's brilliant," he said. "Go find your mother. She'll be tickled pink when she hears what we've cooked up."

As expected, her mother was ecstatic about the idea and fully supported tapping their savings to invest in the *River Rat.* They finished hashing out the idea over supper, and while she and her mom did the dishes, her dad called the Websters to run the idea by Tina and Asher.

"All set," her dad said when he wheeled back into the kitchen. "We're meeting the Websters for dinner tomorrow night. They seem excited about the proposition."

When she got back to her apartment later that night, Wen called Estelle to check in and see how her mother was doing. It had been confirmed that she'd suffered a minor stroke and was, thus far, recovering well.

"My mother's stubbornness and determination may be a blessing in this case. She vows to get back to her normal routine in no time. The doctor said he'd never encountered someone quite like her."

Wen laughed. "I have no doubt."

"How are things on your end?" Estelle asked.

Wen filled her in on the goings-on in Coopersville but held off sharing her exciting news about the tour boat. There were still a lot of details to work out and she didn't want to jinx the plan. It also made her giddy to have a little surprise up her sleeve. One she hoped Estelle would be as ecstatic about as she was.

The following day was balmy, but the wind whipped down the river and it was much shiftier than normal. One minute it blew from the northwest and the next from the south. Coincidence or not, the gusts matched Wen's mood. Variable. She went from dancing along to the beat on her radio to slumping back in her captain's chair and obsessively cracking her knuckles.

Taking over the *River Rat* and bringing Tina and Asher onboard really was a perfect solution. It would enable her to continue to do what she loved and be with the woman she loved. And it would also give her the opportunity to build her business, to be a budding entrepreneur. That was big. It would make her independent from—or at least not completely dependent on—Estelle.

But at the same time, it was scary as shit. For all her carrying on about going to Barcelona and volunteering for the Peace Corps, the reality was, Wen had grown up in a small town and had rarely ventured outside of it. Coopersville may not be fancy or sophisticated, but it was home, and there was a comfort in knowing practically everyone who lived there.

If, and it was a big if at this point, she was able to leave Coopersville in the off-season and join Estelle in New York, what would it be like? How easily would she adapt to an environment that was so different from the one she knew? The city would be full of strangers. And if the rumors were true, not very friendly strangers. Even with Estelle by her side, it would be a monumental adjustment. Loons and the expanse of the river would be replaced by honking horns and traffic-clogged streets. And how would Wen fit in with Estelle's rich and cultured friends? Would they greet her with a warm handshake and then snicker about her redneck roots behind her back?

Deep down, Wen knew it was perfectly normal to have a mild freak-out. If the *River Rat* plan came to fruition and she did move to New York, even if it was only for a few months of the year, it would be a drastic change, especially for someone like her who wasn't at all accustomed to change. And change was scary, even when it was change for the good.

After she delivered her last package, she piloted *Mathilde* back to the marina, secured her in her berth, and made her way to Bella's. Ruby would be about to finish up for the day, and Wen was eager to get her take on the whole *River Rat* thing.

"I think it's a fabulous idea." Ruby laughed. "And not to get ahead of myself, but if you take over Roger's tour business, can you give the boat a new name? *River Rat* is god-awful. I mean, who in their right mind would book a tour on a boat called the *River Rat?*"

Wen laughed alongside her and the tension in her shoulders melted the slightest bit. "You do know they say renaming a boat is bad luck?"

"Yes, I've heard that," Ruby said.

"Although, if the renaming is done properly—smashing a bottle of champagne against the hull and all that—it's supposed to appease Neptune."

Ruby snapped her fingers. "I've got it. I think you should name the boat *Leto*. You know, the mother of Apollo. Kind of a cool play on your last name, and I like the idea of naming the boat after a woman."

"*Leto*," Wen said. "I like the sound of that. I'll take it under consideration, but first things first. I haven't even talked to Tina and Asher yet—my dad and I are meeting them for dinner—and they may not even be interested in the whole thing."

Ruby took Wen's hand and led her to a small table near the window of the now nearly empty café. "Let's remain positive, okay?"

"Okay."

"I assume you've told Estelle about all of this?"

"No, not yet," Wen said. "I wanted to wait until it was more of a sure thing, although I so can't wait to tell her."

"Huh, okay, I suppose that makes sense—to wait until the deal is sealed. So, you're going the surprise route. I'm onboard with that. The whole arrangement would solve a lot of complications for you two and"—she squeezed Wen's hand—"I love the idea of you expanding your empire."

"Empire, ha," Wen said. "That's a bit of a stretch, don't you think?"

"Come on, girl," Ruby said. "You'll own two boats. In my book, that's a fleet!"

She burst out laughing again. "I love you, Rube. You're the best."

Ruby bounced in her seat. "Oh, my God. I have the best idea. You said your dad threw out the idea of expanding the tour business and offering stuff like sunrise breakfast tours and wine and cheese in the evenings."

"Yes, my dad thinks Roger missed the boat—ha ha, sorry for the pun—on maximizing revenue."

"I agree," Ruby said. "So here's what I think. You and I should totally become business partners. You serve my biscuits, muffins, and bread on your cruises and I, in turn, will promote the crap out of your tours at the café. We could do brochures with a discount code, things like that."

Now it was Wen's turn to bounce in her seat. "I like it!"

"Hey, I know," Ruby said, "I can come up with a special beverage or baked good just for you. Leto Lemon Bars, or a special muffin or cookie."

When she left Ruby's café, Wen pumped her fist in the air a few times before jogging home to shower and change for dinner with Tina and Asher.

* * *

Her father was waiting outside the restaurant when she arrived. She bent down to give him a kiss on the cheek. "Hey, Dad."

"You still feel good about the *River Rat*?" he asked.

"I sure do." Wen gave him a quick synopsis of her conversation with Ruby.

His face lit up with a grin. "With you two gals working together like that, the sky's the limit on what you can do."

"It would be pretty cool," Wen said. "Ruby's been my best friend since I was like five. It would be beyond amazing to join forces and build both of our businesses."

"I chatted with Tina and Asher again this morning," he said, "and they are gung-ho about the proposal. They're anxious to find solid, year-round employment." He paused before adding, "And I've got some other exciting news."

"Oh, really. What's that?"

"Your sister called from DC last night and we got to discussing the *River Rat*. She wants to chip in too. Help to pay off Roger's note, but also provide you with a little cash to make needed improvements to the boat and pay for insurance and things like that. Like your mom and me, Laura thinks it'll be a good investment."

Wen had to sit down on the bench outside the restaurant. She couldn't believe her ears. Between her conversation with Ruby and her sister's offer to invest in the business… it was a lot to digest. Talk about a striking turn of events. And talk about having so many kind and thoughtful people in her life. Sure they were giving her money for an equity stake in her business, not giving it to her outright, but still.

"Laura works insane hours at that law firm down there," her father said. "And she doesn't have time to spend any of that obscenely large salary she makes."

They ventured inside and joined Tina and Asher at the table. Before they'd even placed their dinner orders, the young couple had enthusiastically agreed to the plan—they'd run the *River Rat* in the summer and take over the mailboat in the off-season. They spent the rest of the evening devising elaborate plans for how to bring the idea to fruition.

CHAPTER THIRTY-TWO

Estelle closed the book, and the crowd gathered at the small Greenwich Village bookstore erupted in applause.

The store's proprietor joined her at the podium and leaned down to speak into the microphone. "Does anyone have a question for Ms. Crabb?"

A number of hands shot into the air and the proprietor called on them one by one. Finally, he said, "Okay, we have time for one more question." He scanned the crowd and pointed to a person in the back of the room.

The questioner stepped forward and asked, "Your protagonist eludes the police early in the book by sending a decoy down the river. How did you come up with that brilliant idea?"

The bright lights shining over the podium made it difficult for Estelle to make out any of the faces in the crowd, but she'd know that voice anywhere. Wen. What was she doing here? Estelle wanted to run to her, but first she smiled and did her best to answer the question that Wen had posed.

She cleared her throat. "My beautiful girlfriend, Wen, deserves credit for that magnificent plot twist. She's the one who dreamed it up."

A long line of people formed at the table next to the podium and Estelle patiently signed their copies of *In Plane Sight*. Wen waited in the back of the room, the two of them occasionally sharing a smile. After Estelle scribbled *Greta Crabb* for the last person in line, she stood and walked over to Wen.

"Well, this is a nice surprise."

Wen grazed her lips over Estelle's cheek and whispered, "When can you get out of here?"

Estelle scanned the thinning crowd in the bookstore. "How about now?"

"Cool, give me one sec." Wen trotted toward the back of the store and returned a minute later with a large duffel bag and an overstuffed backpack. "The woman behind the desk was kind enough to hold these for me during your reading," she explained.

Estelle eyed her luggage. "Am I to deduce that you're here for more than a brief visit?"

Wen grinned. "Maybe."

"That's wonderful, but how? What about—"

"Let's go back to your place and I'll explain."

They made out like teenagers in the back seat of the chauffeured black car as it wound through the streets of New York. The driver cleared his throat when they reached Estelle's building.

When they got upstairs, Estelle poured them each a glass of wine and led Wen out to her patio.

"Wow," Wen said. "Talk about a view." She pointed to the dark mass of trees that extended in each direction. "Is that Central Park?"

Estelle nodded. "Are you going to tell me what you're doing here?"

Wen set down her wine and took both of Estelle's hands in her own. "I was uh, wondering, do you still need a date to that wedding?"

"As a matter of fact, I do. You have someone in mind?"

"How about a charming boat captain?"

"Is she cute?" Estelle asked.

"In a butch sort of way."

"Sounds like just my type."

"Great, I'll let her know."

Estelle put her hands on her hips. "Wen Apollo. Tell me this instant what is going on."

Wen leaned up against the railing and told Estelle about the *River Rat* and Tina and Asher.

Estelle's heart pounded in her chest. She couldn't believe her ears. After all these months of agonizing about how she and Wen could be together... She'd never given up hope that they would figure something out, but there had been days when her faith had withered. But now, she didn't need to worry anymore. Wen was here with her in New York.

She pinched her own arm. "Just want to make sure I'm not dreaming."

"Nope, not dreaming."

"But what about the weekend of the wedding?" Estelle asked. "I thought you had to coach basketball, and what about your cousin's communion?"

"I found someone to cover my coaching duties," Wen said, "and I promised to take my cousin shopping for a communion gift when I got back to town. That seemed to make up for any disappointment she had about me missing the actual event."

Estelle pulled Wen into her arms and hugged her as tight as she could.

"So, I take it you're okay with me hanging out here for a while?" Wen asked.

Estelle pulled back and kissed her softly on the lips. "I guess I could get used to having you around."

She refilled their wineglasses and they retreated to the plush couch in her living room.

"Now it's me who has to pinch herself," Wen said. "I can't believe I'm actually here. Sitting in your apartment in New York. A very nice apartment, I might add."

"You being here is big, really big, on so many fronts."

"It is. And I won't lie, I'm a little anxious about being in the big city."

"City life will be an adjustment for you, but I'll be by your side every step of the way. In time, I hope you come to love it here as much as I do."

"Maybe tomorrow you could give me a Big Apple tutorial."

"I'd be happy to," Estelle said. "In the meantime, tell me more about the *River Rat* and the couple who's going to help you run it."

Wen scooted back on the couch and crossed her legs underneath her. She became animated as she spoke, and the joy on her face was evident. She was so darn earnest, it was adorable. At that moment, Estelle didn't think it was possible to be more in love with her. Wen looked so beautiful sitting there. Her long blond hair was pulled back in a loose ponytail and her flannel shirt was open wide at the top to expose her smooth, suntanned skin.

"The boat needs a little TLC, but there's so much potential," Wen said. "And Tina and Asher have so many great ideas about how to fix it up. They're going to reupholster all the seat cushions over the winter and give the whole boat a fresh coat of paint. Once we get her spruced up, we've talked about introducing wine and cheese tours and sunrise breakfast tours, serving baked goods from Ruby's café, of course."

"The more I hear about this whole venture, the better it sounds."

"Things just kind of fell into place," Wen said. "Tina and Asher are incredible and so driven. Asher is super handy, and Tina has a good sense for business, plus they're both charming as hell. Add that to the fact that, between them, they speak five languages."

"Sounds to me like the tourists will eat them up," Estelle said.

"I hope so." Wen took a sip of wine. "Anyway, before I left, I also brought them up to speed on running *Mathilde*, because a key element of the whole plan is for them to run the route in the off-season. They spent two full days out delivering packages with me."

"How'd that go?"

"Great," Wen said. "Growing up, Asher worked for his family's fishing charter company, so he knows his way around a boat, and Tina grew up in Coopersville, so she knows how to navigate the river." Wen grinned. "And I left them with meticulous notes. Thirty pages of them, complete with diagrams and even a bar graph."

"I see," Estelle said with a smile. "And what sorts of things did you tell them in these copious notes?"

"Just little things that you wouldn't know unless you'd done the route for a while. Like the fact that Mrs. Key gets lonely and appreciates it if you bring her a book from the library and stay for a while to chat…That you need to check in with Mrs. Grass about her insulin supply because she gets a little forgetful. Stuff like that."

Estelle leaned forward and kissed her softly on the lips. "You, Wen Apollo, are the most adorable, kindest, sweetest person I've ever met."

Wen gave her a goofy smile. "Thanks."

Estelle leaned back against the couch. "I do have one question though," she said. "Have you considered changing the name of the tour boat? I mean, no offense, but *River Rat* is pretty dreadful."

"Funny you mention it. Ruby asked the same question, and Tina said the name *River Rat* made her think of a bunch of guys sitting back and guzzling Budweiser."

Estelle threw back her head and laughed. "I'd have to agree."

"I'm thinking of changing the boat's name to *Leto*." She explained the significance of the name.

"Brilliant."

"It was Ruby who came up with the idea."

"So, is everything with the *River Rat* a done deal?" Estelle asked.

"Yep," Wen said. "First, my lawyer helped me set up an LLC—something he insisted was necessary now that I'd own two boats, including one that would carry paying passengers, and have two employees. Then, a few days later, I went in and signed the documents to assume Roger's loan on the *River Rat* and transfer the title for the boat to me, or technically, to my newly formed LLC."

"I wish I'd been there with you. It must have been a lot to handle."

"It was, and I wish you'd been there too, but I so wanted to surprise you here in New York, and my parents and Ruby were there with me and that helped. I'll be honest though, there was a moment there, right before I signed all the documents, where I kind of freaked out. Wondered if I was about to make a giant mistake, questioned whether I have what it takes to run the *River Rat* and *Mathilde*."

"How do you feel about it now?"

"Better. I mean, I know it was the right decision. I'm growing my business, and more importantly, it means I can be with you. Still, there's a lot of money on the line and people—my parents, Tina and Asher, my sister Laura, Ruby—are counting on me. I don't want to let them down."

"I have full confidence in you," Estelle said. "Sounds to me like you did all of your due diligence."

"I did. I combed over Roger's books for the tour boat. He turned a pretty good profit."

"Profit that you'll only expand on, I'm sure. How could you not with all the fantastic ideas you have about how to grow the business."

Wen stifled a yawn. "Sorry," she mumbled.

Estelle rubbed her back. "You poor thing. You've had a really long day."

"Yeah, and an emotional one. I was so excited about coming here to surprise you and then, as I got closer and closer to the city, I started to panic. Started to worry whether you'd welcome me with open arms."

Estelle stood and pulled Wen to her feet. She wrapped her arms around her and whispered into her ear, "I love you, Wen. You showing up at the bookstore was the best surprise I could have imagined."

Wen giggled. "My plan had been to show up on your doorstep, but then Ruby pointed out that you live smack-dab in the middle of Manhattan and probably had a doorman—a doorman who probably wouldn't let me traipse into the building with my army duffel, at least not without first calling up to alert you. And, I don't know, that didn't seem very romantic."

* * *

"Would you mind if I took a shower?" Wen asked. "After all that traveling, I'd feel better if I were clean before I climb into your bed."

"Climb in my bed," Estelle said. "I like the sounds of that." She pulled a puffy white towel from the cupboard and turned on the water in the shower while Wen stripped out of her clothes.

"Care to join me?" Wen asked as she stepped into the large glass and marble shower.

"Hell, yes."

A moment later, Estelle's naked body came through the shower door and joined her under the spray of hot water.

"Suddenly I don't feel so tired," Wen said.

Estelle picked up the bar of soap and dragged it down Wen's arms and over her chest, slowly lathering her torso before sliding it down between Wen's thighs.

Wen moaned. "You sneaky bugger."

Estelle feigned innocence. "What? I'm just trying to ensure you don't miss any hard-to-reach spots." She rolled the soap over Wen's ass and down the back of her leg.

"My turn," Wen said. She snagged the soap from Estelle's hand and circled one breast and then the other before setting the bar back in its dish.

"Turn around," Estelle ordered.

Wen complied and pressed her palms up against the marble wall of the shower. A moment later, soft bristles stroked her back.

"Oh, my, God, that feels amazing." She hung her head and arched her back as Estelle moved the brush over her muscles.

Eventually, Estelle set down the brush, doused Wen with the handheld sprayer, and turned off the water. She reached out for the towel and handed it to Wen. "There's a spare robe hanging in the linen closet if you want it."

Wen toweled off, slipped into the blue silk robe, and peeked into the bedroom. A king-size four-poster bed sat next to a large window that overlooked the New York skyline.

"Wow, I don't think I'll ever be able to get used to these views." She glanced back at the bed. It was made with military precision and both bedside tables were piled high with books. "Um, honey, which side of the bed should I sleep on?"

Estelle came up beside her wearing a matching silk robe, although hers was white. She loosened her robe and let it drop to the floor. After she released Wen's robe, she backed her up toward the bed, pushed her down, and crawled up onto her. Their lips came together in a hungry kiss, but Estelle pulled back abruptly.

"Wait here. I'll be right back. I've got an idea."

Wen let out a whimper of protest, but Estelle's warm naked body was back on top of her in an instant.

"I picked up a little something when I got back to New York…to help me survive the time we were apart." Estelle held a sparkly pink object over Wen's head. "Have you ever used a vibrator?"

"A few times."

Estelle rolled off her again and said, "I recently read an article in the *New York Times*."

Reading the newspaper was currently about the furthest thing from Wen's mind. "Um, okay…"

Estelle ran a finger down her chest. "The article was about a book called *Vibrator Nation*."

Wen laughed. "Are you kidding me? In the *New York Times*?"

Estelle rolled the vibrator between her hands. "The book is about the history of these little babies." She waved the vibrator in the air. "In the sixties and seventies, it was a huge deal for women to buy them." Estelle chuckled. "Apparently, men were threatened by the competition."

"Of course they were, and with good reason."

"Anyway," Estelle continued, "there was this woman, Betty Dobson, and she went around giving 'sexual consciousness-raising' workshops to women. In them, she stripped off her clothes and showed the audience how to use a vibrator to orgasm."

"This may be weird, but that actually sounds kind of hot," Wen said.

"I thought so too." Estelle didn't say another word. She pulled a small wooden chair into the middle of the room and pointed to the bed. "Make yourself comfortable."

Wen pulled back the sheets, lay down, and slid her hand down to touch herself. "Fuck, I'm already wet as shit."

Estelle held her gaze, placed one foot up on the chair and parted her legs wide. A soft buzzing sound filled the room and Estelle brought the sparking pink vibrator up between her thighs. As soon as it touched her folds, she tensed and raised a hand to knead one of her nipples.

It was the fucking sexiest thing Wen had ever seen. She increased the pace of her fingers and she and Estelle came together. Although they weren't touching, the moment was incredibly intimate.

Estelle put the vibrator in a drawer, turned out the light, and climbed into bed next to her. Wen nestled her head into the crux of Estelle's arm and slid her arm around her waist to pull them tight together. They lay together in the dark. The room was silent except for their ragged breathing and the distant sound of a car horn.

"I'm so glad you're here," Estelle whispered.

"I'm so glad I'm here too," Wen replied. "We're meant to be together. I believe that with my whole heart. There's a reason the stars aligned for us."

CHAPTER THIRTY-THREE

"You're bringing that boat captain to Grace's wedding?" Estelle's mother asked over the phone.

"Yes, I am," she replied.

"Are you certain that's wise? Won't she feel out of place?"

Estelle knew her mother wasn't remotely concerned about how Wen would feel. She only cared about what others might think. Wen hadn't gone to the finest boarding school, and she didn't have a degree from Princeton. Horrors.

"Mother, it will be fine. Trust me."

"I presume she's here in New York?"

"Yes, she is."

"For how long?"

"I'm not sure yet, but for more than a brief visit." Estelle wanted to say, "We're shacking up," but it was probably wise not to push any more of her mother's buttons.

"I see." There was a long pause before her mother continued, "Am I to infer that this relationship between you and this Wen person is serious?"

"Yes, it is. Very serious. As I've told you, I'm in love with her."

"That's all well and good, Estelle, but have you stopped to ask yourself if someone like her is equipped to handle—"

"Handle what, Mother?"

"I'm only pointing out that, as a Gage, you have certain obligations. Social obligations."

"I'm abundantly aware of that. And you underestimate Wen. She can hold her own. She's a very successful businesswoman. In fact, she recently acquired a new boat. A large one that will provide tours on the river."

"I hope you're right, darling."

"I am, Mother. Don't you worry. Someday, I hope you'll take the time to get to know her so that you can see for yourself what an incredible person she is."

"Let's see how things go at the wedding."

* * *

Wen pulled on the long, green taffeta dress, careful not to jostle the perfectly sculpted bun at the base of her head. It had taken the hairdresser over two hours to trim her long blond locks and swirl her hair into its current formation. By her estimate, he'd used half a can of hairspray to hold it in place, but still, she wasn't taking any chances.

Once she had the dress on, she peered into the mirror, pleased to see that her bun remained intact, and she hadn't smeared her makeup. Tonight was the big wedding, and she wanted desperately not to stick out like a hick among the society crowd.

She'd been in New York for two weeks and so far, so good, but tonight would be a big test. Since she'd arrived, she and Estelle had spent much of their time inside, holed up in her apartment. Making love or curled up on the couch, reading. When they did venture out, it was just to wander the neighborhood or stroll through Central Park.

Even though they were smack-dab in the middle of one of the world's largest, most vibrant cities, the surrounding streets had a neighborhood feel to them. Estelle knew all the shopkeepers by name—the pharmacist, the butcher, the dry cleaner—and they often encountered people she knew on the sidewalk. Everyone had greeted Wen warmly, at least to her face.

The main hurdle Wen had encountered in her transition from Coopersville to the big city had been her clothes. At the end of her first week in New York, she'd gone out for a walk alone while Estelle attended a meeting with her publisher, and upon returning to the apartment, another resident in Estelle's building had approached her. The man was not unpleasant, but he'd pointed to a sign that instructed employees to use the rear entrance. At first, anger bubbled up inside of her, but she'd swallowed her pride and thanked him with as much sincerity as she could muster. In truth, she couldn't blame him. He probably wasn't aware that Estelle had someone new living with her, and Wen's attire—Carhartts and a hoodie—did resemble that of the handymen she'd seen roaming the building.

When she'd relayed the story to Estelle, she'd offered to take Wen shopping if she wanted. The idea of Estelle buying her clothes made her uncomfortable, but together they'd reached a solution. A friend of Estelle's ran a high-end consignment shop and she'd agreed to extend Estelle's "friends and family discount" to Wen. Although, even at thirty percent off, Wen had been astounded at the prices and had ultimately allowed Estelle to chip in half. The green taffeta dress she currently wore had come from that store.

* * *

Another chauffeured black car whisked Wen and Estelle to an estate along the banks of the Hudson River where both the wedding and the reception were being held.

Estelle squeezed her hand as they zipped along the Henry Hudson Parkway and asked, "How are you holding up?"

"I'm pretty nervous." In the brief time she'd been in New York, she'd only met one of Estelle's friends, her BFF, Fran. "I think I'd be less of a wreck if your mother wasn't going to be there."

"I promise, I'll be by your side the whole night."

"What should I say if someone asks me what I do for a living?"

"Tell them the truth. That you own and operate a fleet of boats in the Thousand Islands."

"You make it sound so easy," Wen said, a bit more harshly than she intended.

"I'm sorry, sweetheart. I know this is stressful for you. Please know I wasn't trying to trivialize the situation." She looked Wen in the eye. "Look at the bright side, Elton John is playing. How cool is that?"

"Pretty darn cool. I've always wanted to see him in concert. I never expected I'd get to hear him perform at a private event like this."

"Grace has never been one to be outdone. And, just between you and me, I'm not a huge fan of the guy she's marrying. He's kind of an arrogant asshole, one of many who will probably be at the wedding. Try and ignore them. They hold their noses up at almost everyone, even me on occasion, but you can't let them get to you. They aren't any better than you are, just remember that." She gave Wen a soft smile. "You got this."

A man in tails opened the door to the car and Wen stepped out. Her heels wobbled as they walked through the front door of the massive stone estate. Two large ballrooms flanked the foyer and both resembled botanical gardens. Flowers hung from the ceiling and covered the walls and small potted trees were scattered everywhere. One room had tall tables and two bars, and the other was a sea of small round tables set with glittering glasses and silverware, and adorned with colorful floral centerpieces.

Wen let out a low whistle. "Jeez Louise, some florist seriously hit the jackpot."

Estelle introduced her around to a few people before a chime summoned them into an outdoor tent for the ceremony.

After the nuptials, Wen went up to the bar to get herself and Estelle each a glass of wine.

"I don't think we've met," the man behind her in line said. His dirty-blond hair was graying at the temples, and lines were firmly etched in the skin around his kind blue eyes.

She turned to face him and extended her hand. "Wen Apollo."

"Mark Lennox."

Wen recognized his name. He was head of one of the big computer companies. "I'm here with Estelle Gage," she said quickly, in case he thought she'd crashed the wedding to score free drinks.

"Wen. That's an unusual name. Is it short for something?"

She shook her head. "Nope. My dad came across the name in a book and liked it. He decided he would name me that regardless of whether I was a boy or a girl."

Mark laughed. "Stubborn guy, huh?"

"He can be, but he's got a heart of gold."

"So, Wen Apollo. What's your story?"

Wen tensed. "I'm not from around here, but you probably guessed that...I'm from the Thousand Islands. I own and operate a fleet of boats up there." She expected him to laugh and look for someone more interesting to talk to.

Instead, he smiled and said, "Wow, that's impressive. My son is about your age, and he hasn't shown much of an inclination toward work, or really anything but rock climbing for that matter."

Wen stood taller. *He just called me impressive.* "Running my own business is hard work, but it's extremely rewarding." She was next in line, so she turned to the bartender to place her order. Grabbing the drinks, she said, "It was nice to meet you, Mark," and left to find Estelle.

Not long after the reception started, Elton John took the stage. He only sang two songs, but it was still incredible to see him. Wen and Estelle swayed together and sang along to "Can You Feel the Love Tonight?" and then hit the dance floor for "Tiny Dancer."

After he left the stage, the lead singer of the wedding band came to the microphone and said, "Talk about a tough act to follow."

Everyone erupted into laughter.

They all filed into the larger of the two ballrooms for dinner. The meal was delicious, mercifully short, and included the usual wedding rituals. Expensive champagne was poured to toast the happy couple, and the best man's speech was tasteful but funny.

When they wandered toward the bar after dinner, an old classmate of Estelle's came up beside them. Her eyes were red as if she'd been crying and Estelle stepped aside to talk to her. While she was gone, Wen chatted with Fran, and invariably the conversation moved to Wen and Estelle's relationship.

"I've known Estelle since freshman year of college," Fran said, "and I've never seen her this happy."

"That's nice to hear," Wen said casually, although what she really wanted to do was skip around the room.

"You're obviously good for each other, and on top of that, Estelle is different with you."

Wen's voice caught in her throat. "How do you mean?"

"In the past, when she was in a serious relationship, she often lost part of who she was, too often gave up things that were important to her for the sake of the other person. When you two met, initially she was reluctant to begin something with you because she was only just learning how to be her. Although she'd been divorced from Claudia for a year and had been working hard with her therapist, she didn't yet trust herself to enter into another relationship. She feared she'd get lost again…but that hasn't happened with you."

Estelle had expressed this to her, but it was nice to know that Fran saw it too. Before Wen could respond, Fran stiffened. Wen followed her gaze. Catherine Gage was headed in their direction.

Just before the matriarch reached them, Mark Lennox, the man Wen had talked to at the bar, intercepted her.

"Mrs. Gage, what a pleasure to see you," he said.

Catherine greeted him with a smile. "Good evening, Mark." She glanced over at Fran and Wen and then back at him. There was an awkward silence before she said, "I presume you know Francesca Westover?"

"Yes, nice to see you, Fran."

Catherine flicked a hand toward Wen. "And this is…" She coughed as if she'd swallowed something bitter. "This is Estelle's girlfriend, Wen Apollo."

Mark nodded. "Wen and I met earlier. We discussed her business enterprise."

Enterprise. That had a nice ring to it.

"I see," Catherine said.

"In fact," he said. "I want to introduce Wen to my son. I'm hoping she'll be able to light a fire under him."

Catherine bobbed her head in response, as if she couldn't quite believe her ears.

Estelle returned from comforting her classmate, but a moment later she was pulled away again. This time by a woman on the board of the Gage Foundation.

Catherine Gage excused herself, and Fran and Mark went to the bar. When Wen stepped outside to get some fresh air, Estelle's older brother, Russell, popped out of nowhere.

"Hi, Wen," he said. His bow tie hung loose around his open collar, and he was a little unsteady on his feet.

"Hi, Russell." Wen hadn't met him before this evening, but she and Estelle had been seated next to him and his wife during the wedding ceremony. "It's nice to see you again."

"You too," he said. "You wook bootiful in dat dress." He hiccupped and then giggled. "Whoops."

Wen thanked him for the compliment, scanning the patio where they stood. A few smokers lingered off in the distance under a patch of trees, but otherwise they were alone. It was a chilly evening, and although stars sprinkled the clear sky above, most people had opted to stay indoors.

Russell swayed toward her and whispered, "I want to kiss you."

She took a step back and held up her hand. "No, Russell." The smokers were pretty far off. Rather than call out to them, she decided to lure Russell inside. "It looks like your drink is almost gone. Why don't we get you another?"

He held up his glass and inspected it in the faint light. "Good idea." He began to follow her inside but paused to claw at his leg. "Fucking pants itch. I want to take them off."

"Let's get you that drink first." She opened the door and pointed to a chair. "Sit there and I'll go to the bar. What are you drinking?"

He collapsed into the chair and handed her his glass. "Gin and tonic."

With one eye on Russell, Wen stepped over to the bar to order his drink. "Gin and tonic, please. Hold the gin."

She brought the drink back to Russell and searched the crowd for his wife. She didn't see her, but did spot Jimmy and waved him over. He got Russell to his feet, apologized to Wen, and led his brother toward the men's room.

Wen ordered herself a glass of water from the bar and slumped into the chair Russell had just vacated.

A few minutes later, Estelle came up beside her. "I hear you saved the day."

Wen stood and slipped her arm through Estelle's. "What do you mean?"

"According to my mother, you helped defuse a potentially embarrassing situation with Russell. She said you handled my brother with grace."

"Word sure travels fast. But wait, there wasn't anyone else around. How did she know?"

"I have no idea," Estelle said, "but no doubt she's got eyes and ears all over this wedding."

"Russell was completely wasted," Wen said. "He told me I looked beautiful and said he wanted to kiss me."

Estelle recoiled and her hand went to her mouth. "I am so sorry." She looked Wen up and down. "Did he—"

Wen shook her head. "No, he didn't touch me."

"Still, his behavior was reprehensible."

Wen didn't disagree, but she didn't want his conduct to ruin the night, which had otherwise been a lot more pleasant than she'd expected. "What did that woman from the foundation board want to ask you?"

"Oh, you mean Betty," Estelle said. "She wanted to talk about a new program they're working to develop."

"What's the program?" Wen asked.

Estelle smiled. "As you know, one of the foundation's newer initiatives is to improve the lives of women and girls."

"Yes, it's something you've said you're especially passionate about."

"Correct. And according to Betty, there's a new foundation-led effort in Rwanda. Its goal is to work with the community to increase access to education for girls and to bolster women's economic empowerment. She wants me to play a role in getting it off the ground."

"How so?"

"She hopes I'll accompany her and other foundation representatives on a trip to Rwanda. However, unlike many of the other trips I've taken—for a quick ground-breaking ceremony or some other PR event—this one would involve being imbedded in a community for nearly two months."

"Wow, that sounds amazing," Wen said.

"Will you come with me?"

"To Rwanda?"

"Yes. The trip isn't scheduled until next fall. The timing should work well and—"

"Oh, my God, I'd love to go!" Wen bounced on her toes. "Especially for a stay of that length." She wanted to hoot and holler but was mindful that they were still at the wedding, and she had to be on her best behavior. "Rwanda is a place I've read about and dreamed of visiting. The fact that the trip will be focused on work with women and girls is a bonus. It's exactly the kind of work I hoped to do with the Peace Corps."

Before they hit the dance floor again, Wen excused herself to go to the bathroom. As she walked back out in search of Estelle, a woman bumped into her.

"I'm so sorry," the woman said. "I wasn't watching where I was going." She wore a low-cut sapphire dress that set off her light blue eyes. She was tall and athletic and downright stunning.

Wen waved her off. "No worries. And I think it was me who swayed into you." She hoisted her dress slightly and lifted one of her feet. "I'm a little unsteady on these heels."

The woman laughed. "Heels are for the birds. I have no idea why I continue to wear them." She reached up to touch the pendant that rested just below Wen's collarbone. "Your necklace is gorgeous."

"Um, thanks." Estelle's friend at the consignment shop had lent it to her, and Wen had been obsessively checking the clasp all night, petrified of losing the darn thing.

Estelle walked up beside her. "Oh, I see you two have met."

Both Wen and the woman gave her a blank stare. Suddenly it dawned on her. Holy crap. Could it be? Had she just been chatting with the ex-wife?

Estelle confirmed her suspicion. She nodded between the two women and introduced them.

Claudia's jaw dropped open.

Wen managed to keep her composure and extended her hand. "It's nice to meet you, Claudia."

Claudia absentmindedly shook her hand, her eyes never leaving Estelle. After she released Wen's hand, she stiffened and raised her chin. "Stelle, I've tried to track you down all night. Could I have a moment? I need to talk to you…" She gazed over at Wen before returning her attention to Estelle. "Privately."

Estelle's eyes narrowed in on her. "Please call me tomorrow if there's something urgent you need to discuss." She reached for Wen's hand. "Right now, we have a date with the dance floor."

Thankfully, the rest of the evening was drama-free. When the band announced their final song, Estelle's nephew, Cob, cut in to have the last dance with Wen. He stood on her toes, and they twirled around the dance floor laughing.

At the end of the night, they reunited with their driver, and as their car wound down the long gravel driveway of the estate, Wen scooted across the back seat and clipped into the seat belt in the middle to be closer to Estelle.

"Thanks for bringing me to the wedding."

Estelle placed a hand on her thigh. "You, Wen Apollo, were by far the most charming person there tonight. I assure you, people will be talking about you for a long time."

"In a good way, I hope," Wen said.

Estelle brushed her lips over Wen's ear. "In a very good way."

Wen laughed. "The encounters with Claudia and Russell aside, I actually had a good time."

"See, I told you there was nothing to worry about. Most weddings are the same. A happy couple, flowers, cake, dancing, asshole drunk relatives, pesky ex-wives…"

Wen laughed again. In many ways, Estelle was right. The wedding tonight was like many others she had attended. Sure, most weddings in Coopersville had a DJ and a cash bar rather than Elton John and waiters roaming around with two-hundred-dollar bottles of champagne, but many of the other elements were the same. And more importantly, Wen hadn't felt out of place or inferior. And if a wealthy businessman like Mark Lennox was impressed by her accomplishments, maybe she should be too.

It would be naïve to presume that everything with her and Estelle would be smooth sailing from here on out. Their class differences would likely be a source of friction at times, but Wen couldn't let that drive a wedge between them. They'd work through those moments together. Their love for each other was all that mattered. She thought back to the conversation she'd had with Fran earlier that evening. About how Estelle was different with her than she'd been in other relationships. Wen believed it, but she wanted to make sure.

"Can I ask you something?"

"Of course," Estelle said. "What is it, honey?"

Wen summarized her discussion with Fran. "Do you think it's true? That you're different with me?"

Estelle shifted in her seat and cupped Wen's cheeks with her hands. "Yes." She kissed Wen softly on the lips and sat back against her seat. "Without question. And it's made me realize that I am now capable of being in a relationship, a very serious one, without losing sight of who I am and what's important to me." She turned to face Wen again. "That's given me confidence, in myself and in our relationship. When I imagine my future, it includes you."

CHAPTER THIRTY-FOUR

Five months later.

Wen and Estelle packed up the car and drove to Coopersville. It was early spring, and Wen had a lot to do to get ready for the upcoming summer season.

She'd only been home a handful of times since fall—she and Estelle had visited over the holidays and come up for her mother's fiftieth birthday and for Winterfest—and although she was excited to see her parents and Ruby, their first stop was at the marina. Wen wanted to say hello to *Mathilde*. She was due to go into the water later that morning. Only after she confirmed that the old boat had survived the harsh winter did they head into town. Driving down Main Street was like pulling on a well-worn Carhartt jacket. Familiar and warm.

Her lease on the apartment above Ursula's Books had long since expired, but she and Estelle had found a small house on the water to lease for the summer months. Mrs. Gage had insisted they could live on Owl Island, and they'd likely spend much of their time there, but they wanted a place of their own, and logistically, it made sense for Wen to live near the marina. Soon Tina and Asher would turn their attention to running the tour boat and Wen would resume operating the mailboat.

She woke early on their first day back in Coopersville and wandered down to the café to see Ruby. As usual, there was a long line at the counter, but Ruby dropped what she was doing and ran to meet Wen at the door and engulf her in a hug.

"Hello, old friend," Wen said, her words muffled by Ruby's shoulder.

While she waited for Ruby to work through her morning rush, she took two breakfast sandwiches and coffee back to the house for Estelle. When she returned to the café, Ruby joined her at a table and slid a piece of paper in front of her.

Wen picked it up. "What's this?"

"A menu of items I've put together for the *River Rat.*"

Before Wen looked it over, she said, "I forgot to tell you, I decided to take your advice and rename the tour boat *Leto.* We're going to christen her when she goes in the water."

"Good move." Ruby nodded toward the sheet of paper in Wen's hand. "So, what do you think?"

Wen licked her lips as she scanned the menu. "Wow, this all sounds awesome." She looked up at her best friend. "You're amazing."

Ruby waved her off. "I know the tour boat doesn't have a fridge or a stove, so I chose stuff that you could serve straight from a cooler."

"Brilliant, Rube," Wen said. "Guess I better get down to the hardware store to buy myself a giant Yeti, maybe two."

From the café, Wen went to meet Tina and Asher at the storage facility outside of town. They'd been in constant contact over the winter, and Wen couldn't wait to see the work they'd done to the *River Rat.* She whistled when she saw its sleek black hull glistening in the sun.

"Holy cow, it doesn't even look like the same boat," she said.

Asher produced a ladder from behind the building. "Wait until you see inside."

Wen followed him up and into the cockpit. She couldn't believe her eyes. Every surface had been painted and varnished, all the brass hardware sparkled, and the seat cushions were covered with crisp black-and-white-striped canvas.

She pulled Ruby's sheet from her back pocket and held it out for Tina and Asher to see. "Check this out. A menu befitting this gorgeous boat."

After they oohed and aahed over Ruby's menu, Tina said, "I've got a really good feeling about the tour boat."

"Me too," Wen said. "And on that note, if you have time now, I'd like to get your thoughts on the pricing strategy I've devised."

The three of them clambered back down the ladder and Wen pulled a worn notebook from her truck and spread it on the hood. "I read this article about how some Major League Baseball teams are now revenue-managing their ticket prices. Like they charge more when their team plays a good team than they do when they play a lousy team. And they even adjust their prices depending on the weather. Tickets are cheaper on cold, rainy days than they are on warm, sunny ones. I thought we could deploy a similar strategy. Charge more during the peak times and when the weather is nice."

"Makes sense to me," Tina said, and Asher nodded in agreement.

That afternoon, Estelle and Wen donned foul weather gear, heavy sweaters, and wool caps and meandered back down to the marina. The air was crisp, and small ice chunks floated in the water, but there wasn't a cloud in the sky, and the sun made it feel warmer than it was.

Wen patted *Mathilde*'s bow and hopped aboard. Estelle released the boat's lines and joined her at the helm. They puttered through the channel and out into the open water. Wen poked her head out from behind the boat's windshield and closed her eyes as the wind whipped across her face. As much as she'd come to enjoy New York, nothing matched this. Being out on the water. Just the birds and the sky above. And Estelle by her side. The resentment Wen had once held about having to operate the mailboat had now been replaced by gratitude.

When Owl Island came into view, Wen circled it twice and snaked an arm around Estelle's waist. "You know what today is?"

"Of course, it's Good Friday."

"Correct, but what else?"

Estelle shrugged.

"A year ago today, I came to deliver a package and you invited me in for tea."

"Smartest thing I ever did."

Wen nuzzled Estelle's neck and kissed her on the cheek. "You were right, you know?"

"About what?" Estelle asked.

"It all worked out. You and me and the mailboat and everything."

Bella Books, Inc.

Women. Books. Even Better Together.

P.O. Box 10543
Tallahassee, FL 32302

Phone: 800-729-4992
www.bellabooks.com